Lorelei Mathias grew up in a small suburb north of London, and studied English and Philosophy at Birmingham [barcode] living in Melbourne [barcode] London, where she [barcode] r.

D0430837

First published in Great Britain by
LITTLE BLACK DRESS
An imprint of HEADLINE BOOK PUBLISHING

This paperback first published in 2006 by LITTLE BLACK DRESS
An imprint of HEADLINE BOOK PUBLISHING

A LITTLE BLACK DRESS paperback

3

ISBN 0 7553 3272 5 (ISBN-10)
ISBN 978 0 7553 3272 4 (ISBN-13)

Typeset in Transit511BT by Avon DataSet Ltd,
Bidford-on-Avon, Warwickshire

Printed and bound in Great Britain by Clays Ltd, St Ives plc

Headline's policy is to use papers that are natural, renewable and recyclable
products and made from wood grown in sustainable forests. The logging and
manufacturing processes are expected to conform to the environmental regulations
of the country of origin.

HEADLINE BOOK PUBLISHING
A division of Hodder Headline
338 Euston Road, London NW1 3BH

www.littleblackdressbooks.com
www.hodderheadline.com

To my father, for always being there
(even when he's tuned out)

'You've got to live with your product.
You've got to get steeped in it . . . saturated in it.
You must get to the heart of it.'
Bill Bernbach (1911–82)

Contents

Tick Tock

'Oh, come on now. In all fairness, how long does it really take to get from Highgate Village to here? I mean, if you *say* you're going to be here in ten minutes, why do ten-minute chunks keep on zooming by and your ugly red mug still hasn't appeared?'

Realising her audience was growing in size, Amelie Holden sighed and put down her cumbersome shopping bags, coat, scarf, gym bag, overnight bag and birthday presents. She leaned against the bus shelter at Highbury Corner and rolled her eyes at the tramp sitting next to her, who raised his one o'clock can of beer back at her in amusement. Oh sod off, she chided him inwardly. Just because you haven't got to be somewhere in an impossible amount of time. Again.

Why, reasoned Amelie, must the 'Countdown' machinery always lie so? Why must it keep saying Old Street 10 minutes, when time is definitely passing? I *know* time is passing, I can see the seconds skipping by on my watch, mocking Me and My Lateness. And yet still the malicious infra-red display says Old Street 10 – oh no, what's that? 14 minutes! Can time be getting *slower*? Is the bus going *backwards*??!

Amelie fumbled with her bags and fought to locate her mobile. She hastily composed a quick text message, while struggling to keep her eyes at the top of her head so that she could monitor the progress of the bus that would take her into Hoxton.

Clairey – it's not like I didn't really try this time. Truly was going to be on time – early even. But literally been waiting at godforsaken bus stop for invisible 271 for at least 6 years. Be there as soon as humanly poss. If you need to eat, order without me. Will just grab peanuts again. Am x x x

She clicked send but nothing happened. Of course. Her credit was all out and she hadn't had time to get any more.

'Bollocks,' she said. 'Where is the Tardis when you need it?'

A Number 43 pulled up and Amelie had an inward debate about whether to get it and at least be some of the way there, to at least be *moving*. But no, she had made that mistake before and got so lost looking for Hoxton Square from the alien bus stop that she had been even later than if she had waited for the 271. No, this way she would be late but not lost, flustered and overheated.

At least she had the presents all wrapped up; she wouldn't need to get out Sellotape and scissors on the bus. That was something. Oh, but the card. I can be writing the card while I wait, she thought, and began rummaging through her handbag, rifling through tissues and Post-its and make-up, looking for where she had put it. She could feel where it was with her fingers, buried underneath layers of things which she began removing. Squatting for a moment, she reached into her over-stuffed handbag and pulled out a pair of mismatched brown gloves (one suede, one velvet), a notebook (with no empty pages left in it), a pink mini iPod (with a flat battery) and a hairbrush (and its broken handle), and laid them all out on the pavement next to her. Now that the birthday card was more visible, she was about to try and retrieve it when she felt the people around her start to move. Evidently, Old Street 14 minutes had also been a lie. Suddenly, miraculously, the 271 had appeared at the bus stop.

Frantically, she raked all of her things together and began hastily stuffing everything back into her handbag. On the third attempt to zip it up she admitted defeat, left everything hanging, and stood up. Seeing an old lady climb aboard, she realised with astonishment and fury that the doors were about to close in front of her face. And not because the bus was too full. But because this particular bus driver was from the 'I'm not insured if there are any more than two people standing' school of bus-driving, and was refusing to let any more passengers on. As the old lady with her shopping-bag-on-wheels took her seat gleefully, she smiled back at the girl who was next in line: an irate twenty-six-year-old named Amelie Holden, whose bag-laden arms were flapping in the air angrily, watching in astonishment as the doors closed, almost skimming her nose as they did so. In one final attempt to win the driver round, Amelie bashed the window with her hands, but the bus began to pull away.

'Bugger,' Amelie said, stepping back and slumping down on the bus-shelter bench. Sodding, bastard bus drivers, she thought, but didn't say, knowing deep down that she would be on the bus now if she hadn't tried to multi-task at such an ill-chosen moment. Happy New Year! she thought, feeling her two-day hangover surge back into life.

Half an hour later, Amelie was bounding into Shish Bar & Grill, her cheeks rosy and her curly brown hair flying in hyperactive tendrils around her face.

'Sorry, sweetie, happy birthday! Sorry, the bus was a catastrophe. I did try and call but the phone was being unreasonable about credit.'

'Still on Pay as You Don't, are you?' asked Claire, her oldest friend, as they exchanged kisses. Amelie was meeting Claire and her boyfriend Dan for a late birthday lunch, just before they went away on their romantic mini-break to Paris.

'Yep, any day now I'm getting a contract. Any day. Drink?'

'We've got a bottle of Pinot already,' said Dan. 'Grab a glass and join us. We've just ordered garlic bread, so you still have time to browse the menu – just try not to take too long deciding, love. We do have a train to catch.'

Amelie was used to comments like this; they happened a lot. She was painfully aware that if there was an Olympics for Indecision, she would almost certainly win gold medals in all the rounds, particularly coming up trumps when it came to the Choosing Food in Restaurants round. 'No, no, I'll be quick as anything, I promise. I know what I want already, really. Just need to take a look at what else there is.'

Amelie strolled through the menu, thinking she was definitely in a Niçoise Salad kind of a mood. But what were the others having? This made all the difference.

'I'm having a Four Seasons pizza. Dan's having steak,' Claire informed her hastily, knowing that this would make all the difference.

'Well, in that case, I'll have the pasta. Or the lasagne. No, no – the Niçoise Salad. Absolutely. That's me decided.'

The waiter was at their table. They ordered the food, Amelie first. When the waiter, a shy Italian boy of not much more than fifteen, had finished noting it all down, he read it back to them.

'Yes, that's great, thanks,' said Dan. The waiter smiled and started to move away.

'Oh,' said Amelie, suddenly reminded of her two-day hangover by the voice in her stomach that was chanting '*Carbs*' over and over again to anyone who would listen. 'Hold on,' Amelie said to the waiter. 'No. Sorry to be a total pain in the arse, but please can I switch mine to the pizza instead? The Quattro Stagione, please,' as though saying it in the waiter's native language and smiling might somehow be less irritating for him.

Claire and Dan rolled their eyes at each other in affectionate impatience. Dan grabbed Claire's hand under the table and squeezed it warmly. 'So, Amelie. Back at work tomorrow, isn't it?'

'Yes. Don't remind me. While in only a few hours you're going to be in Paris! How jealous am I.'

'Isn't that Australian hot-shot starting this week as your new creative director?'

'Again, don't remind me, please. Duncan and I are dreading it.'

'Oh, it won't be so bad,' said Claire optimistically. 'You never know, a bit of new blood might help the agency. But anyway, how was your sister's New Year's Eve party?'

'Really great,' replied Amelie. 'Shame you guys couldn't make it in the end. Proper, proper alcohol poisoning the day after, though. Spent all of yesterday in bed, and haven't been able to eat a thing until this morning. Don't know what Lauren put in that punch, but it certainly wasn't fit for human consumption – I can still feel it doing odd things to my stomach, even now!'

'Try some of this garlic bread, that should sort you out,' said Dan, munching away and pushing the basket towards Amelie.

'So, any nice men at the party?' Claire asked.

'No, not that I can remember. I'm not looking at the moment anyway,' Amelie said, wanting to shrug the conversation off as quickly as possible.

'But that's when it happens, isn't it? When you stop looking,' Claire pushed.

'No, this year I've made a New Year's resolution,' Amelie said proudly.

'What's that, then?' asked Dan, while Claire looked faintly concerned.

'Well. I've decided not to do things by halves any more. I read this article on New Year's Day which got me thinking. It was saying that, instead of doing lots of little things all at once in your life, it's actually way more constructive to channel all your energy into one area of your life in one go. So, this year is the year of my career, and I'll mostly be doing . . . work. Obviously I'll still see friends and family, but the job will be the main priority.'

Claire and Dan exchanged knowing glances. Amelie

took a sip of wine, felt her hangover breathe a sigh of gratitude, and went on.

'Then, next year, it will be the year of my flat. You know, I'll get the curtains sorted finally, perhaps try a bit of DIY. And then maybe the year after that, I'll look at romance.'

'Amelie, where did you read such bollocks?' asked Dan.

'I don't know. One of the supplements. No, seriously, looking back at all the half-wits and fuckwits I dated last year, not one of them came anywhere near to what Jack and I had going for us. Nowhere near. And when you add up all the time and energy spent choosing what to wear, deliberating over emails, text messages and the rest, it works out as a lot of hours down the drain that I could be putting to more practical use. Especially since I'm nowhere near wanting to settle down anyway.' Amelie paused, took another sip of wine, and concluded her argument. 'So, I've realised, dating: it's just not an efficient use of my time. There's so much I want to do with my life. I don't have time to waste on guys who I know aren't ticking all the right boxes straight away.'

'Amelie,' squealed Claire, 'that is such a twisted load of crap! Never mind what you've been reading; if you ask me, you're still living in the shadow of Jack. Babe, you need to forget him. It's been *three years*. Try a new approach: stop looking for his clone. Stop looking for someone to give you what you had in your once perfect relationship. Just because someone is different to Jack, it doesn't mean they aren't worth a test run.'

'Oh for the love of God, this isn't about Jack! You've not been listening to a word I've been saying, have you?' said Amelie, her eyes lighting up with relief as the food arrived at the table.

*

'It all comes down to you, Amelie.' A few days later, and Joshua Grant's booming antipodean drawl wrestled with Amelie's daydream, bolting her back to the pressures of ad land. Looking up to see one of this month's new creative briefs dancing about in front of her face, she winced as her new creative director launched further into his tirade.

'Holden, we have a problem.' Pausing for effect, he added, 'We present to the client in less than four weeks. So far, all the material we've got to show wouldn't convince even the most desperate, miserable spinsters to hurry up and start dating. It wouldn't save the day if the whole population of the world depended on it!' Pacing around the room, he shifted his speech into fourth gear.

'Amelie, we need something from you that's going to *blow the opposition away.*' Getting carried away now, a faraway look in his eye, he said, 'We need to be convincing people that they're lonely *even when they're not*. We need to be getting inside their hearts, their minds, their souls. Persuading them that they are sad and lonely bastards, with sad and lonely futures ahead of them . . .'

Taking a breath, and eyeing the colourful bedlam of Soho Square through the window, Josh finished with a flourish: 'We need an ad that's going to force people into grabbing a Mr or Mrs Right before it's too late . . . Before they're sprouting slippers, growing mould and sipping Horlicks by the fire into the end of their days!'

Amelie rolled her eyes at her partner Duncan, who was engrossed in an intricate doodle on his layout pad. He looked up and feigned alertness.

'I'm hearing you, Joshua. Really, I am,' she replied. 'We're on the case. But if you wouldn't mind just leaving me and Duncan to it for five minutes, then perhaps we'd be a step closer to devising this work of advertising genius that's going to make or break us.'

Unfazed by Amelie's impudent tone, Josh dropped the creative brief for Fast Love – Britain's latest and most ambitious speed-dating company – on to the desk and smirked. 'Well, four weeks till D-Day, so let's see what that pretty little head of yours comes up with.'

Watching him stride out of earshot, Amelie winced at Josh's condescending choice of words. As she looked on at the sleek black Armani suit fading into the distance, she wondered, for the twelfth time that year (and it was only January), why it was that Josh – the agency's newly recruited creative director – chose to speak to her in this patronising way. By contrast he seemed perfectly capable of being civil and pleasant to the five other copywriters in the agency.

'Just try not to let him get to you so much,' offered Duncan diplomatically, sensing her annoyance. 'All we can do is give it our best shot.'

Duncan could usually be relied upon to supply a fitting verbal antidote for Amelie's turbulent temper, which had a habit of getting her into trouble. While Amelie would sometimes fret about, and over-analyse, the littlest of things, Duncan would happily smooth everything over with his laid-back optimism, diplomacy and a bottomless pit of patience.

But this time Amelie's mood was beginning to take on an energy of its own. As she swept back some strands of frizzy brown hair from her eyes, she began flicking through the creative brief. Obviously we'll give it our best shot, she thought to herself. Joshua Grant may well have been a child prodigy back in Sydney, but that doesn't mean he has to speak to us like we're a couple of simpletons before he's even unpacked, let alone proved his creative worth.

In all her three years working at LGMK (Lewis Gibbs Myers Kirby Advertising), Amelie could scarcely remember a time when she and Duncan had not succeeded in coming up with the pitch-winning idea in the end. With her friend Duncan as art director, Amelie sometimes liked to believe that together they made one of the best creative teams that the agency had. That said, this latest creative brief did appear to have the mark of the devil on it.

'But seriously, Dunc. Just how ridiculous a name is Fast Love?' Amelie enquired, looking up from the brief. 'I mean, exactly how will we get people to take it seriously with a name like that? And tell me, do people actually go speed-dating? I thought it was just an urban myth!'

'Get with the times, Amelie. It's *the* way to meet your partner in these busy career-driven times,' Duncan quoted mockingly.

'Says who?'

'This magazine article in *Glamour*: "My Quick Fix and Why I'll Never Look Back", by "loved-up Gemma from Chiswick". And these searches I'm pulling up now are all radiating praise for it. According to this, SpeedDater UK has hitherto been the most successful brand, but it seems Fast Love is creeping up slowly, poised to take over as the number one. And, as Josh says, I guess that's where we come in.'

'So . . . Just how speedy are the dates? And how many do you get in one night?'

Looking over his notes, Duncan surmised, 'Well, Fast

Love offers three minutes, which is the standard – that's what you get with SpeedDater too. Generally, you get about twenty-five to thirty "dates" per night. Some offer more or less, but Fast Love insists that twenty-three is the perfect amount; after extensive research has confirmed this as the optimum number. Any less and people feel short-changed, any more and the repetition just gets too much to bear!'

'If you ask me, I'd be bored out of my brains after two. But hey, what a bargain. A quid per bloke.'

Duncan picked up Amelie's compact from the desk and began scrunching up his messy crop of blond hair, as though assessing his appearance for its monetary value. 'I'm worth more than a quid, surely?' he jested.

'Well, at that price, Duncan, you would be an absolute steal.'

As the words left Amelie's lips she realised that despite her tone, there was an element of truth to her words. Duncan *was* very good-looking, with his warm smile, well-toned body (through no fault of his own) and chiselled features rivalling even the great Jude Law, but, for reasons his female friends could not fathom, Duncan had never been much of a success with The Ladies. When it came to approaching women, he was invariably held back by the twin evils of inertia and shyness. It was a shame – as all his female friends frequently informed him – he would make someone out there a fabulously lovely boyfriend if he only made the effort to overcome his self-consciousness.

Despite having been good friends and workmates ever since college Freshers' Week, and even though all their friends thought they would make the perfect couple,

Amelie had always said that she and Duncan would never be anything more; that the spark between them had only ever been an intellectual one. Well, unless you counted the in-house firework displays that were sometimes generated by their differences in personality. Strangely, it was these differences between them that glued them together so tightly as a team, and gave their campaigns a creative edge over all the other teams. Because their work was invariably the end product of a ferocious argument of some sort, the resulting idea would always have at its core a dynamic; a spark that would never go out. So much so that the other teams in the agency had learned by now to start getting worried if they heard yelling from their corner. It meant that some 'shit-hot' work was about to be generated from Team Amelie and Duncan.

Amelie, blessed with alarming levels of creative intelligence, also had the relentlessly enquiring mind of a small child. Known to her friends as a loveable but endlessly scatty dreamer, she nevertheless had an indomitable mind that ran according to its own timetable. Duncan would often slope in casually to work at 10 a.m. to find her still at her desk, wide-eyed and caffeinated, having spent the whole night with an IDEA – pushing it as far as it could possibly go. 'It couldn't wait?' he would always ask. And she would always give the same bemused smile.

Not that Duncan wasn't as excited by the ideas as she was – he just believed there was a time and a place for work. For Amelie, ideas also had a time and a place: anywhere (the tube, a nightclub toilet); anytime, (5 a.m. or three minutes before a pitch); anyhow (written in lipstick on the back of a concert ticket stub or a Boots receipt). It was this eccentricity in her that her friends had grown to love (and occasionally hate). Ideas were the embryo of their winning campaigns and, to Amelie, they took precedence over everything – and, sadly, everyone. This was one of the factors that had led to her mounting years of contented singledom. Although she was sociable and outgoing, her last priority when it came to fitting everything in was men.

Amelie jumped. Her Mac was pinging at her to indicate new mail:

Date: 3 January 2005, 10.20
Sender: CWilson@MarshallHopkins.co.uk
To: Holden.Amelie@LGMKLondon.com
Subject: Gay Paris!

Hello, lovely, how is Monday morning treating you?

Just a quickie to let you know that I'm back from Paris. Dan and I had the most perfect, blissfully romantic weekend. We stayed in a lush hotel overlooking the Seine, strolled down the Champs Elysee's, climbed the tower . . . It was amazing . . . Just really great, so much to tell you! . . . Actually, I don't quite know how to put this . . . we even got round to approaching the subject of . . . the 'M' word!!!

Anyway, have to fly but tell you all about it when I see you xxx

Date: 3 January 2005, 10.28
Sender: Holden.Amelie@LGMKLondon.com
To: CWilson@MarshallHopkins.co.uk
Subject: RE: Gay Paris!

Hi, babe, glad you had a great time! I've worked all weekend. Again.

A xxx

P.S. 'M word': Motorbikes . . . Moving house . . . Maltesers? You can't mean, you surely don't mean, Marriage. DO you?

Date: 3 January 2005, 10.30
Sender: CWilson@MarshallHopkins.co.uk
To: Holden.Amelie@LGMKLondon.com
Subject: RE: RE: Gay Paris!

Well . . . you know . . . He didn't exactly come out and say it . . . I think he is treading somewhat carefully. But, let's just say that after this weekend, I think he really might be on the verge of proposing! Isn't that the most maddest exciting thing!

Amelie, trying hard not to choke on her Innocent vanilla thickie, hastily clicked reply and began typing.

Date: 3 January 2005, 10.32
Sender: Holden.Amelie@LGMKLondon.com
To: CWilson@MarshallHopkins.co.uk
Subject: ???&*)%$£$?????

Claire??

Claire. Paris has damaged you in some way, done funny things to your head, yes?

Amelie paused for breath, tapping her fingers nervously on the desk while she fought to think of a more sensitive way to phrase things.

It's what . . . 10.30 . . . on a Monday morning and you come out with this?

What on earth has happened to your old saying that marriage is an anachronistic farce? A relic from the times when it was all patriarchy, knitting and housework . . . when women had no identity outside that of their husbands . . . (they were your words, lady, not mine!!).

This is a wind-up, no?

A few minutes later Claire replied.

Date: 3 January 2005, 10.38
Sender: CWilson@MarshallHopkins.co.uk
To: Holden.Amelie@LGMKLondon.com
Subject: RE: RE: Gay Paris!

Thanks for the encouragement, Miss Havisham.

Nothing has happened yet, OK? But I'm just saying it might be on the horizon, that's all. It's not before time, though . . . I've just turned twenty-seven . . . and you know what they say about 'the timetable'. Can you not – even slightly – hear your own biological clock? I can, and you know what? It's ticking like there's no tomorrow.

This last reply was received by Amelie with rising irritation. 'Biological clock, my arse,' she scoffed, lighting up a cigarette.

But somehow, as she leaned back in her chair and looked out of the window at all the people strolling and lazing around Soho Square in the wintry sunshine, it suddenly seemed to her that an increasing proportion of those who sat laughing together over their lattes and panini were in fact couples laughing over lattes and panini. Successful, beautiful couples in their late twenties. Quite despite herself, Amelie began to wonder how long it had actually been since she'd been in a relationship that wasn't entirely dysfunctional. At the same time, but much further into the recesses of her unconscious mind, a tiny thought flickered into existence. Remembering that her twenty-seventh birthday was creeping up in just under two months, this little thought began to hit upon the idea that perhaps Amelie's oldest friend might have a point.

*

'Well, now that the vodka campaign's finally underway, we can get cracking on this ridiculous Fast Love brief,' Amelie said to Duncan a day later. 'What's say we go for a walk and grab a drink in the long wait for inspiration?'

'That's the best idea you've had in ages,' he said cheerfully, grabbing his denim jacket. 'Meeting Room 4?'

Minutes later they were leaning back on a large brown sofa in The Nellie, the pub just round the corner from LGMK. Being so close to the agency, The Nellie was patronised regularly by most LGMK staff. At any given moment, in any given day, you could expect to find at least one of the hundred staff sitting in the lively Nellie.

Amelie took a large sip of her pint, and her cool blue eyes darted over the creative brief for the twentieth time that day.

' "What is the most important thing that you want this ad to say?" ' she read aloud. Then, in a mocking tone, she read on, ' "That being lonely is no longer an option." '

After a lengthy pause, and a long pull on her cigarette, Amelie commented, 'Surely that's a touch ambiguous . . . are they saying that in today's world it is no longer possible to be single? Or that it's too undesirable an option?'

'Neither. I think it means that with Fast Love being so successful, so unprecedentedly brilliant, that, well . . . it's now no longer *necessary* to be alone. Like . . . anyone and everyone can find their other half to settle down with if they really want.'

Amelie made a retching sound.

Duncan laughed at this. 'You, the eternal cynic, and me, the unluckiest in love . . . Christ, with our combined track record there's no chance of us coming up with a decent angle on this campaign. It's a bit of a joke really.'

'Yeah, maybe we should just sit this one out or something? I mean, I don't even buy into the basic idea of marriage anyway. The rule that you have to find one perfect person to settle down with for ever, in blissful harmony . . . It's all a fairytale. It's not reality.'

She took a big gulp of beer and looked closely at Duncan. 'I mean, just look at my parents. Between them they've had more affairs and flings than they've had weddings. And now my mum, having got married for the third time, totally certain that she'd finally met Mr Right, is discovering that he's just another Mr Wrong, and it's probably not going to work out, yet again . . .' Amelie stopped and looked out of the window for a second. 'I mean, what on earth is so wrong with just being your own person until the end of your days? At least then you won't get hurt or screwed over or humiliated . . .'

'I know,' replied Duncan, his blue eyes thoughtful. 'I hear what you're saying, but part of me still thinks maybe you or I just haven't met the right person yet.'

'Hmmm. I'll believe that when I see it. Anyway,' she said, looking at her watch, 'it's wedges o'clock . . . I'm going to get some, do you want to share them with me?' And with that she leaped up to go and order a large plate of them from the bar.

On her way back to the sofa she considered her last point again, thinking back to her last – and only – long relationship. 'I think Jack was the man for me, if ever there was one. Shame he had other ideas though,' she said as she sat back down on the sofa.

There it was, the stabbing pain to remind her of the

humiliation she had felt three years ago, almost to the day. Coming home early from work with the flu, she had had the misfortune to discover Jack – her best friend and only love – in a tacky, compromising situation with a girl called Penny. Penny, as Amelie later discovered, was a high-flying and beautiful colleague from his law firm, who, Amelie gathered, flaunted her ambition and voluptuousness in equal measure in order to get what she wanted. Prior to Amelie's discovery, she and Jack had been together for three perfect years (in her eyes), and had been living together for one. Although the wound left by this infidelity was a substantial one for Amelie, she now felt anger more than anything else. Anger at how clichéd a scenario it had been. She also couldn't help but wonder why he couldn't at least have had the decency to cheat on her with someone more interesting or dynamic. They knew so many nice, charismatic, talented girls – any one of whom would have been suitable. Anyone but his painfully dull legal-eagle partner. In a strange sort of way, it was the humdrumness of Jack's taste, the sheer lack of imagination behind his infidelity, which, even three years after the event, still left an imprint of humiliation.

'Anyway,' Duncan began, trying for Amelie's sake to steer the conversation away from the potentially maudlin direction it was going. 'At least with speed-dating it's not *only* about looking for your future spouse – it's also about finding someone to go out and have a laugh with. Well, so it seems anyway – not that I've ever tried it. But seriously, maybe that is something to think about for our strategy . . . steer away from it being about just marriage, and portray it in a more lighthearted way somehow. Any ideas?'

Just then the doors to the pub flung open, and a huge shriek of laughter came wafting towards them. Amelie and Duncan turned to see Joshua Grant coming through the doors to the pub, with his new PA hanging off his arm. A petite and pretty blonde named Fleur Parker-Jones, who had recently been promoted from the role of timid agency receptionist to the more demanding, hands-on role of being Josh's PA.

As Duncan and Amelie considered Fleur's lurid pink mini-skirt and matching nail varnish in incredulity, they both felt the phrase '80s time warp' rising to the surface of their minds. While biting into a sour-cream-drenched potato wedge, Amelie watched Fleur curiously, thinking that the recent change in her career appeared to have had a noticeable effect on her outlook, both in terms of her fashion sense – which had now become much more glamorous than before – and her overall demeanour, which was now much less humble and muted than it had been. Amelie lit up a cigarette, her eyes following Josh and Fleur to the bar. Yet another man who seemed incapable of existing outside the realm of clichés, she surmised, noting that Josh already seemed to be leading his new PA a merry dance, apparently entranced by her new-fangled clothes and power-hungry behaviour.

'Oh, how I miss Jana. Lovely, inspirational Jana, and her wonderful exotic earrings,' Amelie thought aloud, lamenting the shockingly sudden departure last year of their previous creative director, Jana Morris.

'I know,' agreed Duncan mournfully. 'I wonder how she's getting on.'

After a brief silence, and a moment spent watching Josh perform one of his trademark surfer grins for Fleur, Amelie sat firmly upright. 'Anyway. Sod him. Let's get our brains together and in gear: love, romance . . . how do we bottle it and sell it in a winning campaign?'

Hours later, Amelie and Duncan emerged from the pub looking deflated; each carrying large jotter-pads bearing scribbles and mind-maps under their arms; the result of a reasonably productive afternoon's brainstorming.

'Well, it's a starting point, at any rate,' Duncan declared optimistically.

'Yeah, I guess,' agreed Amelie on the walk back to the office. 'I'm not altogether convinced it's got what it takes, though . . .' she said, as they walked through the large glass sliding doors to the interior of LGMK, their footsteps gliding over the letters *We think, therefore you buy* – the agency's own lovingly pretentious motto which was engraved into the floor panels.

'You never are. I still think you should consider my idea, though,' Duncan said, pressing the button to call the lift, and leaning against the wall.

'No way. Over my dead body. Not in a million.'

'But – just think about it!' The lift opened and they stepped inside.

'I. Am. Not. Going. Speed. Dating.' Amelie hit the button for floor five, and the lift began its ascent. Looking at their reflections in the lift mirror, Amelie caught Duncan's eyes and added firmly, 'No frigging way, Duncan. Not for all the tea in China or for all the ads in Cannes. I don't care how speedy it is, it would still last an eternity as far as I'm concerned.'

The lift doors opened, and the pair stepped out and began walking to their office.

'But!' yelled Duncan.

'NO!'

'But Bill Bernbach said—'

'I know what he said!' shouted Amelie, painfully aware that they could now probably be seen and heard by most of the creative department.

'I don't see that we have any choice, Amelie,' said Duncan as they sat down at their desks. He looked over at the blank A3 pages on her desk. 'I mean, have you got any actual ideas that we could really imagine running?'

'Just give me a day or so . . . I know I can come up with something, OK?! Leave it with me.'

'And if you don't? What then?'

'Look, Duncan, if you want to find a girlfriend, then go by yourself. There's no way I'm lowering myself to that glorified, institutionalised meat market! At least don't insult my intelligence by dressing it up as "research" just so I can tag along and make you look less desperate!'

At this Duncan looked genuinely dented. 'That was below the belt. You can be a real bitch sometimes.' Then he stormed away, leaving Amelie shocked at the levels her own temper was capable of ascending to, and wishing she could retract what she'd just said.

'Shit,' she said, heading to the pool room and lighting a cigarette. 'Bollocks,' she told herself, thinking about how she seemed to be on a roll, successfully annoying two of her friends in one week, without even trying. She slumped down on to a sofa and inhaled deeply on her cigarette, wondering if maybe there was something wrong with her. Then, on the table in front of her, she noticed this week's issue of *Campaign*. She fought with herself, mustering all her willpower not to pick it up, to ignore what the industry rag had to spout about this week. It was no use. She had to see what brilliant new ads were being featured. Had to see what ideas the creatives in the top ten agencies were churning out. Looking either side of her and clasping the magazine with both hands, she began leafing through it. She'd only got to page two when something caught her eye. To her astonishment, there, at the centre of the page, was a glossy, self-consciously artistic photograph of Joshua Grant, leaning against one of the immaculate white pillars in the LGMK reception. The grin he wore was a confident, happy one; his dark hair was its usual brand of slick scruffiness. Much as it pained her, she had to admit that the photo did him justice – he looked incredibly young. In fact, he *was* incredibly young to be taking over as creative director from a woman in her late forties. In that photo he didn't look a day older than twenty-nine. Looking more closely, she supposed the photo even made him look attractive, if you liked that sort of thing. Deep brown eyes, excessively suntanned, muscly, tall – the obvious surfer-type qualities.

She drank in the headline and cringed. 'Granting All Their Wishes,' it read in big black bold impact type. She read on, her heart in her throat. The article told of how Josh had been head-hunted by the executive board at the financially troubled LGMK, and was instantly dubbed as the man who would save the day, replacing the previous CD Jana Morris who had – much to her humiliation and Amelie's utter dismay – been invited to leave. The article went on to liberally sing Joshua Grant's praises. It told of how he had been a legendary force back in Sydney, breaking more records and winning more creative awards than any of his antipodean contemporaries. Amelie scrolled down, her stomach constricting as she read about how Josh already had in mind many bold new 'Initiatives' and 'Structural Improvements' to set into place in his new post. Oh God – that was management-speak for sacking people, wasn't it? Surely everyone knew that? Feeling even more anxious than before, Amelie realised that her job really could be in serious jeopardy now that this new creative director had arrived. Suddenly the pressure to think of something brilliant for the Fast Love brief was greater than ever.

Right, that's it. I'm cancelling my life for the next four weeks, she decided, opening her bag and reaching for her diary. She flicked through and started to cross out social events here and there. Feeling a wave of guilt, she left in a few for now and snapped the book shut. Sensing lights being shut off around the agency, she realised that she was one of the last people left in the building – again. OK, time to go, she reasoned with herself. She picked up her bag, wrapped her scarf tightly around her, and walked out of the building.

As Amelie stepped on to the pavement in Soho Square and shuffled her feet along, she noticed that the raindrops that had been drizzling over London earlier that day had since turned into a more menacing breed of hail, and there was now a harsh wind in the air. Amelie passed a *Big Issue* seller on her left – the same old man who said hello to her every single morning, without fail. She reached into her pocket and gave him a pound coin and two twenty-pence pieces.

'I don't have time to read it, but here's the money anyway.'

'Big pitch coming up?' the man asked, taking the coins.

Amelie stopped, stunned at his interest, and his intuition. 'Yes . . . actually. For some reason I get the feeling it's going to be one of the biggest pitches of my life.'

Diary of a Reluctant SpeedDater

Work, Friday 7 January, 3 p.m.

Dear Diary,

Hello. So, it's been a while since I've done this . . . you might need to just bear with me a little.

 The thing is this: am being forced against my will to go speed-dating. Something I'd never normally do, not even in my worst, most devilishly psychedelic nightmares. But circumstances are desperate – have contracted severe copywriter's block from somewhere and the Fast Love pitch is in four weeks – so this seems the only thing to do to try and save mine and Duncan's careers from crash-landing.

 Originally I thought it might help us consolidate our research if we took notes while we went along. But then I got to thinking how long it's been since I last kept a diary. I always used to write in one as a little girl, and then, like most girls, I got distracted when real, grown-up life came knocking, and I couldn't keep up with it. Always meant to pick it up again, but then the longer I left it, the harder it got to remember what I'd been up to. Eventually it was abandoned, for which I've always felt a little guilty. So, happy days, here I am again, thirteen years on. Quite a bit's happened but I guess you'll catch up soon enough.

Now, in my humble opinion, speed-dating seems like a terrifyingly crass and unromantic thing to do. Nevertheless, Duncan's convinced there has to be something good about it all – he says it's just like with any other brief for an ad, we have to keep researching the 'product' until we find the benefit, and then we can make an ad out of whatever that is. It's like an old saying by that ad agency WCRS . . . 'Interrogate the product until it confesses'. Total ad-drivel, I know, but there is a certain element of truth in it. So, this diary is going to record and document every step of our 'interrogation'. God help us.

Home, Friday 7 January, 6 p.m.

OK. Just about to go and sell my dignity to the devil and go speed-dating for the first, and hopefully last, time. Luckily Sally, a girl from work who has actually been before, is coming with us. Not sure how to put this – she is coming again out of a quite unironic belief that she might find a guy she likes? In fact, it was she who encouraged me that I might not *have the worst night of my life. Although I'm still convinced it will be hell on earth. Why exactly, it's hard to say. But I know my cynicism has something to do with the whole thing being vaguely reminiscent of school. The*

*institutional way the whole event seems to be organised – it
makes you feel as though you can't organise your love life by
yourself, so you have to resort to getting figures of authority
to do it. I'm still feeling tickled by the confirmation email I
received,* which boldly states that 'Registration starts at
6.30 p.m. Dating starts promptly at 7 p.m.' *And* 'We do try
to include latecomers, but you will not normally be able to
join until after the first break and may miss up to ten dates.'
*Oh, and apparently smoking is prohibited at all times
during the dates! But you are allowed to smoke during the
breaks, thank the Lord.*

*Feel slightly nauseous just thinking about how regi-
mental it all sounds. I know I'm going to hate it. Know I'm
going to detest the – oh shit, that's the bell, Sally is here.
More later.*

The ladies', All Bar One, Friday 7 January, 6.40 p.m.

And they say romance is dead?

*Well 'they' knew what they were talking about. Just had
a quick look around before dashing to the loo to gather my
thoughts. There's already so much to say . . .*

*Just to recap, I arrived here a few minutes ago, to a
dauntingly long queue of overdressed women lined up
along the Charing Cross Road. First impressions as I
walked up the road: male candidates (of which there were
far fewer) seemed an unholy mixture of unlikely desper-
adoes, while by contrast the female constituent appeared
worryingly normal. Stylish, accomplished, attractive. So
my suspicions were proving themselves correct before I'd
even walked through the door: looking around at the sea of
Ben Sherman shirts and sun visors in winter, I knew then*

that romance most certainly was dead, taking with it the archaic idea that women were once able to sit back and be wooed charmingly or courted chivalrously by a range of eligible suitors. I realised then that things now work a little differently. So, with my heart sinking and my teeth gritted, I thought of how much I wanted to keep my job, wanted to murder Duncan for not being there yet, and joined the queue.

Once inside, we were told to sit and wait like a diligent tribe of circus freaks, as they called us up one by one to receive our scorecards and name badges. Name badges. As we waited we had time to examine with one eye our hilarious instruction sheet, and with the other the men on offer – who could best be described as an army of militant defenders of the land that style forgot. Am I being too harsh? OK, so maybe I am, but I've decided my game plan for the purposes of this research is to start off as cynical as possible and see where it takes me . . . Oh, can hear queue forming outside the loo, must go.

Temporary cattle-storage area, All Bar One, 7.10 p.m.

Just sitting on a sofa with Duncan and Sally; each of us clasping our essential speed-dating tools in our hands: crappy branded Biro, badge and scorecard. We're all dying to know what's going to happen next, having been waiting here for an age while they get the dating room ready. All fifty of us. Many Fast Lovers are having to stand as there are no seats left, and it's getting increasingly crowded. It's almost approaching tube-during-rush-hour-style capacity – I wonder, did they plan it that way, just to make us start interacting, getting close with each other, prior to the

*official start time? Either way it's terrible. Like lining up
for an interview, only ten times worse, because not only are
you waiting with the competition; you are also sitting
amidst the interview panel. All circulating together before
the formalities commence. So much for the prompt start at
7 p.m. – looks like we're running quite late.*

*Still, at least it gives me time to jot some things down.
Looking at the info sheet, there is so much to find humour
in, I don't know where to begin. It is, I'm pretty sure,
written without a trace of irony – even the lines about such
a thing as speed-dating etiquette: '*Please treat every date
with respect and don't mark your scorecard until the end of
each date.*'*

*It's funny; everyone is already checking everyone out. The
lads are looking churlishly around at all the beautiful girls in
the room, and you can even see them noting down people's
numbers from their name badges – so they can try and get a
head start on the ones they like. Well, they do have to work
harder, the boys – poor mites. Apparently us girls get to sit
comfortably at the same separate tables all night, while the
lads rotate around us every three minutes. So, as Duncan
quite rightly asked, how on earth are the men supposed to
write out their scorecard 'comments' on each girl without
them seeing? Do they do it while they are walking along to
the next table? That's not going to give them long – each
table is an inch away from the next! Or do they do it once
they've sat down with their new date? Either way, it seems
painfully insensitive and embarrassing if you ask me. No
way is anyone getting a head start on me – I refuse to wear
my name badge until it's absolutely necessary.*

*Duncan's thrilled. We've just informed him that he is
easily the best-looking male here. That's not saying much but*

*he thinks it's great. He's joking that he will have so many
ticks and matches that after tonight the only way to cope
with the post-speed-date administration of them all will be
for him to construct some kind of fantasy group email:*

Subject: Congrats! You picked Duncan

Hi, girls, when's good for you? Please circle dates that
suit you and I'll see you soon!

*Yes, Duncan, whatever. Anyway, we're gradually learning
all the rules and apparently if you don't find any 'ticks' by
the end of the night (you can tick any of three choices – yes,
no, or 'maybe a friend'), you can get a free go next time. This
cracks me up because surely there is an inherent risk here
that you might become addicted and find yourself becoming
a Serial SpeedDater? It doesn't bear thinking about.*

*Oh – the Fast Love chiefs have just said to us that the
reason for all this delay is that they're running into some
technical difficulty. Apparently Camilla, our host for
tonight, has mislaid the Fast Love bell (with which they
signal the start and finish of every single date) and is
running around trying to find it as they can't possibly start
without it. It all sounds good to me; maybe we won't have
time for all the dates now? Either way I'm off for a sneaky
cigarette before the festivities begin.*

Starbucks opp. All Bar One, 9 p.m.

*On much-deserved break. Had to get out of the building so
I could have a breather and reassess. Normally hate
Starbucks but it was the first thing I saw as I came rushing*

out of All Bar One for some air and a cigarette, and it suddenly seemed like the most incredibly welcoming refuge to me after the last hour and a half – ninety minutes of my life which, lamentably, I'll never get back. Anyway, I don't have much time off now, fifteen mins or so, but I decided rather than spend the break sitting among all the other Fast Lovers, I'd creep away and refuel myself in terms of caffeine and sanity.

To be sure, my fears were fully justified: this is Hell On Earth. In fact, it's whole dimensions worse than I thought it could have been.

To illustrate. You know those regrettable times when sleazy men approach you in bars or clubs and are misguided enough to think that you want them to talk to you? The kind you try your damnedest to avoid, and pray they will get the message and go away, often resulting in a charade of either lesbianism or matrimony? Well, take one of those guys and sit him opposite you on a teeny tiny rickety crêpe-paper-covered table with irritating white flaps, which get in the way whenever you move your arms. And make him one of the lesser-end-of-average-looking specimens. But – and this is the worst part of all – furnish him with the belief that you actually want him to be there for a whole three minutes. You want him to probe you deeply with irritatingly mundane questions – in fact, he knows you paid good money to have him do so. And he loves it.

The worst offenders are those who try to break the monotony of the questions by inventing quirky 'I'm wacky, I'm zany' alternatives. My favourites so far include, 'If you were a vegetable, what would you be?' Closely followed by, 'What type of nut would you be?' And, only thirty seconds in, which I thought was terribly restrained, 'What's your favourite sexual fantasy?' Bless them, though – they are just following the 'speed-dating tips' on the scorecard. They've obviously all done their homework: 'It's a good idea to have a few questions up your sleeve in case you run out of things to say. But it's a very bad idea to have a scripted list of questions!'

In my own attempt to break the monotony of the evening, I've begun to masquerade as a variety of different Amelies. I've been everything from a jeweller in Weston-Super-Mare (on temporary leave when questioned), a teacher of A-Level politics and sociology (as soon as it left my mouth I prayed for the bell before a question about current affairs or politics suddenly arose), and finally a firewoman from Essex who grew up on a Kibbutz. Note to self: people will believe anything in three minutes.

I've no idea where these fictional vocations came from, but for some reason I felt genuinely afraid that my brain cells were going to pack up their stuff and leave me if I didn't at least try and create some sort of entertainment out of the situation – however childish. Call me dreadfully impatient, but I just have no inclination to tell the same true stories about myself twenty-three times over in one evening. I'm actually having more fun inventing alternate Amelies. You know, the Me that I might have been, had I made different choices, like if my life was one of those Choose Your Own Adventure books. Five minutes ago I was the lawyer that I once wanted to be. Fortunately, Amelie the Human Rights Lawyer was saying that she was disillusioned by the Bar, that she wanted to do something more creative, so as it happens I think I made the right choice in the end. And half an hour ago I was the (prima) ballerina my mother always wanted me to be, which was sweet. I know it's childish, but it's also escapism of the best kind ... Every three minutes you can pitch yourself as someone totally different ... What could be more liberating? Without this ability to play Let's Pretend, I think I might have gone crazy by now – these events certainly aren't for people who bore easily. Oh, that's my phone ringing. Arse, it's Duncan – time to go and face the final round in this farcical game. Right, more later.

Propping up the bar, 10 p.m.

I'm a copywriter ... get me out of here!

Lost my voice. Lost my will to live. Lost all faith in humanity. Am sitting on a bar stool listening to Aretha, at the end of the most repetitive night I've ever had. Met no 'ticks'. Not even close. Not that I was expecting to. OK – some were bearable. Slightly. I suppose there were some men here who it might have been possible to click with, were we in circumstances less akin to that of a school disco. I guess Number 13 seemed like someone you might get on with, were he not obviously feeling so under pressure to give his best performance in the time given.

In fact, looking back, Number 6 was really quite fit; I have to confess that part of me was slightly looking forward to my turn with him. But due to some strange quirk in the rotating pattern he never actually got round to my table. He's over there now, though, being 'followed up'. However attractive he is, I'm certainly not about to go and join the cluster of cowboy-booted women who are now congregating around him. No, I'm perfectly content sitting on a bar stool with a vodka and orange for company, getting all this down and listening to 'Get Into the Groove'.

Oddly, Duncan and Sally really do seem to have got something out of their experiences this evening. They each gave a generous six ticks, and I think they've gone off to chase them up now, running around the room with all the other Fast Lovers. I can't help being genuinely baffled that two attractive, successful, intelligent friends of mine should be so drawn into this game. Why do I hate it so much? Is there someth—

Amelie jumped as she felt her hair being tugged, and Sally's voice was suddenly ringing shrilly in her ears, 'Amelie Holden – you sad bastard! Stop scribbling now, this instant, and come and join us.'

'Yeah,' came Duncan's equally accusing voice, 'if you're not going to chase up your ticks, at least come and dance! Anyway, isn't this one of your favourite songs?'

Amelie closed her diary, looked at them, and smiled apologetically. 'Sorry, guys, I'm just not feeling it. I'm just finding all this a bit too . . . weird? And anyway, I'm in a flow just now – I've got loads of material down . . . I'm sure somewhere in this we'll have some great ideas for the campaign.'

Duncan shook his head, put down his pint, and looked at Amelie quizzically. 'Am, it's like, ten o'clock on a Friday night. So you've made a few notes. Great. Smashing. Well done. Can't you call it a day now and just enjoy yourself?'

Amelie smiled affectionately at Duncan, wondering how he could be enjoying himself at this bizarrely reconstituted meat market. 'I'm glad you're enjoying it, but I'm just perfectly content sitting here,' she said, adding, 'I'm getting all I need from here.'

'What do you mean, all you need?' asked Sally, 'You're a nutter. How much can there possibly be to write about?' Suddenly noticing that sexy Number 6 had just been released from the octopus-arms of Number 14, she added, 'Um, sorry, I've got to go over there. See you later, hun.' And she dashed away towards the dance floor, striving to make contact with Munky, the greasy-haired biker from Rickmansworth.

Duncan watched Sally walk away towards Number 6, and then looked back to Amelie. 'Come on, Am, just come and circulate a bit. Stop being such a sad geek.'

Amelie picked up her pen again, opened her diary, and said firmly, 'OK, in a bit. Let me just finish this page.'

All Bar One. Still. 10.20 p.m.

What do they all see in this speed-dating merry-go-round that I don't? Seriously worried now. How on earth are we going to sell this? Who is the market?? There is no positive USP as far as I can see. Maybe I'm just not seeing it in the right way, but at this moment in time speed-dating seems to be a toss-up between mind-numbingly repetitive and soul-destroyingly unromantic. If I may, let me rewrite the brief's proposition:

Being lonely has never looked better.

Home (hurrah!), Friday 7 January, Midnight

Thank the Lord, am finally home. Truly cannot believe I made it through all twenty-three dates. And I've now entirely lost my voice, so loud did I have to scream to be heard above the fifty million dates that were all going off at once. Fast Love were clearly milking the room-booking for all it was worth. After waiting for ages in the regular bar area, we were eventually seated in a tiny back room, where there was actually so little space between you and the next couple, it's a wonder anyone could hear themselves think, let alone speak. Between that and the perpetually loud cries of the school bell every three minutes, it's a wonder anyone's communicative faculties are still intact. Oh well, at least I can blame/claim it all on research.

Meant to say, the most haunting moment of the whole night came when Camilla (the teacher-like lady in charge) first rang her school-playground-style bell. Thinking back to the first time we heard the strangely nostalgic sound of the ringing, I remember being instantly swept away, as though teleported, back to some distant place in my youth. As the bell began to ring, my hair was suddenly in pigtails as I, nine years old again, was running around the school playground as fast as I could . . . Running away from Asif, the class fat boy who was pursuing me with his plump kisses. I ran and ran until the lucky moment when the deafeningly loud school bell began to ring back and forth, over and over, penetrating right through my ears, yet saving me from this fate worse than death. Landing back in real time, face to face with a stockbroker named Aswad, I realised with a smile that, seventeen years on, the same bell was ushering in what was, in effect, only a very slightly more mature brand of Kiss-chase.

Kitchen, 4 a.m.

Can't sleep, and since I forgot to eat dinner I've had to break into emergency Ben & Jerry's stash. Was trying in vain to get to sleep just now, but the memories of Fast Love kept spinning round my mind on a loop and keeping me awake. It really was such a surreal evening. Seems a cop-out to use that word as that's the one word which got thrown around in almost every 'date'. But for me it was surreal to the point of disturbing – like it was all a big, terrible comment on the state of romance today. What if true romance really is dead? What if the idea of meeting someone naturally, through chance or fate is just disappearing into an archaic dream, a relic of times past? I think that's the reason I'm so sceptical of all this – because deep down I really do find the idea of speed-dating completely at odds with the essence of what love should be about.

I'm taking it too much to heart. Maybe I'm being too highly strung, being too much of a purist about it, but I can't help wondering, what would Jane Austen say if she were to witness a night like I just have?

A gay friend of mine once told me something which is, lights out, the most romantic true story I've heard this decade. The story of how he and his partner first got together five years ago. Sam – he's one of the account planners in the agency – got terribly drunk one night and told me the story. It's short and sweet – you might not think it's all that romantic, in a traditional sense, but it moved me at the time.

Sam was sitting waiting at a bus stop at about three in the morning one Saturday. He noticed a guy come up to him and sit nearby. A total stranger, but one he unconsciously noted as rather attractive. There was no one else around, and after a few seconds they made eye contact, exchanging shy smiles.

'My name's Dave and I live five minutes away.'

To which the only possible reply, in Sam's shoes, could've

been, 'My name's Sam and I live bloody miles away. Let's go to your place.'

Five years later and the rest is history. Today he's the love of his life, and they are the sweetest couple I know. I even went to the wedding. I guess Dave and Sam prove that sometimes speed-dating can happen naturally, that sometimes you don't even need three minutes.

Work, Monday 10 January, 11 a.m.

So today I had one of those all-too-common tube incidents. The kind where you, in your over-tired or slightly drunken haze, crucially misjudge the amount of space by the tube door, and, conscious of the fact that you are already running late, decide erroneously that waiting one minute for the next train is unthinkable. Far better to clamber on and insert yourself into the thing that looked like a space and then spend the next twenty minutes entirely regretting it. Today was one of those. As the doors closed around me, I realised that the two overweight, middle-aged men I was sandwiched in between were now far less comfortable. And space and oxygen now being as limited as they were, I had no option but to hold my head down, squeeze myself and my baggage in, try to feel as small as possible, and stare at the floor. Realising by this point it was too late to undo the error. Clearly, clearly, there was not enough room for me. If only the doors would reopen and expel me back on to the platform, like some failed experiment and a vital deterrent to any other perspectively challenged latecomers. There wasn't even space for me to hang on to the rail, as that would have meant my stretching out my arms in some kind of loving embrace or passionate declaration with this total *stranger who was no doubt cursing me inside. So instead I had to hold my head down, like some shamed schoolgirl, and feebly press my hands against the carriage door in an attempt to steady myself from the jolts and jars that chugged us bleakly through the tunnel.*

But it reminded me of something I used to think about in my much more idealistic and naïve days. I liked to think that one day I would find my future man just sitting opposite me on a tube carriage. And we would both just know, through some random but amazing act of serendipity. Like in Sliding Doors, *or* Before Sunrise, *or something . . .*

I once stumbled across this ad in Time Out *for these lovely walking tours you can do, where they state the specific carriage of a specific train at a specific time and destination. So that everyone meets, total strangers before they get on, and they all go walking around the rolling hills of Buckinghamshire – Gerrard's Cross or somewhere like that. Maybe it'd be fun to do something similar with random singles . . . Say, people get on to a tube carriage wearing some kind of symbol which indicates they are single. You could call it Tube Dates! Or, on second thoughts, maybe that's just freaky and weird. But I'm starting to think that you can't get much freakier or more weird than sitting down at a table for three minutes, strangers, face to face; two talking CVs, sizing each other up. Sell me yourself in three minutes. Why should I want you above that girl over there? What's your Unique Selling Point? The skill of the three-minute pitch distilled into the world of romance. I don't think I'm ever going to like it . . . but, maybe it's just a microcosm of life and love in general. Aren't we all just pitching to one another all the time about why we should be wanted, why we are worthy of being adored? We're all just products competing against a crowded market, striving for the best strategy, the best* creative.

But at least with dating the normal way (slow-dating?), you get to delve a bit deeper than you can in three minutes. When you 'speed up', it does all come down to the presentation in the end. That's what speed-dating's all about, I guess. The art of the three-minute pitch. Which I was never very good at.

Winging It

A couple of days later, Amelie was at her desk, listening to the loud drum 'n' bass music that was pumping down the corridor from the studio. She was concentrating hard on dodging the rugby ball which kept flying past her and threatening to thwack her around the head. Turning to face Duncan and Max just as it went skimming past her head for the third time, narrowly avoiding crashing into her screen, she shot mock-angry eyes back at them both. They carried on with their game, oblivious. Amelie continued scribbling ideas down on her pad, her brain cells fighting against the cacophony of agency sounds as she prayed naïvely to the God of Concentration. For a happy moment there was a brief respite in the rhythm of the rugby throwing, and Amelie hoped for a moment that they might have finished. But this hope was in vain – Amelie soon saw that the reason they had stopped was to let Fleur Parker-Jones slide past them into the open-plan office. Amelie looked up to see Fleur standing in front of her, straightening out her already sleek blonde mane and clearing her throat officiously. If there had been a door, she would have knocked on it loudly and self-importantly.

'Yes?' called Amelie, continuing to work on her highly important doodle while she spoke.

Fleur leaned against the wall and inspected her fuchsia-pink nails. 'I see you finally managed to drag yourselves back from Café Balans.'

'Not that it's of any consequence to you, but we were actually working in there. Less interruptions, or something . . .' came Amelie's caustic response.

Fleur's face was a picture of tranquillity. 'No, it's not of any real interest to me,' she said calmly, 'I'm just – well, you know, since being promoted and everything, I can't help worrying about poor Josh, stuck waiting on all these urgent briefs, working his arse off while you creative geniuses swan about . . .'

'It's worth noting, Fleur, that some of this agency's best work owes its existence to the breakfast bagels in Café Balans,' said Amelie slowly. 'Dunc and I swear by our Monday morning brainstorms. It's a habit we started at college, and it's a hard one to break.'

Just then Duncan put his hand up to Max to indicate half-time. He turned to Fleur and said, in an attempt to tame Amelie's rising temper, 'What did you actually want to see us for, Fleur?'

'Well, as Josh's new personal assistant, I need to keep up with the progress of each and every campaign. I'm just expressing that interest.' Fleur smiled saccharinely as she wound a string of blonde hair around her forefinger. 'Oh, and also, when you have a moment, Amelie, Josh would like to see you in his office.' With that, Fleur was turning on her kitten heels and marching purposefully down the corridor.

'Jesus,' said Amelie, watching Fleur walk away. 'She's been promoted to Josh's PA for what, three weeks, and already it feels as though she's trying to run the agency.' Amelie looked quizzically from Max to Duncan, adding, 'Anyway, surely it's Sarah's job to keep up with the progress of our work? Why else do we employ a traffic manager?' asked Amelie, standing up and wrapping her blue hoody around her. 'Right, back as soon as I can, then,' she said, but Duncan and Max had already returned to their game.

'You can shut the door behind you, Amelie.' Josh leaned back in his black leather armchair, his brown eyes looking up at Amelie as he flicked his cigarette into an ashtray.

'Ciggie?' He held the pack open towards Amelie.

Amelie was yearning for one, desperately. 'No, cheers. Filthy things, I'm quitting. New Year's resolution.'

'Suit yourself,' said Josh. 'Although I could swear I saw you smoking in the pub the other day.' He looked at Amelie quizzically. 'And in the pool room with Duncan yesterday? But hey, it's *your* lungs,' he concluded, somehow pulling off the self-righteous tone that one would normally expect from an anti-smoker.

Amelie was flummoxed, and more than a little irritated that Josh had been spying on her. It was true, she was trying – albeit failing – to cut down on her smoke intake. But in truth, her motive for rejecting Josh's cigarettes had more to do with a reluctance to break down the pane of ice she had so carefully constructed in between them. She knew it was infantile at best, but she still couldn't help feeling a resistance towards this man who was trying to fill the boots of Jana – Amelie's mentor, whom she had cherished for the last two and a half years. As creative director, Jana had taken Amelie and Duncan under her wing when they were still fresh from advertising college. She had diligently guided their creative development from its humble portfolio beginnings into the ruthless reality of agency life. As such, they would always feel indebted to her, and the thought of welcoming in a new director so soon after Jana's departure was an uncomfortable one, particularly for Amelie.

'Well, you must have imagined what you saw,' she responded factually. 'Anyway, I don't smoke at work. I find it fogs my thinking, you know. Can't get total clarity.'

Josh gave her a confused smile, clearly finding her logic oddly charming. 'Fair enough. So anyway, how is the Fast Love work coming on with you and Duncan?'

Amelie sat down and spread out all of their rough ideas on to the table, talking through them nervously and quickly.

'Right. I see . . .' Josh said slowly, in heavy Bondi drawl. Amelie looked uneasily at him, wondering what he meant; what he thought of her ideas. A long minute passed.

Josh finally spoke. 'To be honest, Amelie, I'm not impressed. In fairness, I'd been hoping you'd come up with something stronger than this.'

Amelie couldn't help feeling irritated by his bluntness. Jana would usually have found a more diplomatic way of saying she didn't love an idea. Josh, by contrast, seemed content to come right out and say it. 'You don't beat around the bush, do you?' she observed.

'No; born and bred city boy, me,' said Josh, and Amelie couldn't help cringing as he went on. 'Amelie – know this about me. I don't believe in sugar-coating criticism, ever. Life's too short. If I don't like a creative route, I don't see the point in dwelling on it for much longer than the word "no".'

Amelie, not a fan of the 'C' word at the best of times, could feel her temper rising as she took in what Josh was saying.

'Right, well, no,' Amelie spoke gravely, striving to fight back the rebuttals that were forming in her mind. 'You're right. I know it's not exactly Gold-winning stuff, but it is just our initial thoughts . . . I think we just need more time and we'll get there . . .' she said, forcing a stoical smile.

'Perhaps,' Josh said a few moments later. 'But, you know, I've been thinking a lot this last week, now that I've had a chance to orientate myself a bit. I've been looking closely at the calibre of work this department has been churning out of late . . . and, to be completely candid, I think the collective quality of work is weaker than it should be. And I think I know the reason.'

Another pull on his cigarette, for dramatic effect. *'Team spirit . . .* It's considerably lacking. Phenomenally so.'

Josh rose out of his chair and began a kind of haphazard pacing of the room. 'So the real reason I've brought you in here is to discuss what you think of this. My idea for how to fuse together the random, disconnected strands of this creative department into one united, unbeatable whole . . .'

'What's that, then?' Amelie enquired cautiously, still reeling inside from his judgement of her creative department's work as 'weak'.

'A team-building weekend.'

Amelie fought hard to stifle a burst of explosive laughter. Spotting her grin leaking out, Josh was defiant:

'I'm serious. A weekend away, where we can all integrate with each other's partners, and connect on a social, spiritual and ultimately intellectual level. We used to do them all the time back in Oz. We'd go to the Blue Mountains or to Palm Beach for a few days – it used to work a treat! By the Sunday afternoon kick-about, we'd all have bonded like crazy.'

Josh looked out of the window, ran a hand through his mass of chestnut hair for the twelfth time since Amelie's entrance, and launched further into his pitch, 'So, my thinking is that by the end of the weekend we should all be able to function as one big creative force. Much more integrated, tighter, invincible . . . well, compared to the disparate, subdued partnerships we seem to have here at the moment. So. I'm proposing a weekend away for all of you guys, at Wing Manor Inn, where we can all take part in a variety of team-building exercises, in a fun, social setting.'

'Wing? Where on earth is Wing?'

Adopting a sage tone, his brown eyes focused intensely on Amelie's, Josh went on, 'Wing is a very special place. No, not many people have heard of it, but my distant English rellies used to have a cottage there. It's a beautiful, remote farming village just south-west of Leighton Buzzard, in the rolling green hills of Buckinghamshire. My Aunt Margaret says the country manor house is an excellent venue for these kinds of occasions. What was that cheesy saying they used to have? Something like "Wing, Tring and Ivinghoe . . . three little villages, all in a row . . ."'

'I see,' said Amelie, smiling but not quite sold. 'So, when do you propose to host this event?'

'Well, I was thinking of three weeks from now. That way, everyone's morale should have been boosted enough in good time for us to have a shred of a chance at beating the other agencies to this Fast Love business!' Josh's voice elevated in excitement at this prospect, as he stated, 'Amelie, every creative team at LGMK is involved in this speed-dating brief now. The pressure's on; we *have* to win this pitch.'

There was a long pause while Josh looked at Amelie and held her gaze, waiting for a reaction to his master-plan, and lingering as though there was something else he needed to say. He didn't say it, whatever it was.

Amelie broke the silence. 'Well . . . It sounds interesting, I guess. But what does all this have to do with me? Why have you called me in here?'

'Well, I'm not sure, really . . . I just had this sense that I should run this all by you first, before Fleur sends the memo round to the whole department. To see what you thought, get you on side, for want of a better phrase . . .' He trailed off, a peculiar faraway look in his eyes again.

'But why me?' asked Amelie suspiciously.

'No reason really, I don't know . . . I guess being new, I got the impression you were kind of chummy with most of the departments here . . . and as someone who's also been here a while, I thought maybe you'd be the right chick to test the water with, or something.'

Amelie winced at his reference to herself as a chick, and also to what was fast becoming another of his annoying habits – a perpetual reliance on colloquial sayings or clichés to illustrate his points. 'Right,' she said cautiously.

'So, d'you reckon people will go for it?' Josh fished.

'Well, if I'm brutally honest for a second . . . it seems to me to be a bit of a tacky, Americanised approach to things.' Then, seeing Josh's disappointed expression, she added, 'But it could be a laugh, I guess. If it worked for the Aussies, then why should we be so different? Anyway, throw enough free booze and food at people and I'm sure you'll have them eating out of your hands. In this "Wing" place of yours.'

Cringing inside, Amelie added half jokingly, 'Oh, and you could always get Red Bull to sponsor the whole thing – get people really full of energy, and then . . . then you could call it *"Red Bull Gives You Wing"*.'

Smiling a 'So that's why they hired you' kind of smile, Josh said, 'Right, that's settled, then.' With that he leaned forward to press a button on his desk.

'Yes, babe?' Fleur's saccharine voice flooded through the intercom. A wave of scarlet flushed momentarily across Josh's cheeks.

'Fleur,' he spoke sternly into the microphone, 'the Wing memo.'

'Yes, it's sitting in my outbox, ready to go.'

'Please can you send it round a.s.a.p.?'

'Certainly, precious. Consider it done.'

Clearing his throat, apparently uncomfortable with the increasing number of pet-names coming through the intercom, he added hastily, 'And please could you bring me in some more coffee, this mug has gone cold again. In fact, can you go to Starbucks for me?'

'Yes, Josh. Anything else, love?'

'That will be all thanks, Fleur,' at which a discreet giggle could be heard through the intercom. Amelie rolled her eyes to the ceiling so that Josh couldn't see, and then got up to leave. 'If that's all, then am I free to go?'

Josh looked distracted. 'Sorry? . . . Yes, sure. Thanks for your thoughts. Best get your head down now and come up with something decent for Fast Love, hey?'

'I'll see what I can do. Don't know what the other teams have up their sleeves, but Duncan and I have got something of a plan on the go,' Amelie said, a cheeky glint in her eye as she pulled the door behind her.

Cut and Paste

It's a few days after the mayhem of Friday's dating with speed. Have just been to see Josh, who, by the way, seems to get stranger and more annoying by the day. Also just been chatting to Duncan about Friday. Turns out that, after assessing all of his 'ticks' for a further three minutes in the bar afterwards, that was all it took him to realise that they too were in fact 'crosses'.

However, for the sake of research, and for it to be a fair test to speed-dating itself, we've decided that we ought to follow things up to some extent – until the next Fast Love evening which Sally and I are booked on in a few days – God help us. So, now that the event has officially been 'opened' (to use the correct terminology), we're going on to the Fast Love website to see who our matches are. For a giggle I'm going to tick every single one of the guys that I met and pretend that I liked them all, and see how many matches that generates. Here goes . . .

52

Work, Wednesday 12 January, 12 p.m.

Duncan isn't speaking to me. I got three times as many matches as him. I can't believe it. Seventeen matches. Which means seventeen of these men thought they could see themselves with me. Which is really quite alarming when you consider the saying 'like attracts like'.

Work, Thursday 13 January, 9.30 a.m.

My inbox has been getting lots of action already. It's actually getting a bit over-excited from all this new-found male attention. If only I was. Duncan thinks it's hilarious, but personally I don't know what to do with them all. Fifteen emails in one morning. Do I write back? Horror of Horrors, do I have to see them again if I do? Looking through the follow-up emails I've received so far, they all tend to follow a strict format:

a) Open with a question about the night, and a quick joke about how rushed it all was!
b) Obligatory reference to getting very pissed this week and being hungover a lot
c) Tentative invitation to go out properly for a drink soon

There's a couple I just had to cut out and keep:

Hi, Amie-lee,

Are you the cute one with blue eyes and mad pretty brown hair? (If not, sorry, no offense.) If so, what did you reckon to speed dating? . . . there were some quite fit birds there I thought (including you) although there weren't half some rough dogs too. And I don't know about you but I had the mingingest hangover the next day?!! hard to keep track of how many you're putting back when you're speed-dating – its all speeded up even the drinking! And, I prob. shouldn't tell u this but woke up in the middle of the nite with sick on my duvet, and on my mate's sofa – no idea how it got their???? Maybe it was the zambooka afterwards. What do you do again? I know it's something legal – something to do with Copyright?

Speak soon Raymond x

Lovely stuff. Or there's the slightly more evolved smooth-talker, Ian. I can't say for certain, but I think he may be the mildly attractive one – the one I never actually got to have my three minutes with on the night.

Amelie,

Did you enjoy the other night? I didn't really, if I'm honest – had more fun last time I watched paint dry! We never got round to each other ☹, but you seemed nice ☺. More interesting than the others. Did you meet your Mr Right? If not d'you want to meet up sometime?

☺ Ian ☺

A few more emails have come through since. Wrote back an evasive but friendly reply to them all – have decided the best thing to do now is to subtly ply them for information as to their motives and their aspirations regarding speed-

*dating . . . it's a little tricky to keep up, though, when (at the
risk of sounding like a complete bitch) some of them seem
like they're from another planet, or worse . . .*

Hullo Amelie

How are you?

Was so over the moon to hear from you, because
sometimes you get matched up with people but then
girls never reply to your emails. So I'm glad you did. I
just knew I felt a big spark between us. Did you have a
good night? I thought it was surreal but fun. Don't
remember much to be honest, except that you seemed
nice enough. Is your hair naturally that radiant colour?
Did you buy that lovely top especially? I thought it really
suited your figure. When would you like to meet up?

How is your little jewelry empire going? Did you find a
venue for your second shop yet? Have you found much
time this week to get to the beach?

When will you next be down in the big smoke? Let me
know, it'd be nice to go for a drink soon. I'm pretty free
at the moment. In my experience I think it's best to act
on these things sooner rather than later, strike while
the iron's hot if you know what I mean – so yeah let me
know where you're at.

All Best

Jon

Starting to worry – is this now getting more complicated than I'd imagined? Are all my fictional Amelies coming back to haunt me with a vengeance? Why did I have to make up so many stories? Some of these guys actually might not be that bad, and yet I've no idea who's who out of any of them; they're all just a mish-mash of numbers and names. Now can't help feeling slightly guilty for playing this game.

One other disconcerting thing, though: after they see you've ticked them, suddenly it's like these floodgates swing open and in rushes a tide of life stories. It's like – I've got you now; I'm going to talk and talk at you; tell you all about me and my life! And the worst part is, I can't remember what any of them look like at all, so it's basically like some random guy cornering you in a bar and presenting a fully-fledged polemic at you all about who they are. Enter Marius, who bounced back in seconds with this pre-prepared autobiography:

Dear Amelie,

I'm a midlands boy. I was born in 1976 into a massive family; in a tiny village called Upton-over-the-Wey. Our family goes way back actually – Dad always gets the family tree out to show off when guests come to stay. The Tandys have been going to the school in our town for five generations. We all went to school there, and then to sixth form college and then I was the only one to go to uni. I did Computing, then spent a few years on an I.T. helpdesk, helping idiots on the phone learn how to turn their PCs on and off, then gave it up to do Web Development which I've been doing ever since. Now close to earning over 100 grand a year: nice work if you can get it. I've just managed to buy. Nice not to be throwing money down the drain on rent cheques. I live in Morden on my own. Used to live in a squalid shared house with uni mates, six of us sharing one bathroom – never again. Never seen so much mould. I work in Wimbledon nearby. How's the **ballerina** lifestyle? Sounds hard work from what you were telling me. Don't expect you get much time to go away on weekends, but if you ever do my parents have a lovely cottage we could go to? Let me know and I'll whisk you away from it all! And the family would love to meet you!

Where do you live? **What did you say you're performing in at the moment? Can I still have seats in the stalls?** I'd also like to take you for dinner sometime – let me know how you're fixed and perhaps we can diarise something soon.

Marius
Tandy Web Development UK
www.TandyWebdevelopment.co.uk

Feel strange mixture of charmed and afraid. He seems like he'd be quite nice (in a web-developing kind of way), but it's all just a wee bit speedy and keen for me (in a bunny-boiling kind of way). All that stuff about meeting the parents, just from my one very generic, lukewarm email? I mean, all we've shared is three blurry minutes together and I get the creepy impression he's already told his mum, dad, siblings and cousins all about me. OK, must try and be more open-minded now – that is just the way it works with speed-

dating – I guess every part of the process happens more quickly than normal.

But the trouble with all of these guys is that, once they reach the end of their cut & paste sermon, they all then want all the same answers out of you. So what do I do now? Keep it going? Answer their questions? Make up stories again? But – I can't remember who I told what now, so that could result in severe confusion. God forbid – do I have to meet with them?? At what point is this research getting out of hand and becoming a bit cruel on them (and myself, come to mention it)? Where must I draw the line?

5

Alarm Bells

Date: 17 January 2005, 11.35
Sender: CWilson@MarshallHopkins.co.uk
To: Holden.Amelie@LGMKLondon.com
Subject: news

Can you meet me for a drink tonight? Something important to tell u. Meet u in All Bar 1 after work?? Let me know x

'Sounds ominous,' Amelie muttered, replying, '*Cool, cu then x.*' Then she felt her stomach constrict as she realised she had just agreed to a return to the scene of Friday and all its horrors. Nevertheless, not having heard from Claire in a while, she decided she was prepared to make this sacrifice for her sake. Just then her phone rang, halting the conveyor-belt of farcical memories which had begun to rotate around her mind.

Who can that be? Amelie thought, looking at the

display and seeing it was an unknown number that had come via the switchboard. 'Ah lovely, another design agency on a sales pitch,' she said to Duncan, who nodded sagely.

Tentatively, she answered, 'Hello, Amelie speaking . . .'

'Awright, Amelie. It's Maffew,' came an unfamiliar cockney voice.

'Sorry? Matthew . . . Matthew who?'

'Maffew Hunt. You know. From last Friday. All Bar One.'

'Oh. Right. Hello,' Amelie said, her eyes dilating with confused surprise.

'So, d'you fancy catching up over a drink?'

Amelie pulled the receiver away from her and examined it, as though she was taken aback by the speed at which Maffew was operating, wondering whether she had missed something.

'Well. I'm kind of busy at the moment, to be honest, what with Easter coming up and that, so er . . .'

'Right, well, when you're not so busy, gimme a shout, isn't it.'

'Yes. Yes, it is indeed,' replied Amelie numbly, before adding, curiously, 'So . . . um, how did you get my number, just out of interest?'

'Well, it's LGMK you said, isn't it? I just rang 118 and then your main switchboard.'

'Oh, right. Of course.' *Like you do.* 'I'm sorry, actually, Matthew, you've caught me at rather an awkward time. Could you call back? Thanks.' She hung up, shuddering to herself as Duncan collapsed with laughter.

'Easter?!' exclaimed Duncan. 'Easter coming up? It's bloody January!'

'What else could I say? I couldn't think on the spot like that!'

'Who was it?' asked Duncan, his voice full of concern. 'Your face was a picture of horror!'

'Honestly? I have no idea. I mean, technically, we've met. I suppose. But he could be anyone really.'

'Oh it sounded priceless. You should have put him on to speakerphone! Next time, promise you'll put him on speaker?!'

'GOD forbid there should be a next time.'

Duncan looked worried. 'What if he calls back?'

'Oh he won't, surely. He'd have to be stupid. Didn't you hear the raging disinterest in my voice?'

After an hour or so of silence, Amelie and Duncan were becoming absorbed in their work when the phone rang again. They exchanged nervous glances. Seeing it was reception ringing through, Amelie said calmly, 'It's fine, it's just Chloe.'

Amelie picked up the receiver. 'Hello, love. You all right?'

'Yeah . . . listen, hon, are you busy at the moment?'

'Well, kind of brainstorming, so, no . . . why, what's up?'

'Well,' Chloe paused for a few moments, 'are you – expecting anyone? Anyone – by the name of Maffew?' There was another pause as Amelie overheard Chloe mumble something away from the receiver. Amelie began to look puzzled, when Chloe's voice came back: 'Sorry, yes, a guy called Matthew Hunt says he's here to see you. Won't say what agency he's from . . . and . . . I don't think he's a freelancer or a photographer, as he hasn't got a book with him. So, I'm afraid I don't know *what* he is really . . . Shall I send him up?'

'Oh good God. Oh good God, no, please don't!'

Duncan was staring at Amelie, his blue eyes brimming with curiosity. Amelie mouthed, 'It's *him*,' to Duncan, who promptly burst into laughter. Amelie mouthed, 'Shhhhh!' to him and pulled the receiver closer to her ear. 'Um, listen, I don't know *what* this guy is doing here . . . but I don't want you to have to deal with him – I'll pop down and sort this out. Don't worry, I'll be there in two ticks . . .' and Amelie hung up.

'Wow, Am, your very own stalker. How trendy. I want one,' teased Duncan as Amelie stood up to leave the room, affectionately toppling Duncan's baseball cap from his head as she walked past him.

Moments later Amelie stepped out of the lift on to the ground floor. Before venturing out into the immaculate white, open-plan reception area, she crept behind one of the white pillars so she could steal a glance at this strange, most militant of SpeedDaters. As she had no real memory of meeting him, she had no idea what he could possibly look like. There were only two certainties about him. He knew where she worked, therefore he must have been one of the rare specimens whom she'd told the truth to. Therefore, at least she didn't need to try and retrace which industry she had said she was in – be it the Birmingham Royal Ballet, jewellery-maker extraordinaire, or the Chelmsford Fire Brigade. The second certainty, she realised, was that she must surely get rid of this person as soon as possible. Anyone who went to this much effort, unencouraged, to chase a girl he had barely spoken to must surely be unhinged in some way, she felt. Either that, or just very, very romantic.

Amelie entertained all these different thoughts as she stood watching the tall, thin man sporting a tango-orange ski-jacket who was simultaneously scratching his bald head and idly leafing through the *Sun*. In wonderment, she stood and watched as he scratched away more zealously. Then, with horror she stared as he stopped scratching and began to examine the flakes one by one as they trickled down into his hands. Then, without even checking to see if he was being watched, he blithely blew on his hands, sending shards of scalp flying all over the white leather sofa on which he was slouched.

Dear God, thought Amelie, suddenly feeling stoically religious. Please don't let this be him. Or, if it is, please make it clear to me, how can this person be interested in me? What could I *possibly* have done to encourage him?

Just as Amelie was pondering this conundrum in her head, she felt someone brush past her, making her jump.

'Amelie?' Josh said, loudly enough for anyone in reception to hear. 'Why are you hiding there, behind that pillar? Is this your new thinking spot?'

'Me?' Amelie laughed awkwardly, noticing the man in the orange ski-jacket look up and begin to shift about in his seat. Bugger, it's definitely him, she realised.

'Oh, me? I'm not hiding!' she laughed. 'I was just – just, checking myself in this mirror here,' she said, indicating the full-length mirror that was only just within viewing distance. 'Anyway, I was just on my way to greet a free-lancer, as it happens,' she said firmly, as though that was the end of that conversation. With that, she marched across the room towards scalp-flaking tango man, and said, 'Why, Matthew!' flinging her arms around him. 'Thank you for dropping by at such short notice!' Maffew looked thrilled at her display of affection, and began to go slightly red as he noticed Josh staring at him suspiciously.

Amelie was keen to deal with this man as efficiently and speedily as possible. If this was their second date, Amelie decided they would still need to keep it to a strict three-minute curfew. She said firmly to him, 'So, shall we quickly pop into this meeting room? I'll just get you a coffee from the machine. How do you take it again? White with one?' she said as she bundled him into the small empty meeting room adjacent to reception, and closed the door tightly behind him.

Josh was still staring at her quizzically when she turned back round to face him. 'What?' she said defensively, while walking towards the coffee machine. 'He's here to talk about Fast Love; he's done some interesting research for me.'

Josh shook his head in bemusement as Amelie stepped into Meeting Room 2 and then closed the door behind her.

Minutes later Amelie and Maffew were sitting together in silence, perched politely on plastic chairs three feet apart, their untouched plastic coffee cups steaming synthetic coffee into the already noxious air.

'So. D'you fancy meetin' up sometime?' began Maffew.

Amelie edged her chair fractionally further away. 'Oh. Well, we've "met up" now, haven't we? I mean, here we are?'

'Yeah. But I mean for a proper date, like?'

'Oh. Well. I'm a bit busy at the moment . . . I can't really see when I'll next be free . . .' Then, remembering the brief, Amelie added, 'Um, how about we just chat for a minute? Let's see. Where do you work?'

'Slough.'

'Oh – that's nice. What do you do there?'

'I work with books.'

'Oh really, you're in publishing? That must be fun.'

'Well, yeah, it is. Although, no, I'm not really that involved. Actually, I don't really like books. They're kind of boring, you know? Although, I don't know how I know, since I've never read any of them. Can't remember when I last read one. Maybe it was some Dickens thing at school, but I couldn't finish that so I dunno if that counts. No, I prefer DVDs me; computer games and that. They're much easier. You know, when I've been working hard all day the last thing I want to do is to force my brain to *work* at something. You know?'

'I know,' said Amelie, suppressing a smile. 'So, if you don't have any passion whatsoever for books, what are you doing working in publishing?'

'Well, I only do in a very loose way. I pack boxes. I work at Amazon.'

'Right,' Amelie said, suddenly very aware of how much work she had to do, and well, nothing against Maffew, but she was beginning to question how far she really needed to take this being friendly-for-the-sake-of-research.

'Well, this has been great, Matthew . . . but . . . I'm afraid I'm going to have to get back to work. Thanks for dropping by.' She smiled forcefully, willing him to comprehend what she was saying, for him to start getting ready to leave. When he didn't budge a muscle, she smiled apologetically and added in her most humble voice, 'Listen, I'm sorry. I'll have to be quite open with you now and say that I'm afraid I can't quite see this going anywhere.' When Maffew's face sank, she added, feeling a piece of her soul wilt as she did, 'I'm sorry, it's not you . . .'

'I know . . . it's me,' he finished, as though this was a phrase he was jaded with pre-empting. He stood up to leave, picked up his orange jacket and hurried away, leaving Amelie staring at the untouched cups of steaming plastic coffee, and feeling wretched with guilt.

Some hours later Amelie and Duncan were at their desks. Duncan was doodling absent-minded stars all over his lay-out pad while gazing out of the window. Amelie was half watching Duncan, and half studying in depth the texture of his faded Converse trainers. Fortunately the memory of the uncomfortable Maffew encounter was slowly fading. As Amelie analysed the fraying split ends of Duncan's green laces, she suddenly recalled something she had once read in a book about advertising. The theory that for any advertising creative, approximately a quarter of your time is spent staring at your creative partner's shoes. At the time she had thought it was just a silly myth, but now she was starting to see the guy's point.

'Well, we're not getting anywhere, so I say we call it a day and come to it fresh tomorrow,' Amelie suggested, waking Duncan out of his daydream.

'Yeah, good plan. Oh God, is that the time? I've got to go anyway,' said Duncan, looking at the clock on the wall. 'You up to much tonight?'

'Meeting Claire. Why, what are you up to?' Amelie asked, noticing Duncan blush slightly.

'Not sure . . . might be going out,' replied Duncan coyly, his eyes darting around the room, straining to avoid her gaze, as he sometimes did when trying not to give anything away.

'What do you mean, you're not sure?' Amelie looked closely at his flushing cheeks. 'Has Dunky got himself a slow date?!' she teased.

'Don't be daft. It's just dinner with Max and his girlfriend Audry. He just also happened to mention that she may be bringing her sister along as well. But it's nothing.'

Max was Duncan's good friend and colleague, who worked at LGMK as an account manager. Having been together with his own girlfriend for six years now, Max was often trying to set Duncan up with his various female friends, to varying levels of success.

'What, the oh-so glamorous sister Sara-Jayne who's been a fashion buyer in New York for ages?' Amelie probed, climbing into her coat and rearranging the clutter on her desk.

'That's the one. SJ, she likes to be called. She may actually be moving back over here,' Duncan replied, as they began walking towards the lift.

They strolled past all the work-spaces in the creative department, and past the ball-pond 'inspiration zone' which had recently been installed, courtesy of Josh. As they walked past Josh's large corner office, Amelie saw that the door was slightly ajar. Through the gap she could see Josh, sitting at Jana's old desk, in Jana's old office. Amelie noticed with sadness that it hadn't taken him long to remove most of Jana's old furniture. In its place, he appeared to have installed his own gallery of eccentric back-packing paraphernalia from around the globe. Scanning the room, Amelie saw that the left-hand corner was entirely taken up with a gigantic, psychedelically painted didgeridoo. Next to that there was a large bongo engraved with authentic aboriginal carvings. Finally, adjacent to this, hanging across the bay window overlooking Soho Square, was the most striking installation of all: a purple and red batique hammock straight from the Khao San Road in Bangkok. Amelie rolled her eyes derisively at it all, watching Josh as he leaned over the lay-out pad on his desk, scribbling intensely as though in thrall to an idea. Looking away, Amelie walked towards the lift and whispered to Duncan under her breath, 'Why's he brought all that stuff in? Such an exhibitionist.'

Duncan shrugged and countered, 'I think it's cool – it kind of makes for a shrine to the simple life! Anyway, you've been travelling, haven't you? Why are you criticising him for hanging on to all that stuff? Didn't you hear him say we're all welcome to go and sit in the hammock whenever he's not there? I bet it's a great little thinking spot, don't you?'

'I guess,' mumbled Amelie as they stepped into the lift. 'Sorry, Dunc, I just don't think I like the guy. Don't like his attitude.'

Duncan shrugged indifferently, and seconds later they both stepped out on to the ground floor and walked into the reception area.

'Bye, Chloe! See you tomorrow,' called Duncan to the agency's timid new Australian temp, who had been recruited to cover Fleur since her promotion to creative PA.

Chloe looked up guiltily from the epic email she was typing to her friends back in Melbourne, and brushed the blonde hair from out of her eyes. 'Oh, hey! See you tomorrow, have a good evening.' She smiled, and then picked up her headset as the phone started to bleep. 'Good afternoon, LGMK,' she answered, mock-rolling her eyes to the ceiling, as Amelie and Duncan smiled sympathetically and walked through the revolving doors.

'Walking to the tube?' asked Duncan.

'No, I'm meeting Claire in All Bar One, remember?' she replied as they turned out of Soho Square and into Frith Street. It was dark already, and a harsh January chill was in the air.

'Oh, Am, are you sure you don't want me to walk with you? He could be out there, lurking behind a lamp-post, waiting to jump out at you!'

'Who?' asked Amelie innocently, having already forgotten about the events of the day.

'Maffew – your stalker, of course!'

'Oh – don't be moronic! He'll be over me by now. Speedily met, speedily forgotten, I'm sure.'

'Call me if you need me,' Duncan said, his face doing its best to be grave and serious, let down by the churlish grin leaking out. Once at Old Compton Street, they said goodbye and went their separate ways, Amelie cheekily wishing Duncan good luck for his 'slow date'.

Amelie walked along the busy streets of Media Soho, past the rows of cafés and bars streaming with people, reclining in chairs, lounging on sofas; chattering busily and animatedly over their G and Ts and Chardonnays. She shuffled her feet along, unconsciously noticing again how divided into couples the people in the cafés seemed to be. She didn't care, she decided, lighting a cigarette, and hugging herself from the cold. She was happy being single. Stalker or no stalker, she was happy, successful, independent and free.

*

When Amelie arrived at All Bar One, Claire was sitting at their regular table by the window; minding two full wine glasses and a bottle of Pinot Grigio. As Amelie walked through the door, she noticed that Claire did not seem her usual composed self. Today she appeared more agitated than normal – nervously drumming her fingers on the table and looking at her watch.

'Sorry I'm late; got held up at work again,' Amelie said as she fumbled with her jacket and scarf.

'Yeah, yeah, and the rest,' Claire teased. In all their years of friendship, Amelie had never quite managed to master the arts of punctuality and time management; always blaming this on her artistic streak.

'Anyway, cheers!' she said, smiling and raising her glass as Amelie sat down and did the same.

They clinked their glasses together. 'Thanks, sweetie. So, what is it that you have to tell me? The suspense has been chipping away at my sanity!'

Claire gave a sly grin.

'Is it that promotion you've been working so hard for?' Amelie asked.

Still silence, but now there was a slightly smug grin dancing on Claire's lips.

'It *is*, isn't it?!' exclaimed Amelie. 'I knew it! Oh, you're such a star; I told you you'd get it. So, what did that girl Katie do when the news broke? She must have been so gutted and jealous!'

Claire said nothing. Merely picked up her glass in her left hand and slowly lifted it towards her face.

'What? Why aren't you saying anything? What is it? I'm right, aren't I?'

Claire grinned sheepishly and wiggled the fingers on

her left hand against the glass. She appeared to be waiting for Amelie to react; her eyes sparkling almost as much as the large jewel on her finger.

'Oh, sweet Lord!' Amelie cried. 'Is that what I think it is, on your finger? Oh my God, Claire!'

'Dan proposed last night!' Claire said, grinning broadly. 'I know what you think; what you're going to say. But honestly, Am, I've never felt so sure about anything, ever. I knew he was thinking about it after Paris, and I wasn't sure if I was ready . . . but then suddenly something inside of me just snapped. I just knew that I was ready. I *am* ready, more than I'll ever be; and I just see no point in holding back any longer!'

'Oh, Claire, I don't know what to say,' Amelie blubbered, looking dumbstruck. 'But you know I'm happy for you, don't you?' she said, seeing Claire's face begin to look overcast. Amelie stood up and went to give her friend a warm, celebratory hug. 'It's brilliant. Really. I was just kind of blown away at first. But . . . I can't think of a better bloke for you, Claire. You really do deserve all the best.' Amelie shuddered, adding, 'Ewww, listen to me, coming out with all the clichés!'

'Sometimes that's all there is left to say,' said Claire. 'So you're not going to give me another torrent of feminist, anti-marital abuse?'

'Well, part of me wants to,' Amelie admitted. 'But the other half of me is sort of creeping round to accepting the idea . . . that maybe the other day you had a point. I *was* being a bit bitter, and maybe even envious of how happy you two are together . . .'

'Oh, you silly muppet . . .' Claire teased.

'Well, that, and the absolute truth that I'm clearly

destined to be a sad spinster till the end of my days . . .'
Amelie added wryly, before standing up and walking
towards the bar.

'Where are you going?'

'Getting us a proper drink. Champers, my darling, is
definitely in order!'

'Oh, excellent, thanks!'

Minutes later Amelie returned with a bottle of Moët,
cracked it open, and cackled with laughter as it sprayed
Claire in the face.

'To you and Dan,' toasted Amelie, and they clinked
glasses and took large sips.

'So, I take it the wedding's a long way off? This is one
of those long engagement deals, right?' Amelie probed
tentatively.

'Well, actually, that was my second announcement.'

'Oh?'

'Well, we're both just dead keen to get on with it. Now
that we know it's what we want . . . well, it might seem
impulsive, but we just thought, what the hell, let's do it
a.s.a.p., before we change our minds or something!'

'Serious?' Amelie asked, feeling her stomach fill with
hyperactive butterflies.

'Yep. So . . . we're getting married in three and a half
weeks! Just in time for Valentine's Day! Isn't that mad? We
didn't want anything too elaborate, so we don't need
months of excruciating planning. We just both fancied a
quiet, modest affair. Nothing too expensive or flash, you
know. So we've just decided to book it as soon as we could,
so that there's no turning back!'

'Oh my God, that's so exciting!' Amelie said aloud,
meanwhile thinking to herself, Claire *would* tell me if she

was pregnant, wouldn't she? Suppressing this horrific thought, she asked, 'Do your parents know yet?'

'Yeah, they're both delighted. I think Dan's mum's pretty chuffed too. Oh, and it also means a last-minute hen weekend – sorry not to ask you earlier, but can I book you, not for this Saturday, but the one after? I think Lydia from uni is organising it – nothing flash – we'll just pop down to Brighton for a big girlie night . . . it may involve something silly like a Pink Lady theme . . . I'll let you know . . . but say you can come!'

Amelie reached into her bag for her diary. As she opened it and checked the dates, she sighed with relief. 'That's lucky – it's not the same weekend as Josh's silly team-building weekend at least! Yep, count me in! So, where's the actual big day going to be? With three weeks' notice there can't have been much choice of venues, can there?'

'No, we decided it would be lovely to hold it down at his parents in Penarth – it's this completely beautiful mansion by the sea. There's a wonderful dramatic cliff that juts out over the estuary – we thought we could have the service in the local registry office, and then hold the reception in the house and gardens.' Claire looked at Amelie as though she was searching for reassurance in some way, before adding, 'It might sound a bit under-whelming, Am, but honestly, it's just sublime there, you have to see it! And at short notice that's all we could manage.'

'I think it sounds perfect. I can't wait . . . that is, if I'm invited?!' Amelie half joked.

'Well, of course. And you must bring Duncan too, I haven't seen him in ages.' Claire looked at Amelie purposefully and added, 'I do wish you'd realise how lovely he is,' a meddling look appearing in her eye.

'Of course I'll bring him, if he's free,' Amelie said, ignoring Claire's insinuation.

'Oh, and there's one other thing. Little, tiny thing,' Claire began. Then added slowly, 'I was wondering whether you might, you know, consider being . . . my blushing bridesmaid?'

Amelie looked uncomfortable and began playing with the bits of shredded tissues in her coat pocket. 'Oh, well . . . I'm not really sure about getting all glammed up and über-girlie like that. I don't think I really have it in me,' she paused, shifting about awkwardly in her chair. 'Are you sure I can't just come and watch? I mean, I wouldn't want to be a hypocrite . . . you know my stance on marriage . . .'

'Oh, Amelie, it's hardly selling your soul to the sodding devil, is it?' Claire interrupted, growing irritated. 'And it's not as though I'm asking you to do it in a church . . .'

'God forbid!' Amelie exclaimed.

'Please, Ammie. It would mean so much to me. There is no one else I'd want to be up there with me as much as you.'

'Oh, I know, I know. I'm sorry, I guess I'm just stuck in a rut of cynicism after my parents' continuingly disastrous attempts at getting married . . . I'm sorry. Of course I'll be there for you. Just don't expect me to catch the bouquet and follow in your footsteps, OK?!'

'Of course, of course. Thank you, thank you! You won't regret it. Who knows, you might even enjoy it!'

Hours later, they were polishing off their drinks in the same seats, feeling the effects of the alcohol become more prominent.

'Lord, is that the time?' Claire asked, looking at her watch. 'I've got an early meeting in the morning, I'd better be getting back.'

'Yeah, that champers has knocked me out; I'm knackered now,' Amelie agreed.

'Want to stay at mine?' Claire asked as they pulled on their coats. Then, after a minute of walking, Claire added, 'God, listen to us! When did we become so sensible and boring?'

Amelie laughed. 'You're right; a few years ago we would have gone on drinking and finished up at a club – meeting or no meeting!'

Claire giggled. 'I know. It's scary, this middle-age thing creeping up on us ... Hey, do you remember that silly "Middle-Aged-Ometer" that Lydia, Lisa and I used to have up on the sitting-room wall in our student house? We'd probably both get really high scores on it now! Still, I bet Lisa and Lyd would do far worse than us now, what with them both being married and with houses already. God, where *does* the time go?' Claire kicked a stone along the street as they walked. 'I'm not exactly helping the situation by going and getting hitched, though, am I?'

'Well, no, but these things happen, I guess,' Amelie teased, linking her arm with Claire's.

'Want to share a cab?' Claire asked, hailing one down.

Amelie thought about this a moment. 'No, actually, I think I'll just walk a while and take the bus.'

'Sure?'

'Yeah. So I'll see you at the weekend, then?'

'OK.' Claire leaned over and gave Amelie a warm hug. 'Take care, babe, and good luck with the brief from hell!

I'm sure you'll crack it any day now. And maybe even meet the man of your dreams along the way!'

'Oh, I think I already have,' she said, amusing herself with the memory of Maffew. When Claire looked intrigued, she added, 'Oh no, just kidding. But thanks; I'm going to need all the luck I can get with this one. Anyway, have fun planning the wedding! I still can't believe it.'

They kissed each other on the cheek, and Claire climbed into the taxi. 'Hampstead, please,' she said, pulling the door shut and waving to Amelie as the car drove away.

'Bye, then,' Amelie said, even though Claire was long out of earshot. As Amelie started strolling to the bus stop, she couldn't help feeling a sense in which she had just said goodbye to her oldest friend, to a piece of her youth. Despite her best efforts to fight back the mental clichés, she couldn't help but begin to feel that in some way, Claire was drifting towards the other side of an invisible line.

Seeing a 139 bus begin advancing up Oxford Street towards her, Amelie broke into a run, reaching it just in time. She climbed aboard and swiped her Oyster card, taking a seat near the rear of the bus and resting her head on the window. As the bus pulled away, she watched the lights and bustle of London sweep by in a misty haze, and tried to let the news of the evening sink in.

Twenty minutes later she awoke with a start, seeing the graffiti-adorned walls of the Abbey Road Studios pass by on her left, alerting her to the fact that she was nearly home. She robotically hit the stop button, picked herself up and rubbed the sleep from her eyes. No doubt her contact lenses would be stuck to the surface of her eyes again. She sighed, looking forward to a session of careful nudging and trying-not-to-tear, in an attempt to remove the flimsy little circles of sight. Oh, the perils of vision, she mused.

At the corner of Abercorn Place, she stepped down from the bus and lit up a cigarette. Inhaling deeply, she began walking up the road to her flat in Violet Hill. Once inside the flat, she picked up the pile of mail and started idly sorting through it on her way to the kitchen. 'Hello, Malibu,' she said, bending down to pick up the ball of white fluff that was her new kitten. 'How was your day?'

'Mine was OK, thank you,' she said, switching on the kettle and collapsing on the sofa. She stared round at the walls of the flat, all adorned with photos, pictures and paintings collected from her many travelling adventures during her early twenties. Photos of herself and Claire at school, of her student days at college, and with friends, travelling around Asia and South Africa during the year after graduation. All of which seemed distant halcyon days to her now, of a time when everything and anything was possible; anything apart from growing older and settling down.

The kettle made a hissing sound. Amelie yawned and went to make a cup of tea. As she drank, she thought about how, in just under a month, her oldest friend was going to be getting married, and not long after that, probably starting a family. Suddenly everything was going to be very different. And there it was again, like a balesha beacon flashing in her mind – the thought that, deep down, maybe she had had enough of this single life. Although she relished in the spontaneity and the independence it brought, she was growing tired of the loneliness that always played along in the background. Amelie was starting to wonder whether maybe she wouldn't mind having someone to come home to. Someone – with two legs rather than four – who would be able to make her a cup of tea and talk back to her about her day. For the first time since getting over her break-up with Jack, Amelie felt the tiniest bit lonely and incomplete.

Love Bites

What will the Cupid junkies think of next? Have just found out about something which could possibly make a refreshing alternative to speed-dating. Apparently there are these nights you can attend called 'Dating in the Dark'. They sound fascinating. I pulled up some searches on the Net about them. What happens is you sit around a table and have dinner with a group of strangers. You chat and get to know each other, just as you would at any regular dinner party. The only difference is that you can't actually see anyone. It sounds a great idea to me. You get to know people genuinely for who they are, with far less danger of being judgemental. Then, when the lights come on, you get to put a face to all those different disembodied voices – see who your perfect match is, and whether or not you fancy them.

It sounds intriguing to me but I do have one hesitation. I worry that under the limited lighting conditions, it will be even harder than normal to maintain grace and co-ordination in the table-manners department. I can see myself now – merrily chatting away in the dark, but secretly waiting in abject terror for the moment when the lights come on, worrying about what they would reveal: most likely that most of my dinner had missed my mouth and found its way into my lap and all over my chest. As the lights come on, I gaze into the eyes of my perfect conversational match, and in return he gazes back at me, looking thoroughly repulsed and unimpressed.

Thinking about it, catching even a flicker of disappointment in their eyes could be a really crushing experience. It could set you back weeks in confidence levels, surely? On second thoughts, I don't think this is a good method after all. But it may still be worth testing out – if nothing else, perhaps it will show speed-dating in a better light; help me crack the campaign . . .

Work, Tuesday 18 January, 11.30 a.m.

Oh sweet Lord. Duncan has just shown me some-thing which is whole dimensions worse than both Dating in the Dark and Speed-Dating put together. Apparently, the people of Britain are now so lonely and so busy that they have begun to resort to what can only be described as the world's trashiest dating craze yet: 'Fast Food Dating'.

The idea behind this initiative is that a bunch of hungry singletons congregate in the refined, atmospheric foyer of the Regent Street Burger King. They are then paired with a 'dinner date' for the length of time it takes them to eat a complimentary Flame-Grilled Whopper Meal. Apparently this actually happens, and they are planning to go nation-wide with it. According to the organisers, this is now 'the most efficient way to find love, when you're a bit pressed for time'.

Call me a dreamer, but surely we are not really so busy and career-driven that we need to resort to Burger Dating? Can the txt generation really not be bothered to put in the hours? I mean, there was once a time when romance was a slow, tense affair, involving tortured silences over elegant dinners, atmospheric walks by a river or a lake, wandering through a labyrinth of does-he-doesn't-he dilemmas and will-she-won't-she complexes ... And even though all that stuff can be agonising at times, surely it's all part of the process of finding the one you love, isn't it? These days the quest for true love is turning into a frantic mish-mash of scorecards and pens, kisses over ketchup, marriages over mayonnaise ... How long before McDonald's joins in the festivities with its own brand of McLove? Has Cupid got bored of us all and gone off to play on an X-Box somewhere?

And another thing. Years from now, when two 'ticks' do tie the knot and settle down, what are they going to tell their grandkids or kids, when the day comes for them to tell the story of how they met?

'Daddy met Mummy in a bar one night – even before the bell had rung to signal their three minutes were up, Mummy knew that he was the one!'

I mean, is that what we'll tell our grandchildren?

'Mummy met Daddy over toad-in-the-hole in the dark? It was Love at First Bite!'

Is that what we'll say?

Work, Tuesday 18 January, 3 p.m.

Not involving ketchup or eating with the lights off, suddenly speed-dating is starting to look ever so slightly more appealing. My inbox is still enjoying a steady stream of follow-up banter. However, there is one problem with all of them. Nice though some of the men seem, I truly cannot remember what any of them looked like, and I haven't the vaguest idea who was who. So I've decided that it may be best for me to cease all contact with them and start again – only this time I'll be much more methodical. Duncan, meanwhile, has given up on his ticks and taken up Lottery instants, which he says are far more satisfying, and much more financially viable. Between you and me I think he might be becoming addicted, but I'm sure it's nothing to worry about at this stage. Must keep an eye on him, though; he does have a compulsive personality.

Sally, on the other hand, has already been on a couple of follow-up dates with her ticks; although none of them have turned out to be worth the 'extra time'. So far her conclusion is that three minutes is most definitely not long enough. Granted, it's sometimes far too much time for the really unlikely candidates – but for the ones you aren't sure about, you definitely can't squeeze in a fair assessment in three minutes. According to Sally, there's a risk that some people come off looking much better than they really are. So much so that when you go on a follow-up date with them, it's really little better than going on a blind date, as you know so little about them, beyond what you managed to remember from their hectic ninety-second monologue.

Not wanting to waste time emailing her ticks and learning their cut-and-paste life stories, Sally was very forward and arranged drinks with them straight away. Sadly, upon closer examination, all of them turned out to be disasters. The first guy – Webmaster Marius – turned up completely legless, reeked of cigars, and spent the whole evening spluttering about what Sally had always thought was a place in Indonesia. Poor Sal spent the whole time trying to think up excuses to get away. She phoned me whilst on the date, to check up on 'Howard', her newly fictionalised brother who was in hospital having his chin operated on. Apparently I told her he had taken a turn for the worse, as she started sobbing at me down the phone and told me she'd be there right away. Next time I'm under strict instruction to call her at a fixed point in the evening, just in case she needs another 'family emergency' with which to extract herself from excessive discussions about Java. When it comes to blind (or at least visually impaired) dates, us girls simply have to stick together.

Another guy was Ken – her 'Top Tick' – and therefore one she had reasonably high hopes for, according to the jottings on her scorecard. To her initial delight, Ken gave a double take on meeting her – something she was quite encouraged by. However, to her dismay, it soon became apparent from their conversation that the reason for his double take was that Ken had actually got his names and ticks muddled up, and Sal was not the tick he had in mind. After an awkward ten-minute chat he made his excuses and went to the men's room, never to return. When my time came to call her, she was already alone, waiting diligently for him to return from the lavatory.

Amazingly, she is thick-skinned enough to want to go again. I don't know where she gets her determination from. Or why she even needs to resort to such measures – she is charming, pretty, bright, successful – really a lovely all-rounder. But she keeps on saying to me that her time is running out, that Mr Right isn't going to just come up to her in accounts one day, or suddenly be sitting next to her on the bus . . . 'I can't spend the rest of my life holed up inside my flat, waiting for the balti delivery dude or the postman to be the man of my dreams,' she chants.

So apparently she should get out there and look for him – make love happen – as it were. Not sure I'm convinced by this argument, but then maybe my sister Lauren is right, and I am too much a prisoner of my own excessively romantic outlook. Or maybe Sally has a point that could be made into an angle for the Fast Love campaign? The idea that life is too short, 'Don't just sit around waiting for Mr Right', etc. But surely that's too obvious, it must have been done to death a thousand times before. No, I have no choice but to go again and look for a better hook than that.

So as I'm being forced to go again for the sake of my career, and with Sally being more determined than ever to find HIM, we have decided to get proactive this time, and find ways to avoid the mistakes of last time. Duncan has, amazingly, started seeing Max's friend Sara-Jayne. He now thinks he's too good for Fast Love and, not wanting to be unfaithful to 'SJ', has declined the invitation to go again. So this time it's just us girls together. Tomorrow night at our second (hopefully last) Fast Love event, we've decided to get tactical. Of course, it goes without saying that to really improve our chances of success, what needs addressing most is the calibre of men. Short of a miracle, though, the following tips will have to suffice. However, it is worth noting that the next event we are going on is actually called a Media/Creative special, hopefully involving a cast of fifty other People Like Us, which is slightly encouraging.

So, in order to get our money's worth, Sally's come up with some guidelines. Any truly committed SpeedDater should try (where possible) to abide by these rules: (NB, Sally works in accounts and has much more time on her hands than us creatives so I've only been able to make marginal suggestions.)

Sally (and Amelie's) Essential SpeedDating Tactics

*a) **Concentrate**.*
This is absolutely key. (Amelie in particular – try not to look quite so bored)

*b) **Take better, more detailed notes**.*
If necessary, follow a code or legend of some sort that can be deconstructed afterwards (TBC). e.g.s so far:

Jude = chiselled
Jonny = nice hair
Brent = irritating d***head
Norman = dull, slightly geeky
Michael = possibly into child porn
Mackenzie = funny
And so on.

*c) **Remember their actual names**.*
Also fundamental. Take care to remember who is who. If we are going to take part in any follow-up dates, we don't want to risk meeting up with a Brent or a Norman. If

necessary think up mnemonics on the spot, or associations that will help you remember them.

d) *Think up some daft questions for emergencies.*

Uncomfortable silences on a speed date are somehow even worse than the regular kind. So we need to have some ammunition up our sleeves. Not quite so stupid as the ones we got hit with last time, involving out-of-season vegetables, but just a few nice variations to be able to play with. Oh – but it's also vital that we don't double up on these – we are probably going to be meeting the same men after all.

e) *Try to look like you are enjoying yourself.*

You don't want them guessing your game after all (again, Amelie in particular).

OK, that ought to do it. Here we go again.

7

Saved by the Bells

When Amelie arrived at Langley's Bar in Covent Garden, there was no tell-tale queue filing out on to the road as there had been that first night at All Bar One. Where was everyone? she wondered. Where was Sally? Had she got the venue wrong? Surely she wasn't *that* late. Checking her watch and her confirmation email, she realised with growing fear that she might possibly have ever-so-slightly missed the registration time. Her throat began to constrict and her Marks & Spencer's ready meal began to feel unsettled in her stomach. What would the organisers say to her? Would she be publicly shamed for her lack of time-management skills? Be declared unfit for dating with speed? She took a deep breath and descended the spiral staircase before her, found the door marked 'Private Event', and pulled it open.

'So anyway, if I could just have everyone's at TENTION PLEASE. Thank you. Ahem. Good evening, ladies and gentlemen. Welcome to tonight's Media and

Creative Fast Love event at Langley's Bar here in London's Covent Garden. Thank you all for coming. Now, I do need to just say a few words but I'll keep it quite brief. Myself and Marty here are your hosts for this evening, so if anyone has any questions, please don't hesitate to come up to us. We're here to help make this a night to remember!'

Shutting the big chrome door behind her as quietly as humanly possible, Amelie's eyes collided straight into those of the chief Fast Lover for the evening, who was standing on a podium making the introductory speech. Amelie looked around her and saw that the bar was already packed out with candle-lit tables-for-two. Scanning the room, she observed the purple velvet curtains that were draped over the walls, the scarlet rose petals that were scattered over the bar, and the 'romantic' elevator music that was playing dimly in the background. Realising that she had entered at exactly the worst moment possible, Amelie tried to hide behind one of the purple veils, but it was too late. She had been seen – by everyone in the room, who, in one united movement, turned to study the latecomer in curiosity, with her curly brown hair matted to her face from the rain, and her cheeks flushing to an irrational shade of scarlet.

The lady on the podium, whose peroxide-blonde hair was pulled into two tight pigtails, put down her clipboard officiously. Affecting a broad smile, she said in a thick Brisbane accent, 'I guess you must be here for this evening's Fast Love event which has just started?'

'Hi, yes I am, please,' replied Amelie awkwardly, in front of the whole room of eager Fast Lovers; loathing herself for having stayed, sloth-like, to watch the end of

The Simpsons and having therefore failed to be on time and avoid suffering this chronic humiliation.

Pigtails made a big show of having to step down from her podium so that she could administer the latecomer. The other daters in the room looked at Amelie in amusement. She wanted to turn back and run home as fast as humanly possible, but she could see Sally looking at her with an uncomfortable mixture of sympathy and fury, and this held her feet to the ground. Pigtails – whose name badge indicated that her name was in fact Anna – looked down at her list and said, 'And what was your name again?' in that way that Amelie always found so irritating.

'I haven't told you yet,' she mumbled, before adding more audibly, 'it's Amelie. Amelie Holden.'

'OK, Amy, let me just have a little look here.' She rested a magenta-nailed finger on the guest list and scrolled manually through the names. 'Here is your scorecard and pen in the meantime, so you can be filling out your name and signing your name badge. You're Number 26, OK?' she said as she handed these items down to Amelie.

'Now, the dates *are* all good-to-go, so you will have to miss out on a couple, I'm afraid. Actually, let me think.' Anna's round face strained. Her hazel eyes squinted together, as if to illustrate clearly that she was suddenly, as she put it, *thinking*. She looked at the twenty-five dates that were awkwardly waiting to kick off, and then studied her watch. Shaking her pigtails she said gravely, 'Yes. No. I'm sorry. You will have to wait until the first interval now. It's just too disruptive for the other dates.'

Amelie tried to look crestfallen. 'Oh, OK. Sorry to be a nuisance. I'll just grab a drink and wait at the bar for a bit. Thanks for your help.'

Anna went off to finish her speech. Gleeful, Amelie went to the bar and ordered a champagne cocktail to celebrate having missed – if her instruction notes were anything to go by – 'up to seven' dates.

Back on the podium, Anna continued. 'Now, you should all have in front of you a scorecard, name badge and Biro. And as you all should know if you've read your speed-dating instruction sheets, the Fast Love scorecards are heaps simple to use – you'll soon get the knack of them. Simply mark down your date's name and a little bit about them. And also make sure you mark up whether or not they are a "yes", "no", or perhaps "someone you would like to see as a friend".' Anna stopped and looked around excitedly at her audience, all of whom seemed to Amelie to be fidgeting nervously and growing increasingly impatient.

Still Anna went on. 'And then tomorrow morning when the event is opened online, you'll all be able to enter your ticks in the Fast Love members' area, and see who your matches are!' Anna smiled at the couples in the room, eyeing them affectionately as though they were a tribe of needy, unfortunate children planted temporarily in her care.

'Now, I hope you're all feeling sparky, because fortunately, this evening it's rather a full house, and you'll all be going on as many as twenty-seven dates! Girls, you'll be rotating tonight, so the men stay seated where they are during all the dates. We might be slightly down on men, I think, so ladies, you might find yourselves with a gap or two, but you can use this time to catch up on your note-taking!'

Amelie sipped her cocktail and noticed Anna's skimpy tank top with the words *You've got to be quick! **Fast Love*** emblazoned across it. Amelie felt a sudden wave of relief, thinking that if this was the slogan that Fast Love were running with at the moment, maybe her job wasn't in such jeopardy after all.

Just then she noticed a tall, slim man with mousy-brown hair and glasses standing near the podium and looking uncomfortably from his watch to Anna. This must be Marty, the second-in-chief Fast Lover for the evening, she deduced.

Getting the hint from her sidekick, Anna picked up her pace.

'Um, just a few small notices now. Please could you ensure that you've turned off any mobile phones or pagers. And we regret that there'll be no smoking at all during any of the dates.'

Feigning sympathy, Anna added, 'But if you do find that you must smoke, we provide short breaks in between every seventh date or so for this purpose. And we'd prefer it if you went outside to smoke, just to keep the air in the room clean. But please ensure that you are back here in good time for when dating reconvenes.'

Looking round the room and smiling, she finished with, 'Now, without further ado, all I have to say is, let the dates begin!'

With this she lifted the big brass bell up high in the air and shook it hard, back and forth, over and over again. As Anna slowly reached a diminuendo, so too did the ringing in everyone's ears, a busy murmur filling the room as the dates kicked off. Amelie couldn't help but listen intently as the 'How are you's and the 'Is this your first time?'s and the 'Did you come alone?'s darted frantically around the room.

'So, what made you come speed-dating, Kevin?' Amelie

overheard Number 3, a tall brunette in a bright yellow top ask her date.

'Well, Frankie,' said Frankie's date, who was concealed from Amelie's view by one of the deep purple curtains, 'being a model, I tend to find that girls just like me for my body.' Then, after a dramatic pause he added, 'I want them to know and like me for my mind.'

Amelie tried in vain not to spit out all of her Strawberry Bellini.

'Yes. Of course.' Frankie smiled sympathetically. Glimpsing Frankie's expression from out of the corner of her eye, Amelie could tell that Frankie hadn't come close to buying into Kevin's pitch at all. Although Amelie was itching to see what Kevin really looked like, it was pointedly clear from Frankie's face that he was, in all probability, not a stunner.

Moments later Amelie caught sight of Sally, who looked resplendent in a brown devoré top, and was clearly already enjoying herself. She flashed a disapproving look at Amelie for her being late and having to sit out this round. Amelie grinned back at Sally, and shrugged innocently. She was *here*, wasn't she? It wasn't as though she was completely copping out. Besides, this way maybe she could get a new angle on the event by seeing it all from the perspective of the bar rather than actually taking part herself? Last time there was no time to actually stand back from it all and watch the performances together as a whole formation. Yes, being late was a stroke of genius. She took out her journal and began jotting down observations.

Amelie soon became bored of this. She put down her pen and her eyes began surveying the room again. Seconds into her survey her gaze met with a pair of handsome brown eyes that appeared to be staring right at her. Checking behind her nervously, Amelie realised two things. First, this man was definitely staring straight at her, and right past his own date, who was talking inanely at him about *Sex and the City*. Second, this man was very, very good-looking – and in that quirky, pretty way which always made her feel weak at the knees. She took in his dark blond wavy hair and muscular physique, smiled back at him, and wrote down in her journal, *Have spotted outrageously gorgeous Orlando Bloom type. Is obviously a plant.*

Downing the rest of her drink, she went outside for a cigarette.

Amelie was just stubbing out her cigarette and opening the packet to get out the next one when she sensed somebody appear right behind her.

'Don't suppose you have a light, do you?'

Amelie looked up and saw Orlando Bloom looking down at her from his majestic height of six feet five, clad in a rugged brown leather jacket.

'Oh. Yes . . . sure.' Amelie fumbled in her handbag for a while. Not being able to find the lighter that she had, only *minutes* ago, put away, she began rifling through a mass of old tissues and make-up and Post-its and pens, smiling and praying inwardly that Orlando wasn't instantly put off by the scattiness of this genre. Remembering that he was obviously a plant from Fast Love to lift the standards of the male contingent, she relaxed into the search and took her time, which was usually the best approach anyway. Finding the purple lighter, she smiled and offered it to the plant.

'Thanks. I'm Charlie, by the way.' Then, looking down

at his name badge, he gave an embarrassed laugh and added, 'But I guess you can see that already.'

Amelie laughed, and replied in a mock-condescending way, 'Yes. Hello, *Charlie*.'

Charlie pulled on his cigarette and leaned against the brick wall. 'So . . . how much is this like being at school?' he joked flirtatiously. 'I mean, grabbing a sneaky ciggie behind the bike sheds before the bell rings again?'

'I know. It's quite exciting really. A little naughty, even,' said Amelie, running her hand through her hair to check that it wasn't all still matted to her forehead from the rain.

'You haven't told me *your* name yet,' said Charlie. 'You, the notorious and beautiful latecomer, the naughty kid who is too cool to wear her name badge . . .' He trailed off, and then a light flashed in his brown eyes. 'Oh, but hang on, I remember, you had to tell the whole room when you came in late, didn't you?' Yes! It was Amy, wasn't it?'

'Amelie, actually.'

'I know, I was only kidding. I knew it was Amelie because I remember thinking – excuse my cheesiness – how much I loved the name. I take it you saw the film?'

'Yeah, I loved it. It has a great soundtrack too.' Amelie leaned against the wall behind her and Charlie turned to face her.

'Yes, it does, doesn't it! And Jean-Pierre Jeunet is one of my favourite directors. Brilliantly quirky. Have you seen any of his other films – *City of Lost Children* or *Delicatessen*?'

'Um, no, not yet,' said Amelie. 'I've been meaning to see *Delicatessen* for ages, though. You know your films, don't you?'

'Yeah, I'm a bit of a buff, but I have to be . . .' Charlie

looked down shyly and then said quietly as though it was some kind of confession, 'I'm an actor.'

'Oh, don't be apologetic. I work in advertising. I guess that means we're both pretentious in our own way,' said Amelie, thinking to herself that there was every possibility now that this lovely looking, charming man might even be a bona fide genuine person, and not a plant from Fast Love.

Charlie looked at her admiringly and took a drag on his cigarette. 'So, I have to ask, what brings you here? What's a stunning wit like you doing in a place like this?'

Amelie laughed and stubbed out her cigarette with her shoe. 'Well, I could ask you the same question . . . But I won't. No, seriously, I really didn't want to come; I've been dragged here by a friend in need of moral support.'

'So I guess that's why you looked so over the moon when you heard you'd be sitting out the first round,' said Charlie. Then, stubbing out his butt, he added, 'Well, since you didn't ask, the reason I'm here is because I've dated one too many actresses . . . and with the circles I move in, there was no chance of me ever meeting any nice non-actresses – well, all except for the girls that work at my flatmate's accountancy firm – and I seriously doubt that I'd be able to hit it off with anyone with that much passion for numbers.'

'What's wrong with actresses?' asked Amelie, intrigued.

'Oh my God, what's *right* with them! They're all so self-involved! They need you to caress their self-esteem *continuously*, to keep telling them they've lost weight, that their performance gets better every time you see it . . . Honestly, I got to feel like I was some kind of ego drip!'

Amelie laughed nervously, not having been expecting

quite such a tirade, but nevertheless satisfied that this was a good enough reason to try speed-dating.

'So what's the last thing you've been in? Or is that a sensitive question?' she asked, but they were rudely interrupted. The bell was ringing to signal the end of break-time and the start of a new round of dates.

'Ho hum. Back to the rat race,' said Charlie, looking disappointed.

Amelie looked up at this gorgeous, available and seemingly flawless man who was smiling down at her, and couldn't help smiling back. It was funny; in a way, she had met this man quite naturally, as they hadn't even had their fixed date yet, and already she had found talking to him so incredibly easy and relaxed, like they could have stayed out there all night and never gone back in. So if he's not a plant from Fast Love, she reasoned, he must surely be a psycho of some sort? A sado masochist. A militant Christian. Or maybe even a plant from a *rival* speed-dating company. Yes, that's it! Seriously, there must be something wrong with him, she thought. There *must* be a flaw, otherwise why would he be so keen to talk to her? Either way, she made a mental note to ensure that she planned her questions well and made the most of her three minutes with this one.

Charlie shook off his coat and opened the door to go back in. 'Well, I'd much rather stay out here and smoke naughty cigarettes with Amelie, but I think we'll get put on detention if we don't go back in now,' he said playfully. 'And you've already got a black mark, so I think you shouldn't take any more chances, missy.'

'Yeah, you're right. Better go and face it. But I'm sure we'll meet again soon,' said Amelie.

Closing the door behind them, Charlie looked at his watch and replied, 'Yes, in approximately forty-five minutes' time, if I'm not mistaken.'

Amelie grinned as she realised the mental effort it must have taken him to work out the time of their date just from knowing their two badge numbers. How oddly flattering, she thought as she went to take her seat opposite a distinctly unattractive man named Kevin.

Next up after Kevin, the model who craved mental stimulation, was a stockbroker, who, with a firm handshake, introduced himself as, 'Donnie. Current salary in excess of two hundred K. And then there're bonuses. How do you do?'

Three extra-long minutes later, Amelie found herself sitting face to face with the stunt double of Manuel from *Fawlty Towers*. As she put down her pen and took another large swig of her third drink, 'Carlos' gazed into her eyes and said, 'We 'ave met before? In a previous life?'

Amelie struggled to keep a straight face and to think of an interesting reply. 'Perhaps, who knows . . .' was all she could manage, with a smile. 'So, Carlos,' she said, remembering she had work to do, 'what do you think of speed-dating?'

'Well,' he thought for a moment, 'I think it eez good . . . it should help spread a leetle more love in zee world, *si*?'

'So, do you think it will last?' she was asking Gerald from New Zealand four minutes later. 'Can you see it spreading around the world?'

'Well, perhaps,' said Gerald, a stout man with a warm smile and receding blond hair.

'Although it's not really the most romantic thing in the world, is it? Still, maybe it's a good way of finding out about the world, about people. I mean, from a sociological point of view it's sort of fascinating.'

'Yeah, I see what you mean,' said Amelie. 'So, are you a sociologist?'

'No, I'm a movie director. You know, I'm actually starting to think all this might make great content for a short. Or maybe even a feature-length picture, if you could get a good enough script.'

Amelie laughed in agreement. 'Maybe you should be taking notes tonight, for research.'

'Yeah, good idea.' Gerald looked at Amelie and you could see the tick forming in his eyes in approval. 'Do you know what else I've been thinking? It's quite a London thing this, isn't it? I mean, you couldn't imagine it needing to happen somewhere really far up north like Newcastle, could you? Everyone's already got social skills up there. It's almost like Southerners have become so stuffy and rigid that they've lost their natural ability to talk to strangers, unless they know they're authorised to do so!'

'Yeah, you might be right,' said Amelie, her eyes wandering over to where Charlie was sitting. 'Well, if you need an actor to play one of the SpeedDaters in this film of yours, that guy over there is your man.'

'Oh yes, Orlando over there? Yes, I thought he seemed like a performer of some sort,' commented Gerald.

The bell rang and Gerald looked disappointed. 'Well, it's been really nice talking to you, Amelie. Enjoy the rest of your evening.'

Amelie smiled and agreed that it had been nice. He seemed like a sweetheart; maybe a little out of her age range, but charming and intelligent all the same.

Three dates later, Amelie was feeling increasingly

jaded, and couldn't stop herself from monitoring Charlie's dates as they progressed around the room. Suddenly she wasn't so bothered about interrogating her dates for their motives any more. She began to feel more and more excited about her date with Charlie. They had only met for a few minutes, but there was definitely a connection between them; definitely a spark – even before they had had their 'first date'. Counting the dates lined up between herself and Charlie, she noticed with dismay that many of the girls awaiting their moment with him were noticeably attractive. She couldn't help but feel exasperated at the rigid structure of the evening – at last she had found a guy she liked, found a guy she clicked with, but it was against the rules to go and talk to him!

Two dates later, Amelie was feeling her trademark stomach ache that she always got before a big date with a nice man. Only this time the date was only one metre and three minutes away and she could already smell his Ralph Lauren aftershave. She felt nervous and excited and was barely listening to the man opposite her as he told her about why the new *Star Wars* film was going to be the best one ever made, even better than the original trilogy. Tick, tock. Tick, tock, she thought. I only need to smile and nod for another forty seconds and then it's my date with the lovely Charlie.

Thirty-nine seconds later the bell rang and Anna's voice came on to the microphone. 'Break-time, everyone! This will be your second break for the evening. See you all back here in fifteen!'

Fuming inwardly, Amelie decided she might as well use the time to check on her appearance, so she got up and went to the ladies', picking up Sally en route.

'How're you getting on, Sally Cinnamon?' she asked as they went through the doors to the ladies' toilets.

'Oh, pretty well. I've ticked about seven so far.' Amelie tried not to look entirely taken aback as she closed the cubicle door.

Toilet banter: therein lies the real truth about speed-dating. Amelie had been in her cubicle only thirty seconds when the cacophony of amusing comments began. Three minutes later she was still in there, transfixed by the hilarity of the stories, and the myths that were already spreading.

'Have you *seen* Number 12! His body is to die for!' squealed one voice.

'Yeah, but did you see the wart on his neck? No thank you!' replied another.

'Call me picky, but is no one else feeling just a little bit cheated by the amount of accountant and IT geeks here? They've obviously lied in their applications and smuggled themselves into the Media/Creative night, haven't they?! Sneaky fuckers,' exclaimed a girl with a thick Scottish accent. 'I mean, don't you think the organisers should be more careful about reading the occupation box? I didn't spend twenty-five of my hard-earned squid so I could meet more accountants and webmasters!'

'Yeah, me neither,' came a dissatisfied voice from Walthamstow. 'Pass me the lip gloss, Soph. Thanks, love. I mean, this one guy said to me he was an IT consultant, but that he *wanted* to be a film director. As if that made it OK!'

'Yeah, I know,' came a disaffected voice from Hoxton. 'I wanted to meet people who work in the media and have similar interests as us . . . not repressed, closet creatives who are stuck in soulless City jobs. Imposters!'

Suddenly a new, aggressive voice joined in, 'Oh for God's sake, girls. You can't really be *that* shallow, can you? They're just people at the end of the day.' Amelie came out of her cubicle and realised it was Sally, who had suddenly decided to make some sort of a protest. Why, exactly, Amelie wasn't entirely sure, but she felt she ought to stand and listen by way of support.

'I mean,' Sally continued, 'why does what you do *have* to entirely define who you are? They might be nice people underneath their professions, and you're not even giving them a chance. They could even be The Ones.'

Stunned, awkward silence followed this unexpected diatribe. Sally looked around the toilets at all the girls doing their make-up. They were each either looking down at their cowboy boots or playing with their name badges, not sure what to do next. Eventually Louisa from Walthamstow broke the silence.

'So . . . anyway, did anyone have Number 16 yet? Derek – he has the squeakiest voice! Definitely gay, but trying to suppress it.'

Laughter all around. Sally rolled her eyes and walked out of the ladies' room, Amelie following closely behind, wandering at what point Sally had had such as epiphany about the way she saw other people, and feeling surprised that just coming speed-dating could make you think so deeply about your place in the world, and how you relate to others. On second thoughts, maybe it was just that Sally really hated her job. Perhaps *she* was one of the said repressed creatives. Walking into the bar, Amelie wasn't sure which was closer to the truth.

Back in the toilets, the ladies carried on reapplying their make-up, and checking that their appearances were as good as they could possibly be. 'Is this your mascara, Lou?' asked Sophie.

'Um, no, but you have it, sweet. Hey – did anyone ever hear about The Girl With Twenty-Seven Ticks? Wonder what *her* secret is?'

At long last the bell had rung for Charlie and Amelie's date. Since Amelie had sat down, Charlie's eyes had fixed on her and barely moved an inch.

'So,' asked Charlie, a playful grin on his face, 'are you anything like the Amelie in the film?'

Amelie laughed. 'Um, well, I don't look anything like her, but I guess my personality is kind of similar . . . in some ways. My friends would probably tell you I am. I can be quite "quirky" at times, but maybe not quite as loony as her.'

The pair were just getting into their date, when, after only forty seconds, the bell rang again, making them jump.

'Ladies and Gents.' It was Anna, taking centre stage again. 'I'm terribly sorry to interrupt your dates, but we seem to have mislaid one of our males. Has anyone seen Number 32? Male, Caucasian, tall, blond, glasses, dressed in a crimson Ben Sherman shirt?' Anna looked around hopefully.

'No? Well, he was here during the last round, according to Number 12, and the first round, according to Number 7. But he seems to have failed to return from the toilet since the break.'

There was a gentle murmur as all the dates in the room collectively shrugged and appeared not to know anything about Number 32. Finding the idea of a speed-dating fugitive on the loose around Soho all too amusing, Amelie sniggered as quietly as she could. Charlie grinned cheekily at Amelie and jutted his foot out under the table, nudging her foot in a disciplinary display of affection.

'So,' continued Anna, her face full of concern, 'if anyone does have any information regarding his whereabouts, please do let myself or Marty know. Until he returns, ladies, I'm afraid you'll be another man down, so if you wouldn't mind just having a rest for three minutes or talking amongst yourselves. Sorry, guys, you will be able to resume dating in just a moment. And we'll give you some extra time for all the time I've just taken up. Thanking you.' Ring, ring.

'Wow, one less date to have to sit through. Brilliant,' said Amelie as the dates rebooted.

'I wonder where he went, though,' said Charlie. 'Imagine just bolting like that. I guess he must have looked round the room and decided no one was his type and saved himself the bother. Anyway, forgive me for sounding a little sick for a second now, but I just wanted to say I've been really looking forward to our three minutes.'

Amelie grinned, feeling rapturous that he was thinking the same as she was. 'Yes, that is cheesy. But I'll forgive you, seeing as you said it so nicely.'

Charlie put his elbows on the table and leaned closer.

'Do you ever wonder what people can get away with on these "dates"? I mean, speaking purely hypothetically, of course. Do you think if two people really hit it off, like, if they *really* fancied each other, to the point where they just really wanted to have a quick snog on the spot, would that be against the rules?'

'Oh no. I think that would be completely unacceptable,' said Amelie. 'Can you imagine Anna letting that happen?

She'd be over there in a flash, breaking them up, telling them to go and sit in a corner or something.'

'Yeah, you're right. No putting out on the first date; it's just not the done thing, is it?' Charlie was looking at Amelie intensely, his brown eyes dancing.

'So,' said Amelie, her eyes focused on his. 'You never told me – what was your last performance?'

'Oh, you'll be so impressed. I played a dead man, in a play by Harold Pinter at the Hampstead Theatre. Apparently I play dead really well. Great feedback from the director and everyone else. A "natural" they said. Between you and me, though, I'm a bit worried I was too good . . .'

Amelie laughed. 'You're worried you'll be typecast now?'

Charlie nodded. 'I've played some bigger parts since I left drama school. But it's so up and down. You can be next to Derek Jacobi on a West End stage one day, then down the Watford Harlequin shopping centre handing out flyers for Carphone Warehouse the next. Things have been even quieter this year, which is worrying. Although I'm up for a part in the new season of *Doctor Who*. I'd go *mental* if I got that.'

'Oh my God, will you get to be a dalek?' exclaimed Amelie excitedly. 'I love the daleks! I mean, I'm no sci-fi geek, let's just make that clear now, but when it comes to the daleks – I mean, Jesus, there's just something about them, isn't there? Maybe it's a nostalgia thing; my sister Lauren and I used to love watching it when we were kids.' Amelie thought to herself that discussing daleks with an Orlando Bloom lookalike was the last thing she had foreseen for her second stint at speed-dating; but she was enjoying herself all the same.

'Well, they *are* pretty cool, even if you're all grown-up,' said Charlie, clearly thrilled at her taste in aliens. 'But no, I'm not up for a dalek role. I think it's one of the new exotic kinds of aliens.'

Amelie looked impressed and smiled. Charlie looked at his watch and saw that their time was running out. 'So, here's a thought. D'you think you'd be allowed to give me your phone number? Or is that also against Fast Love protocol?'

'Well, let me think,' said Amelie, but suddenly the bell was ringing again and there was a large ginger woman standing next to her.

'Shift up, love. It's my turn.'

'Just a second, *love*.' Amelie looked up at bolshy Number 24, and picked up her pen and scorecard. Then she wrote down next to Charlie's number, 'Mackenzie, Jonny, Dalek. Lovely' and, despite herself, gave him the first tick of the evening. As she stood up, Charlie smiled and stretched out his arm to try and take her hand. She declined, not wanting to make a big show in front of the increasingly irate Number 24. 'See you again.'

'Definitely. Lovely.' Charlie smiled and followed Amelie with his eyes as she moved down to sit with her next date. Number 24, meanwhile, looked neglected and cleared her throat.

Half past ten and five dates later, Amelie was exhausted, bored and ready to crash. She had enjoyed herself far more than last time, and would have preferred to have spent many more minutes with Charlie than five. But, even though she had been looking forward to meeting up with him after the formal dates were over, after rotating around so many more dates and identical conversations, she now felt as though she had the personality of a forgetful goldfish and was ready to retire.

Scribbling some notes on to her scorecard about Derek the Christian Media Salesman, she realised with elation that it was finally time for her last date of the evening. Bidding Derek farewell, she rubbed her weary eyes and dragged herself round to the other side of the white pillar to where Number 28, her final speed-date would be waiting for her. Rounding the corner, Amelie drew back the purple veil that was concealing the mystery man's identity. When she saw who was sitting there, the colour drained instantly from her face, and she had to grab on to the pillar to stop herself from fainting.

'Hello, Amelie. I didn't see you there.'

Seeing a Ghost

Just when I was starting to see the good side of speed-dating. Just when I was starting to think that maybe it wasn't so bad after all. The unthinkable happens.

Of all the godforsaken fuckwits in the world, who should be my final speed date of the evening? Who should be tucked discreetly behind a pillar all night, spying on me, knowing I would have bolted on sight if I had seen him any earlier? Well, none other than The Reason There is Evil in the World, Bastard Git King of the Arseholes himself, Mr Jack Halliwell.

The selfish Jack Halliwell whom I caught cheating on me with his high-flying lawyer colleague three years ago. The arrogant Jack Halliwell who took my heart, broke it into a thousand pieces, and then left it there, shattered on our living-room floor. The beautiful Jack Halliwell, whom I swore I could only get over if I never ever saw him again as long as I lived. Damn this ridiculous job and this cursed brief; I wish I had never gone back again for more sadistic research.

But how completely weird that he was there. What a terrifying coincidence.

My God, he looked so different – so totally withdrawn, unshaven, pale – and so skinny! He had none of the chunk on him that he was starting to develop those last months we were together. In fact, maybe that's why I didn't spot him sooner. He looked so different to how I remember him. Not that I even want to remember him! Even now, just seeing him again three years later, all I can feel is the exact sensation of pain I felt on that miserable January afternoon. My stomach hurts in exactly the same place. I want to yell the same things. I want to cry in exactly the same way.

It gets worse, though – it wasn't enough that I just had to spend the longest three minutes of my life in his company. Oh no. The arrogant arse also had the audacity to use this time to try and gaze intensely into my eyes, to try and tell me that it never worked out with Penny . . . That all this time since then not a day has passed when he didn't entirely regret what he did. He went on to say that it meant nothing to him, the fling with her . . . it was just that he and I had rushed into things too soon, moving in together straight after college . . . and so he went on, with all the predictable rest.

More than anything, though, he had the cheek to say that he still missed me, that he still couldn't stop thinking about me. He said he'd wanted really badly to get in touch with me but hadn't been able to figure out what to say or where to start . . .

But then came the worst part of all.* He let loose a massive torrent of crap about how it was obviously fate playing a hand in getting us together tonight. That it was destiny that had brought us together again after all this time. He knew that would hit a chord with me, being the hopeless fatalist that I am. For a second I felt a twinge – that maybe this was the reason I'd been given the speed-dating brief in the first place – and maybe this was why I'd chosen to go again tonight. All because we were meant to be reunited – it was a preordained truth, written in the stars. But then, just as he was writing down his phone number and suggesting we meet up, the bell rang. Realising in a flash what utter bullshit this was, I told him to stick his scorecard up his arse. There's no way I'm giving him a second look, let alone a second chance. No way in hell.

* Depends how you look at things. You might say that the worst part of the night was getting home and realising that in my destitution I completely forgot to remove my speed-dating name badge after the last date, and thus humiliatingly, travelled the whole tube journey home with: 'Hello, my name is Amelie. You've got to be quick!' plastered across my chest. Which is always nice.

Divorce Genes

'Amelie. Amelie, it's me. Please pick up, I know you're there.'

Amelie was lying in her room, the curtains closed, the lights off, and the music from *Lost in Translation* playing on a loop. She had no idea what time it was, or even what day. All she knew, from deep under her duvet, was that she hadn't felt this bad in three years.

'Amelie. You left in such a hurry last night, I was really worried about you. Hope you are OK, sweets. I'll come over if you want and we can talk about it. You seemed to be enjoying the night from what I could see. You looked like you were hating it far less than the first time, so I don't know what happened . . . Anyway, give me a call, OK? Speak soon, hon.' At the sound of Sally hanging up, Amelie rolled over and buried her head under her pillow.

*

'OK – hold it right there, missy. There's no way in the world you'll get me in that!' exclaimed Amelie in reaction to the ostentatious magenta ball gown that Claire was holding up.

It was twenty-four hours later, and Claire had finally managed to extract a broken Amelie from her pyjamas and take her out for some Ben & Jerry's, a facial and a spot of wedding shopping at Selfridges. Fortunately, the memory of Jack was beginning to be less vivid, and she was starting to remember what it felt like to be Amelie – scatty, successful singleton – again.

'OK, how about this one, then?' Claire held up a much simpler, sleek Karen Millen dress.

'Mmmmn, that's a bit more do-able. The others are either too girlie or too mumsy, I'm afraid.'

Claire looked heartily relieved. They had been looking for hours. 'Thank God. So will you try this on?'

'Yes, but I much prefer the blue to the peach or pink. Besides, they would clash horribly with my hair.'

'Fine, let's try it, then.'

While Amelie began undressing in the changing room, Claire began to gently probe for gossip.

'So . . . little miss SpeedDater . . . didn't you say there was one guy that you actually took a shine to the other night? Well, before the Date With Doom, that is?' asked Claire, grappling with the intertwined coat hangers in her arms, slowly managing to separate them.

'Well, I guess so,' Amelie called through the changing-room curtain. 'Although I'd kind of forgotten all about it after Jack appeared . . . Yeah, I guess there was this one guy. Charlie – a really cute actor. It all seems such a blur now, but I think we really hit it off. Even before our scheduled three minutes . . . But I'm not sure I can stomach seeing anyone at the moment, my head is all full of Jack again . . . plus I've got so much work to do.'

'Oh, Amelie, that's such crap. You should definitely give this guy a go. You're just being a wuss. It would do you good. And you never know, the more you see the guys from the Fast Love event, surely the more chance there is that you'll be inspired and come up with the goods for the campaign?'

'Oh, I so wish that was true. You know, Josh is really turning into a bit of a psychopath about this pitch – he's on everyone's case about it. I'm telling you, Claire, if I have to listen to his ridiculous Rolf Harris 'Can you tell what it is yet?' impression again, or hear his disastrous attempts to play the didgeridoo one more time, I swear I shall go mad!'

Amelie stepped inelegantly into the blue dress and continued. 'But anyway, Sally has forced me to register my ticks online. Although I'm pretty sure the only reason she kept ringing to harass me about it was so that I can find out this weird Christian bloke's email address for her!'

'How do you mean?' asked Claire, sounding confused.

'Well, you see, if you tick everyone, which I did again for the sake of *research*, what happens is, you automatically get sent everyone's email address who ticked you. And Sneaky Sal has discovered a sort of speed-dating loophole. If you don't tick anyone after the event, Fast Love assumes it's failed you, so it lets you go again for free. Sort of like with insurance, I guess; when you don't make a claim, you get to hold on to your no-claims bonus. Um, can you pass me those strappy shoes, please?'

Claire passed the black kitten-heels under the curtain while Amelie continued. 'So, Sal has decided that, since out of all her ticks, there was only one guy there that she really liked, it wouldn't be worth her submitting her ticks, as then she'd lose her free go next time! But, with me ticking them all, chances are I might get Derek. Apparently Derek hasn't done his ticks yet, so I don't know if we're a match. But if I do end up with his address, Sally reckons she's just going to email him on the sly, and save her free go for next time in the process!'

'Sneaky! Am, are you all right in there? What's taking you so long?'

'I'm OK, I'm almost there, just having bra issues . . . one sec . . . So anyway, I *did* tick Charlie and most of the others online to see what would happen, and he came up as a match and emailed me straight away. I haven't emailed back yet, and he's emailed me again already, which I'm just a little put off by!'

'Oh you and your silly complexes, Amelie,' Claire said sternly. 'How many times do I have to tell you? Just because a guy likes you and is keen and wants to know you, it doesn't make him a freak. He sounds nice, from what you've said. It sounds like you got on really well. And if he *is* being over-confident, it's probably just an occupational hazard that all actors suffer from. Give him a chance. Put it this way, if he was acting all disinterested, you'd want to see him, wouldn't you?'

'Well, yes. I suppose.'

'So just pretend he is, and go on a date with him!'

At last, Amelie pulled across the curtain to the changing room, and Claire gasped.

'Oh wow, Amelie, you look gorgeous! Honestly, it really works – it really brings out the blue in your eyes.'

Amelie turned to face the mirror and studied her reflection critically. Modestly, she admitted, 'Well, it does sort of work, doesn't it?' She swayed from side to side and scrunched up her hair, letting the wild brown curls fall down in soft muddles around her shoulders.

'Yes, it's magic, Amelie.' Then, after a pregnant pause, Claire added, 'Does it not make you feel, even for a second, I don't know . . . a little bit tempted, like you can one day see yourself on your own wedding day, in the future?'

Amelie shrugged nonchalantly just as a wave of melancholy drifted across her eyes. 'I've told you, I'm never getting married. You know that; there's just no point to it. Not for me, anyway. Not with my divorce genes. Besides – look at me, I'm no blushing bride; it's just not my style. Sorry, Clairey,' she said, beginning to remove the dress. Moments later she added awkwardly, 'Oh, I've just remembered, I promised Dunc I'd pop by the office in the afternoon and see how the campaign was going.'

'But it's a Sunday, Amelie!' exclaimed Claire in exasperation.

'I know, I know. But we've finished dressing up now, haven't we?'

'I suppose. OK, go on, then,' said Claire, a note of disappointment lingering in her voice.

Amelie quickly dressed herself and then picked up her bags and coat.

'Sorry I have to dash off – I didn't realise how late it had become.'

'That's all right – I know you and time-keeping aren't the best of chums.'

'Bye, sweet.' Amelie leaned forward and gave Claire a hurried kiss, before leaving her standing there, bearing the blue dress over one arm, and a bewildered expression on her face.

Amelie hurried down the busy escalators in Selfridges

and walked out on to a rainy and flustered Oxford Street. Pulling on her coat, she picked up her pace to keep up with the bus she needed to catch to take her home. She turned back to face the bridal mannequins looking out of the fourth-floor windows, and felt a pang of guilt for fleeing so suddenly and leaving Claire there. The rain dripped down Amelie's face, and she held her head down, fearing that any passers-by should see her watery eyes. As she stood in the crowded queue for the bus, she sensed her eyes welling with more tears; unfathomably emotional tears. Shaking her head in frustration at herself, she climbed aboard the 139.

Now her phone was ringing incessantly. She looked at it, saw that it was Jack calling her again, and switched it off. Definitely time to get a contract phone, and change numbers in the process, Amelie decided. She slumped down into a seat by the window, feeling choked and fragile and hating herself for it. Plugging into her iPod and putting on her favourite Doves track, she began to rummage through her bag for her journal.

139 bus, Sunday 23 January, 4ish

Sitting on the bus home after running out quite strangely on Claire from a shopping trip. Feel like I've just been a total bitch – lied to her about needing to go to work, and have no idea why. Don't know why I'm in such a state lately. I know I sound like Elizabeth Wurtzel on a bad day, but I really do feel as though there is some kind of dark cloud following me around at the moment, and the slightest thing will set me off into tears. And the sad truth is, no matter how hard I try, I just can't get Jack out of my head. Don't know what it is about him, but seeing him again just brought everything back, reminded me of how amazing it once was with us. What if I never find someone that I click with that much again?

Hearing him say that he still feels it, even after all this time, it makes my insides want to eat themselves up. Haven't been able to eat anything remotely solid since then. All that's passed my lips in the last thirty-six hours is half a pot of Ben & Jerry's, on Claire's instruction, and even that still feels like an unwelcome guest in my stomach. And I have to confess that at my most depressed, subhuman point yesterday, I kind of gave up on self-control altogether. Found myself delving in the innermost chasms of the loft, hunting for all 'our' music, which in a rare moment of strength I had buried deep, years ago, amid piles of hoarded memorabilia. Why I still hold on to all that stuff now is one of life's mysteries, when it can surely only serve as emotional torture, but I never have been any good at throwing things away.

Anyway, there I was, legs crossed on the freezing, musty attic floor, surrounded by old clothes, junk and mothballs, tears streaming down my face as I listened to all 'our' old songs again. It took me right back to the heart of the good times, but in the most painfully bittersweet way. The real low point came when I put on that Dylan album. The one Jack used to play to death in the car. Because he only had it on cassette, every road trip we made, to Brighton, Cornwall or wherever, without fail, out the trusty, knackered tape would come. He'd crank it up to its maximum tinniness, and then there we'd be, cruising along the motorway, listening to the wobbly old recording, singing at the tops of our voices because no one else could hear us; the sun gleaming through the window at us and warming our shoulders through the sun-roof. Playing silly car games, eating dirty garage pasties, and chattering away like the soul-mates we were. Listening to the CD equivalent only yesterday, the sound was more refined and far less crackly, but still it made me remember exactly how it felt back there in the car – reminded me of that naïve feeling of security; that visceral certainty that we'd always be together, could never imagine ever being apart. Well, up until the inevitable moment in every long journey, when his rusty blue Beetle would reliably break down, and we'd get into a silly fight while waiting for the AA to come and dig us out. But it never lasted – we'd always be kissing again by the time the car was back in action, inseparable and unable to take our eyes off each other again.

So I couldn't help allowing myself to wallow yesterday. It's just too hard not to; his face is so vividly etched on to my mind. It's weird how some music can just bottle an emotion like that, keep it so tightly concealed that, years later, like a time-capsule, it can just rip your heart right open again. Anyway, after a few hours of listening to his lovingly crafted 'Amelie's mix' CDs, I'd just about reached that miserable stage of getting one of those cold, nasty crying headaches, complete with hyper-red eyes, puffy cheeks and self-loathing. It was exactly this point when the door went. Of course, at the sound of the doorbell, my heart did somersaults from thinking it would be Jack. Then from praying it wouldn't be. And then from rushing to tend to my face and eyes and apply some hasty make-up just in case it actually was. And then finally my heart sank again properly when I saw Claire's face on the other side of the door. Lovely Claire, come to excavate me from my well of self-pity.

Bless her, I'm glad she did; it's good to be back in the world again. But, even though I'm feeling slightly better now, I still can't stop thinking, What if I really am meant to forgive him? What if bumping into him again after three years really is fate's way of telling me that there is such a thing as a 'one', and that Jack is it? Maybe I was too harsh on him? I mean, I really can't imagine finding anyone like him again, that just 'gets' me so well. Should I give him another chance?? Wish I knew . . . Wish I'd never gone to that stupid event; wish to God I'd never started this evil ad campaign.

Suddenly aware of the fact that the old man next to her on the bus was avidly reading every word of Amelie's thoughts, Amelie shut her journal abruptly. Turning up the volume on her iPod, she leaned her head against the window for the rest of the journey home, watched the clouds sweep by, and tried to be invisible.

Hungry for More

'What can you say? Nothing, apart from "The guy's a genius,"' Charlie informed Amelie three days later as they strolled out of the Electric Cinema in Notting Hill. Amelie had finally decided to jettison the Jack-related mixture of feelings, phone calls and emails which had been orbiting her for the past few days, and she had emailed Charlie back in reply to his offer of a date that would be more than three minutes long. Then, after a brief foray into email flirtation, Amelie had agreed to meet up with him again, to let him take her to see *Delicatessen*.

'It was a great film, I admit,' said Amelie, smiling. She was basking in the realisation that she had finally broken the back of her depression; at last she could see that there was fun to be had in the world again. 'Very eerie,' she added, 'I'm really glad I've finally seen it. Thanks for taking me.'

Amelie smiled, feeling full of life again and looking contentedly up at the sky. Even though it was January, the sky was clear, and it was an unusually mild evening; both Amelie and Charlie were carrying their winter coats by their sides while they walked along the road.

'Hey, how about we go and get a little bite to eat?' said Charlie. 'I know a great little place up the road which would be lovely on a night like this. Except, um . . .' He turned to Amelie, his face suddenly overcast, and said meekly, 'Amelie, I'd love to buy you dinner now, really I would. But I'm *so* skint this month; I haven't had paid work in such a ridiculous length of time I don't want to think about it. Do you mind if we go halves?'

'Christ, I thought there was really something wrong then, you looked so serious.' Amelie giggled. 'No I don't mind at all; I hate people paying for me, it makes me feel all nervous.'

The sunshine returned to Charlie's cheeks as he took Amelie's hand in his and they began walking down Portobello Road.

'I think we're going to get on rather well.'

Half an hour later they were seated around a large round table, shielded from the cold by a bizarre kind of miniature marquee, on the roof terrace of a bohemian little café in Portobello. There they were, ready to tuck into a candle-lit dinner for two of mixed fajitas and sangria, looking up at the stars and nestling up to the outdoor heaters for warmth. Before long they were deep into an animated discussion about the merits of art-house cinema. Unbeknownst to them, this romantic setting came with an asterisk of sorts. Being such a sociable and popular venue, the terrace tables at the Grove Café were always in high demand. So very limited in number were the places there that a table for five with only two customers was still – if you read the small print – just an unfulfilled table for five. Little did Charlie and Amelie know that, just as they were starting to relax into their indulgent 'Fajita Fest for Two', three starving Italian lads were mounting the spiral staircase towards the terrace, needing to be fed, watered and seated. On their arrival the waiter gave no hesitation in placing them in the next available seats, which happened to be on Amelie and Charlie's table.

'*Ciao! Mi chiamo Paolo*. And this is Franco *e* Raphael. You do not mind if we join you?'

The other two Italians, apparently less fluent in English, smiled nervously while their outgoing friend did the talking, and Amelie did the nodding.

'Of course not, please come and join us,' said Charlie, looking a little disappointed not to have Amelie all to himself, but accepting responsibility for having brought her to such a zealously sociable venue. Pulling their chairs up to the table, Paolo and his friends came to join them. The trouble with this set-up was that Charlie and Amelie, being still quite nervous around each other as first-daters, had chosen a more casual, opposite-each-other positioning, rather than the more intimate, next-to-each-other seating plan. This left Paolo with no alternative than to sandwich himself awkwardly in between the pair, while the other men sat in the remaining two seats on either side. Suffice to say, all five were now much closer to each other than Englishness would normally deem appropriate.

Paolo, blissfully unaware of this, leaned into Charlie and winked at him.

'You are married, *si*? The *signora* is *molto bella, si*? You are very lucky man. And you are very much in love, yes? It shows, *si*, it shows very much.' Franco and Raphael nodded in acquiescence.

Charlie opened his mouth to protest in some way, but Paolo went on. 'We will have some champagne to celebrate.' He lifted up his arm to attract the waiter's attention.

'*Scusi, per favore*. Please can we have a bottle of champagne for five, and three servings of the pesto linguine?'

Moments later, the five of them were toasting to '*l'amore*' and sipping Veuve Cliquot. As it turned out, Paolo was a successful filmmaker from Milan who had just finished making a movie all about unrequited love, so it gave him great joy to see true love blossoming before him. After a while, Charlie and Amelie decided to play along, hide their left hands under the table, and pretend that they really were newly-weds.

'Yes, we were married in Vegas. Very romantic, you know, surprisingly so,' said Charlie.

Half an hour and numerous filmmaking anecdotes later, Amelie and Charlie felt replete. Sighing, they admitted defeat over their gigantic fajita platter.

'Shame,' said Charlie, arranging his cutlery in the closed position. 'Delicious fajitas, but I guess we did gorge ourselves silly on popcorn earlier.'

'Yeah. I hate wasting food when it's this good,' agreed Amelie, knowing that she never usually had much of an appetite on a first (or second, depending on how you looked at it) date. Especially not on a date with someone she liked as much as she liked Charlie right at that moment. Dressed in a casual white shirt, scruffy Levi's and a black tailored jacket, he looked even more handsome to her than he had done on their first meeting.

While Amelie was admiring Charlie, Paolo was admiring the plentiful leftovers of the Fajita Fest on behalf of his Latino stomach and that of his two hungry friends. Charlie, meanwhile, was watching the whole scene in amusement, thinking to himself that perhaps tonight wasn't going quite as he had planned.

Moments later, all three plates of the minimalist pesto linguine portions had been demolished, and yet none of the Italians looked in any way satisfied. So it was that when the waiter came over to take the fajita platter away, Paolo's beady eyes were still glued to the sizzling leftovers. Observing this with amusement, Amelie suddenly sparked up.

'Oh, just a minute,' she said to the waiter, 'I don't think we're quite done yet, thank you.' She grinned at the Italians and said, as though it was the furthest thing from Paolo's mind, 'Here's a thought: we're not going to manage any more of this lot; do you want to try some? No point in wasting it, is there?' Amelie pushed the plates towards the three hungry men.

Paolo was rapturous, as were Franco and Raphael. Each leaned forward tentatively. In an affectation of humility, they took timid, polite portions, mumbling that they would just try 'un piccolo'.

'Delizioso,' stated Paolo ten minutes later in satisfaction. With a broad, grateful smile, he ceremoniously wiped the platter clean with the last bit of tortilla.

'Si, grazie,' said Franco, and Raphael nodded.

Charlie, by now desperate to whisk Amelie away some-where so he could have her all to himself again, motioned to the waiter to please bring the bill. When he came over and offered the five of them coffees, the Italians agreed immediately, but Charlie declined. Amelie looked at him quizzically.

'I know a lovely little place that does coffee round here,' he said.

'Oh, sounds good,' she said as they put their money down and got ready to go.

'Well, guys, it was lovely meeting you,' said Charlie.

'*Si*, and you. Many thank-yous for the fajitas! And may you have a long and happy life together,' said Paolo warmly, both Franco and Raphael smiling and nodding.

'Thank you. And you,' said Amelie back to them, grinning as Charlie took her hand and led her down the spiral staircase to the street.

Back on Portobello Road, and in fits of explosive giggles, Amelie grabbed Charlie's arm affectionately and asked, 'So where is this lovely coffee house of yours? I'm only going there if it comes free with a squad of very thirsty Spaniards, OK?'

'Oh, no can do, I'm afraid,' said Charlie, deadpan. 'It was actually my place I was talking about. I live just down the road in Lancaster Gate.'

Amelie scolded herself inwardly for her naïvety. How long had it been since she had been on a proper date? Obviously way too long. Hoping she didn't look too stupid, she said, 'Oh, I know, I was kidding. I do, on the other hand, know a nice wine bar down the road if you wanted to keep going.'

'Oh, that sounds nice; I'd love to. Only I have an early audition tomorrow and I need to stay fresh; it's for a part I'd give my right buttock for. So I should really be getting back before long.' He paused, looking pensive, and turned to her. 'But listen. I'm not being funny. And I'm not trying to manipulate you, honestly –' Charlie stopped and put his arm on Amelie's. 'The thing is, I don't know about you, Amelie, but I've really enjoyed being with you this evening . . .'

'No, me too. I've had a really nice time.' Amelie nodded and looked up at him.

'And I really don't want it to end. I'd love to carry on talking to you. Over coffee. At mine. I really do just mean coffee. I'm sorry if I sound cheesy now, but the thing is, I think I'm really starting to like you. A lot.'

Charlie paused, his eyes loaded with expression. Amelie looked away, avoiding his gaze. 'There's something about you, Amelie; I noticed it the moment you came in the other night. I can't put my finger on it, but – OK, I just heard how corny I sound, so . . . I'll leave it there . . .' Charlie trailed off, looked down at Amelie with his deep brown eyes. 'Obviously it's entirely up to you.' Feeling his hand go limp in hers, Amelie looked up at him and wanted nothing more than to give in to his performance word for word, to be swept away by it; be swept away by him.

Ten minutes later she was eastbound on the Hammersmith and City Line, scribbling away in her journal:

Seriously fun evening. Lovely, lovely guy; def. want to see him again. He sure can deliver a line, though – he very nearly had me for breakfast. Actors. Am fast becoming aware that they can convey a three-minute pitch better than anyone.

When You Least Expect It

The next day Amelie and Duncan were sitting at their desks, their heads bent over their pads of paper, scribbling away industriously. At last the cogs of the creative wheel were churning their way into some sort of motion. The walls around them were garlanded with scraps of paper depicting half-finished drawings, copy lines, random words and jottings here and there. Similarly, the floor was a patchwork of half-empty coffee mugs, takeaway packaging and loose sheets of paper bearing cryptic black marker-pen scribbles.

'OK,' Duncan said, pausing to look over at Amelie. 'So really what we're saying is, don't wait around.' He began sketching, Rolf Harris-style, while he talked. 'So. Here we have Harry the pizza delivery guy, carrying his Four Seasons.' Duncan cocked his head as he drew Harry and his fictional pizza box, parking up his motor-bike.

Amelie was shaking her head at Duncan, not quite

following his train of thought; instead fearing that she was losing him down another tangential abyss.

'And here we have Billy the postman, tottering along with his pile of envelopes and packages, even before the sun has come up.' Duncan scribbled away, slowly bringing Billy into existence.

'And then finally . . . Oh.' Duncan stopped, running out of ammunition. 'Am, who else can there be?'

'I don't know what the fuck you're on about, Duncan.'

'Yes you do, Amelie. Just play along with me here. Humour me, if you will. You know, what other kinds of people are there that just come in and out of your lives?'

Amelie sat up, suddenly listening. 'Do you mean without even leaving the house?'

'Well no,' said Duncan, 'I was thinking of all the other chance meetings that we have in daily life – in the home and when we're out and about.'

'Oh I see what you're getting at.' Amelie's blue eyes opened wider as she began to understand. 'You're saying we should take a look at the day in the life of one lonely soul – in this case, let's say a woman. We paint a picture of her average day. We say that, of all the people she meets, not one of them is just going to come up to her; not one of them is going to be her perfect match or turn out to be her other half. Not without her putting in a bit of effort first.'

'Yeah, that's sort of what I'm getting at,' said Duncan.

'OK,' said Amelie, suddenly inspired, 'so what about drawing a man next to her on the tube? Someone she admires for a second; has penetrating eye contact with. In a flash thinks he could be The One, plans their wedding day in her overactive imagination . . . but then he just jumps off at the next stop, and she never sees him again.

The reality being that love doesn't just come to you these days. You have to get out there and look for it.'

'Yeah, that's it!' said Duncan, pleased that Amelie was finally taking a seat on his thought-train. 'But what words can you think of to go with that visual, copy queen?'

'Um, I'm not sure. Thing is, I still think maybe this basic idea is too obvious. But let's draw it up anyway.' Amelie took a sip of her black coffee. 'Um, what about having three beautifully shot photographs of all these so-called "opportunities": the pizza guy, the postman, the man on the tube. And then just the words "Not The One" in really subtle type underneath them all? Or even just the words "Not Him", repeated three times, until you get to the final panel which would give you the sign-off about Fast Love. I guess that's what we need to say in this ad, without being too aggressive about it. We need to show people that instead of waiting around for Mr Right, where you least expect him, they should go speed-dating and get on with it.'

Amelie paused, picking up her pen, while Duncan listened, looking pensive. 'And maybe you could play on people's perceptions of speed-dating?' she added. 'You know, the way in which lots of people could never imagine needing to go to such lengths, like they think they're too good to go speed-dating, even though they're still sitting around being lonely and depressed. So you could make the end line something like "Find Love Where You Least Expect It". I mean, as in speed-dating, that's the last place some people would look. Or is that completely obvious and rubbish?'

Just as she said this, Amelie's phone beeped with a text message. She picked up her mobile and opened the inbox.

Ciao, bella! Come sta? had v cool time last night, despite bein usurped by greedy Italian tribe . . . hope u got home OK . . . fancy meeting up soon for that coffee? Charlie x x x

Amelie smiled to herself and reread the message a few times. She thought about replying, but then put the handset down. Her head was too busy crafting campaign ideas at the moment to be able to craft the perfect text for a guy like Charlie, she decided. A guy whom, she had to admit, had been on her mind a considerable amount since the previous night. Yes, she decided; she would reply later when she had more time to think.

Duncan looked at Amelie thoughtfully and carried on talking; 'Yeah, I get what you mean. I think we may be on to something here. Not sure about the words, but I think there's something in it.'

'Really?' asked Amelie, mentally filing Charlie's deep brown eyes at the back of her head for now. 'Um, no, I still don't think it's fresh enough really. It's not saying anything new. But, let's give it a whirl anyway.' Amelie paused, thinking. 'I suppose what we're really telling people is, "Go on, make your own luck. Tell Cupid to get a move on . . ." '

'Now there's a thought!' Duncan screeched, throwing down his pen in excitement. 'Give Cupid a real character, a real three-dimensional part to play in all this – that might be a solution! Yes! We could do a kind of cartoon, a comic strip with Cupid puffing along in running shorts, trying to get into shape as he's let himself go a bit!' Amelie and he burst into laughter at this idea, as Duncan started drawing again.

'That's a neat visual,' Josh Grant's voice broke in suddenly.

Amelie jumped, not realising that they'd been overheard all this time. Her face looked a little flushed at Josh having just strolled uninvited into their creative space.

'Sorry to interrupt you, guys. But I just heard your idea as I was walking past, and when I hear a good idea I have to point it out. Occupational hazard.'

Josh strolled closer towards them. 'Have I ever told you how I know when an idea's a good one? I know it's good when I start to feel annoyed that I didn't think of it first. So, well done.' Josh smiled warmly, pulling up a chair to sit down, and Amelie couldn't help feeling pleased at his praise, despite herself. Duncan, meanwhile, was thinking to himself that maybe this new creative director really wasn't so bad after all.

'But don't just leave it at Cartoon Cupid; charming though he is.' Josh grinned. 'Listen. If you file down all your thoughts about how to execute this idea, I think you might have something really solid at the heart of it. Something you can make a great campaign out of.' Josh looked around the room at all of Duncan and Amelie's half-formed concepts and scribbles.

'Do you know what this whole creative idea boils down to? Once you've stripped away the baggage? What you're really saying is that, contrary to popular belief, you *can* hurry love. If I was you, I would hang on to all your other thoughts so far, but also think about how you can make that proposition the centrepiece of your campaign.' Josh stood up and began walking about, while both Amelie and Duncan listened, suddenly transfixed.

'I mean, in real terms, for your audience of thirty-something singletons, this is a cultural revolution! All these years they've all been patiently believing what they've been told, that you should wait for love to happen when you least expect it. So, you need to think about the strongest possible way to communicate this realisation; that times have changed now, and that with Fast Love, you *can* hurry love along. We've been misguided all these years! Newsflash: you can go out there and find it for yourself! Hell – who knows if speed-dating actually *works*, that's not the point. The point is, we need to persuade them of this new realisation, and in doing so, convince them that it works, and to get out there and try it!' Just then Josh's mobile began to vibrate and play the tune of 'Baby Love' by the Supremes. 'Excuse me, I'd better take this. Anyway, good luck. I'll catch up with you later,' he said, and wandered away.

Amelie leaned in excitedly towards Duncan.

'I've GOT it!'

'What? Tell me!'

'A TV script.' Amelie stood up, her blue eyes sparkling. 'OK, this is off the top of my head now: we open on a back alley. Atmospheric music, haunting, creepy.' Amelie started pacing the room. 'We see two men in black cloaks, shades, trilby hats, looking shadily at one another. One of them gets a message on their walkie-talkie and nods to the other. A car pulls up, a black Mercedes, and they get in. Their driver nods to them and they drive off.'

' "Which is it?" One of the men asks. "Collins?"'

' "They got Collins already. It's worse than that. It's Ross."'

'Moments later they pull up to a shopping mall in Albequerque, June 1967, where crowds of people have gathered, impromptu, to see Diana Ross and the Supremes sing. As the men in black race into the mall, the chirpy sounds of "You Can't Hurry Love" can be heard. The audience are lapping it up: school kids, young and innocent teenagers, men and women of all ages, etc. The men in black jump through security and on to the stage, and grab hold of Diana Ross.

' "Come with me Ms Ross."

'Cut to them moments later, bundling an irate Ross into the back of the van, next to Phil Collins who, unshaven and sweaty, has clearly been there for some time, and looks distraught, but pleased to see Diana. Little do they know, they're being taken away to a prison of some sort, punishment for having misguided the world for decades.

'Fade out to a voice-over, saying something like, "Who says you can't hurry love? *No one*. Fast Love – Britain's best-loved speed-dating company. *It's time you got out there and hurried love along*."

'OK, so I *badly* need to tweak the naff endlines, but it's a start, maybe?'

'I love it Amelie!' Duncan exclaimed through his laughter. 'It's just so far-fetched, so stupid! It'll definitely get people's attention! You could do some really daft outdoor posters to back it up as well!'

Just then Amelie's work phone was ringing. With the image of a billboard sporting a forlorn-looking Diana Ross forming in her mind, Amelie giggled as she picked up the phone. 'Hello? Amelie speaking.'

'Hi, Am. It's me, Jack.'

Her heart leaped into her throat. In the mayhem of the moment she had forgotten that she was still meant to be screening her calls for Maffew and Jack; the latter of whom had kept up his assaults on her mobile phone.

'Am! What's wrong with your phone? I've been trying and trying to get hold of you!'

'Oh . . .' Amelie shook her head, annoyed with herself for having answered. 'There's a reason why I've been avoiding your calls. I didn't mean to answer. In fact, I'm un-answering this, if I may. Bye, Jack.'

Just as she tried to hang up the receiver, she could hear him protesting earnestly. Reluctantly, she brought the receiver back to her ear.

'Please, Amelie, please don't hang up. You must have wanted to talk to me deep down. Surely you can't keep avoiding me for ever.'

'No. And yes, I can, Jack, I managed it for three years. It's been a great three years. Why stop at three?'

Sensing that Amelie might want some peace, Duncan crept out of the office and headed out to the newsagents. After ten minutes he came back into the office with a Cadbury's Caramel for Amelie and five scratch-cards for himself. Amelie was still on the phone, looking increasingly distraught and emotional. Duncan mimed concern, and she smiled back meekly, mouthing a thank-you for the much-needed chocolate.

'OK.' She sniffed and rubbed her eyes. 'I know. Look, this is really difficult for me. You can't just reappear for one minute and expect—' She stopped, and listened for a moment while he continued to talk. Before long, she had heard enough. 'No. Listen. I really have to go now, I'm really busy . . . No. I really don't think that's such a good idea. Honestly, I'd rather not . . .' She stopped, while Jack persisted with begging, through his sobs. Eventually it was too much. 'Oh, look, if it will get you off my back for a minute, then all right. I'll meet you for a coffee. But one espresso at the counter and that's it, OK? And strictly to catch up as old friends.' Amelie paused, regretting it already, while Jack expressed his gratitude at her response. 'But not until next week. I'm too busy until at least next Tuesday. OK, let's meet there, then, sixish. Fine. I really have to go now. Bye, Jack.'

She hung up, feeling a shaky mixture of fragile and angry. 'Fucking fuckwits!' She looked over at Duncan who was entirely absorbed in his rapidly growing pile of used scratch-cards.

'Oh. My. God.' Duncan, now entirely oblivious to Amelie's relative trauma, looked up and cried, 'Yeesssssss!!!!' He looked at his numbers again and then back up at Amelie. 'I've only gone and sodding won again! I've just won sixty-five squid, Am! Can you believe it?'

'No, I can't believe you bought another five today, Duncan,' she said sternly. 'Men! They don't know when to stop, do they?' She stood up and turned off her Mac. 'They can't ever be happy with what they've got, can they?! Fucking fuckwits.'

'Oh, I'm sorry, Am . . . Listen, it's five-thirty. Let's go for a drink, celebrate a great day's thinking. I'm buying.'

'Yeah, good idea,' agreed Amelie, smiling. 'I need a drink, I do. Meeting Room 4?'

Slippers and Hammocks

What a week. Just got in after speed-date follow-up number two: Gerald. Now, I'm not usually one for being judgemental, although let's face it – the industry of speed-dating itself must thrive upon it, or at least actively encourage this trait in people. In fact, perhaps they have a lab somewhere where they are, as we speak, trying to isolate the judgemental gene so that people will be more inclined to be picky and choosy and go speed-dating? Or maybe I'm over-tired and should get some sleep. But one thing I've realised from doing all this is that if you can't be judgemental on at least some level, quite frankly, you're not going to make it in this game. If you're looking for love in the Fast Lane, then good judgement and time management really are good qualities to have on your side.

Anyway, I'd decided it would be worth trying out one

more Fast Love follow-up date, seeing as Gerald and I did kind of get along on the night, to an extent. So we went to see The Motorcycle Diaries, *which I've been meaning to see for ages. It was fantastic. Admittedly, the lead guy in it was completely adorable. But it was the incredible scenery that really got to me – made me really miss travelling, made me miss the 'open road' again – so much so that when I got home I had to consciously restrain myself from going rummaging in the loft, so I could don the old backpack, thongs, beads and headscarf once more and become a tree-loving hippie again. But I didn't. Instead, maybe I'll just settle for a sleep in Josh's office hammock when he's not around.*

But back to the date. Gerald and I had a pleasant enough evening, and some really interesting conversations. But I don't think I'll see him again. It's a shame, but in truth there was no spark. The other thing is, though – and as I said, I'm trying my hardest not to be judgemental here – I do worry that a man named Gerald just might not be holding the key to my happiness. I mean, much as I try, I say 'Gerald', but it just comes out as 'slippers'.

Charlie, on the other hand, is one guy I really could see again. Haven't seen him since I left him by that lamp-post in Notting Hill looking like the cat who hadn't got the cream, but we've been texting and emailing quite a bit. And he's just called me up, over the moon with excitement because he's getting to perform on stage again next week. He's playing the lead in a rerun of a play he was in last year: Arcadia *by Tom Stoppard. I said I'd go and watch, and then we'll go out for a drink afterwards. Have to confess, I'm really looking forward to seeing him in action . . .*

Unfortunately, seeing Gerald again didn't trigger any

new sparks of inspiration for the Fast Love campaign, even though I'd hoped seeing another real-life SpeedDater might have somehow helped. Really trying not to panic, but as far as I can see, Duncs and I are still no closer to having a great angle on the campaign. And we've so many other briefs to be getting on with now that I don't think there's even time to start pursuing any new avenues any more. So, despite enduring two exhausting nights on the speed-dating merry-go-round, which adds up to a frightening total of fifty Dates With Total Strangers, I still can't quite pin down the essence of it. Still can't think of a simple, strong idea to base an ad campaign on. All we have to show so far is a rather silly TV script involving an endangered Diana Ross, and some equally shady outdoor ideas. Josh and Duncan think they're sound, but still something in my gut is saying they're not winning ideas. They're good, but they're not great.

Josh is still really winding me up. At first I thought it was just my aversion towards his attempt to fill Jana's shoes, but now I think it's just him. He can be kind of arrogant at times – jumping in uninvited to the middle of a creative session; flippantly offering his opinion, however slating or irreverent. And, despite the fact that Duncan now thinks he's the best thing since the Atkins diet, I'm still not convinced Josh has the creative talent and star quality that everyone has been raving about. Haven't seen him come up with one great idea yet. And I have to say, I find his support of my Diana Ross concept a little disconcerting, when it is obviously quite ridiculous . . . surely he can't imagine it actually running, can he?

Anyway, from Fast Love to lasting love . . . I can't believe it; tomorrow is Claire's last big night out as a single lady, so we're all off to Brighton for the hen night. Should be a nice crowd going; lots of her mates from university and a few old faces from school. As I feared, there is going to be a dress code. The email invite said to Think Pink – as in, we all have to go as a Pink Lady. Much as I loathe dressing up, I guess it will be fun to have the old crowd from school together. I remember as clear as yesterday the days when we were all running around the playground in little denim-jacketed gangs, pretending to be exclusive members of our own, newly branded 'Magenta Girls'. We were going to go as Magenta Girls again this weekend, but Claire didn't want to exclude all the newer friends who wouldn't quite understand this crucial difference in shade. So, for the sake of not being cliquey, we are going as traditional Pink. Claire is going dressed as Sandy after the make-over, while I'm going as Rizzo. Look out, Brighton, is all I can say.

But after that, it's the Coffee With Jack, which I'm 99 per cent dreading. I guess I'll just see how it goes. And hopefully this weekend will take my mind off it. Maybe I can meet up with Charlie the day before, just in case I decide that he's even more wonderful than anyone I've ever met, and I really fall for him, so that I'll be all distracted and besotted about Charlie by the time I see Jack? A kind of diversion, to stop me doing something stupid? Actually, thinking about it, he'll probably be tied up in rehearsals all week. And, as far as I know, love doesn't usually work quite that fast . . .

So I guess I'm just going to have to face Jack with a clear head; try to be as strong as I can. Really hoping, praying, that he won't be looking too good. Please, God or whoever it is, don't let him be wearing one of his beanies –

won't be able to handle that. In fact, let's hope he has a horribly busy day in court, so that he's looking all haggard, overworked and prematurely aged by the time he gets to me.

What am I saying? He always looked gorgeous. Always looked picture-perfect, no matter how long and gruelling his day in court. Let's face it, it was my appearance that would always be the first to rapidly degenerate during a stressful day. Jack, by contrast, would always retain his model-like stature. Maybe that's why I wasn't enough for him. Maybe that's why Penny – always the antithesis of me – immaculate, stylish, thin, accomplished (but not a creative bone in her body) . . . maybe that's why they were so perfectly suited. Maybe he thought I'd 'let myself go' the minute I'd got comfortable with him. Wait, did he think that? Is that why he ran off with her? Wish I knew. I never hung around long enough to find out; didn't want to know at the time. But every so often, that little bit of unsated curiosity really bugs me – it kills me that I still don't know why someone who was both my best friend and my first love could just do that.

What am I doing, tormenting myself like this? Hate him for dredging up all these childish feelings of inadequacy. Was so, so fine before he came on the scene again. OK, whatever happens next week, I promise to try and resist his superficial charms, drink my coffee quickly, and focus on his demonically evil inner self.

Truly cannot believe that soon Claire is going to be permanently attached to a whole man of her own, complete with all the mind-boggling behaviour that comes with them. What a haunting thought, that tomorrow night we're all going to be celebrating her last days of freedom. Talking of *which, I still can't get the backpacking vision out of my head. Am off to sleep, to dream of hammocks, tropical beaches, sarongs and sweaty Brazilians leading me a merry salsa . . .*

Magenta Girls

Twenty-four hours later, Amelie was pushing her way towards the ladies' in the heaving, noisy Escape bar on Brighton's sea front. Having fought her way to the mirror, she leaned towards it to examine the relative damage to her appearance following the drunken antics of the night so far. She had been at the bar with Claire and a group of their closest friends for a few hours now, after they had enjoyed a delicious three-course meal in a vegetarian restaurant on The Lanes.

'Oh, sweet holy mother of God,' Amelie sighed, pulling out her make-up and beginning to tend to her face and eyes. Only as she did this did she start to notice the alcohol levels inside of her welling up and making her feel intoxicated and dizzy.

So far, the evening had been a blurry mixture of drinking games, drunken renditions of *Grease* classics, dancing competitions and nostalgic reflections on the girls' school days. Most of the girls Amelie knew well, except for

Claire's university friends whom she had met only a few times before. One thing commonly prevailed among them all: a fact which grew increasingly pertinent to Amelie as the night wore on. Every single one of the girls was in a long-lasting, stable relationship. Even those who weren't married and settled were at least already one half of a happy, functional and secure couple. Suddenly Amelie felt another shudder run through her as she queued up to wash her hands. This time not an alcohol-fuelled shudder, but one triggered by the realisation that in just two weeks' time she would be watching her best friend walk up the aisle towards a life of marriage.

Amelie decided to repress this mildly disturbing thought for now and head back out to the bar. She pushed open the doors, revealing the sound of the increasingly bawdy chants of 'For she's a jolly good fellow, she's a jolly good fellow . . .'

Reaching the table just in time, she forced a huge grin on to her face, threw her arms around Claire, and yelled, 'And so say all of us!'

'Right, who's for another round of slammers?' she challenged the group, to a chorus of eager acquiescence and squeals of delight.

And then, four hours later, there were two. After closing time, all the other girls had gone back to the hotel, while Amelie and Claire had chosen to go on to an all-night café for bagels. Leaving the café two hours later, feeling hazy and replete, they leaned on each other, carrying their Pink Lady wigs as they staggered up Ocean Parade towards the beach.

'You're *sure* you remember the way back to the hotel from here?' Amelie asked Claire suspiciously.

'Oh yeah, it's just up here and on the left, I'm positive,' Claire stammered, falling weak at the knees and having to grab hold of a lamp-post to steady herself. She giggled ludicrously, put her peroxide Sandy wig back on over her own wavy blonde hair, and began slurring.

'Ye know what, Amelie? I luurve you, I do. You're the bestest friend I've ever, ever had!' She stopped walking and then suddenly collapsed in a heap on the pavement, trembling, and breaking into sobs; tears coming from nowhere and rolling down her cheeks.

'Hey, what the hell's wrong?' Amelie stopped and sat down next to Claire, embracing her and stroking her hair. 'What's the matter, sweetie?'

'It's suddenly dawned on me. All at once. What the fuck am I doing? Really?' she spat out hysterically. 'What the buggery-bollocks! In two weeks . . . fourteen days! I'm not going to be a whole me any more. I'm going to be just one half of something . . .'

'But one half of something amazing!' Amelie corrected.

'But you don't understand, I'm just so scared!' Claire slurred. 'What if . . . what if maybe I just can't go through with it, like I've made a huge mistake and can't go back?' Claire was on the beach, staggering awkwardly along the pebbles and lighting up a cigarette.

'Where did you get those? I thought you'd given up ages ago!' Amelie exclaimed, visibly shocked. 'And Sandy doesn't smoke!'

'The naughty Sandy does! And it's my hen night for fuck's sake. If I can't smoke now, when can I?'

'Well, indeed. Just don't tell me off next time we're out, OK?' Amelie took Claire's arm and they began walking down the beach towards the shore.

'Anyway, my lovely, it's never too late,' Amelie reasoned, putting her Rizzo wig back on as though that would help matters. 'But that's not the point. I know you, and I know you've made the right choice. You have to go through with it. If nothing else, because I say so. You're just getting cold feet, it's all normal.'

'Oh, but Amelie, I just don't know!' she wailed through sniffs and sobs, shaking from the cold. She stopped walking and looked at Amelie. 'I – I look at you and I think, I don't know . . . in a way I envy your freedom. The way you can just go anywhere, do anything, be anything, you want. I'm about to leave all that . . .'

'No you aren't!' Amelie argued, hardly recognising herself any more. 'Claire, you're still free in every other window of your life; it's just that the romance bit of it will be more sorted, that's all . . . But that's perfect, because Dan's the one for you. Why would you want it any other way?'

'But I'm really scared that I'll feel choked and old before my time, and suddenly –' Claire's voice was growing more and more frantic as she spoke through her tears.

Amelie sighed and put her arm around her friend comfortingly. As Claire sobbed, Amelie squeezed her tight and stroked her hair.

'You know this is basically the tequila talking, don't you? But what you're saying is all really normal; to be expected, even. Tomorrow you'll feel differently. I promise.'

Claire took a deep breath and her tears began to diminish in frequency. They were close to the water's edge now, and they could hear the waves lapping the shore as they sat down on the pebbles.

'But, Amelie, I still feel jealous of you being so independent and free, and I don't know why I keep thinking like that.' Picking up a pebble and throwing it out to sea, Claire went on, 'Surely it's really wrong of me; unfair of me to think these terrible thoughts. Maybe I shouldn't go down the aisle feeling like this?'

Amelie picked up a bigger pebble and threw it out even further. 'But you don't feel like this. You're just drunk,' she said with rising impatience.

Claire shook her head, her green eyes desolate. Amelie stood up, looked around at the moonlit beach, and threw down her wig. 'Let me tell you once and for all, Claire Josanna Wilson, you do not, repeat *not*, want my life, or any part of my stale, depressing, pestilent, singleton freedom. It's over-rated, it sucks, and, to be honest, I'm thoroughly bored with it all!'

Claire looked shocked, and pulled off her Sandy wig as though this would help her digest what Amelie was saying. 'Really?'

'Yes, really. Believe me, Claire, you definitely don't envy me. I know I always pretend like I'm happy being free and single, going from one stupid, half-arsed relationship to the next, never quite committing . . . but I think I'm starting to see that maybe that's all been a kind of performance; that it's not really what I want. It's like all this time I've been pitching myself as aloof, super-cynical, hating the speed-dating, and criticising everyone for trying all these crazy new ways to find love. Thinking I'm too good for it all. When in truth, I'm way more of a sodding romantic than any of them put together! And if I think about it, I can't imagine anything worse than *not* finding that someone. That one amazing person that could be worth so much that you would want to spend the rest of your life with them . . .'

Claire looked startled and seemed to visibly sober up. Her eyes were wide with concern, transfixed on this altered Amelie, as she went on, 'As much as I want to cringe saying this, what you and Dan Alexander have now is how it's meant to be. From where I'm sitting, you guys are the real thing.' Amelie stopped and looked at the stars, her mind fixed on something. 'Oh my God!' she looked over at Claire, an infantile grin on her face. 'He's your Danny Zuco!' Suddenly the irony in this was too much to bear. Amelie begin to laugh hysterically, and her voice rose in pitch as she grew more excited. 'Hey, you're Sandy, and he's your Danny! You're meant for each other!!'

Claire laughed through her tears, her eyes lightening up a little.

'Seriously, Clairey, you are doing the right thing,' said Amelie. 'And you will definitely feel better about it in the morning.'

'Promise?' Claire sniffed and brightened.

'Promise,' Amelie assured her, pulling herself and Claire off the pebbles. 'Now. Let's get back to that hotel room. The others will be wondering where we are. Plus, we've got a mini-bar to raid.'

They walked up the pebbles towards the road, arm in arm. At the top, where the beach met the pavement, they hugged, holding on to each other for what seemed like hours, thinking everything over, and reflecting on how long they had been friends. Eventually, Amelie pulled away, stepped out on to the Brighton street and hailed a taxi.

14

Life's a Pitch

A strange few days have gone by. Slowly getting back into work again, having re-emerged from my first ever hen experience largely unscathed. Well, all except for the strangely subhuman hangover that's been following me around the last two days. But it was worth the liver damage – a thoroughly fun and nostalgic time was had by all, and it was lovely to see Claire in her element. Even if the night did end with me in the surreal position of trying to persuade her that marriage was a wonderful thing!! Alcohol certainly does paint surreal pictures . . . def. must start cutting down on my intake, any day now.

But, re. other news, I've just got in after seeing Jack, and am now feeling more than a little fragile. We met in Little Italy. We were meant to meet in Camden, but I had to work late again and couldn't get away in time. OK, I was two hours late. But that came as no surprise to Jack, who's better equipped than anyone to deal with my lateness.

He was perched on a stool when I arrived, smoking a cigarette and leafing through a newspaper. I spotted him before he saw me, so I stepped back on to the kerb before going inside, just to compose myself from all the sprinting, and to examine him from afar. I stood outside, staring at him as he raised his cigarette to his mouth and inhaled. Watched as he ran a hand through his dark-brown hair and looked anxiously at his watch. Standing outside in the cold, looking through the glass at the man who was once the love of my life, I had to admit that despite everything, he was looking good. That said, I decided I would be strong. There was no way I was going back into that world, however handsome he still was. No matter what he had to say, no matter how he made me feel, I had absolutely decided that Jack Halliwell was staying in the past. I pushed open the door; saw him flinch and look up to see who had entered.

He smiled nervously and stood up, held out his hand, and I smiled confidently back at him. 'Hello, stranger. Sorry I'm so late.'

He shrugged as if to say he expected nothing more. Then, like the gentleman I don't recall him ever being, he took my coat, and we both sat down.

'I thought you didn't smoke any more. You said the other night –' I began, in an effort to start the conversation off on a light footing.

'Well, I started again,' he confessed, as though ashamed of his diminishing self-control. 'Seeing you again, it reminded me of how much I liked it. And I guess the child in me sees it as a slight rebellion against Penny, who never let me.'

Once we'd got past this wince-inducing reference to

Little Miss Home-Wrecker, the small-talk began to flow smoothly enough. So far so good, I thought. Until moments later, when, still being so wired from all the day's caffeine I realised that the absolute last thing I wanted was another coffee. So when Jack asked the waiter for a glass of Pinot Grigio, I found myself following suit. And then, when the waiter suggested that it would be cheaper to share a whole bottle, Jack agreed, chirping, 'Well, we might as well; we don't need to drink it all.' Not having remembered to eat anything since breakfast, it didn't take me long to hit dazed and woozy territory, and soon I was enjoying myself and laughing out loud at Jack's ridiculous jokes. Meanwhile the sensible fraction of me began grieving the promise I'd made to myself only minutes before: that this meeting was to be nothing more than 'a quick espresso at the counter, in and out in twenty mins'.

After some time, Jack looked at me a little too intensely and said, 'You know what's funny? I even miss your lateness. Your scattiness, your ditziness – I really missed it. Penny was so organised, always early for everything, one step ahead of the game, she used to say. It started to get boring in the end. I realise now, Am, your quirks are what give you such an inimitable charm. That was definitely one of the things I loved about you. Well, still do . . .' Then he looked at me, his big eyes blinking hopefully, expectantly.

'Oh come on, Jack,' I countered quickly. 'I drove you mad. You know I did. You're just looking back with rose-tinted aviators. Besides,' I added delusionally, 'I'm not scatty any more; I've grown up since then. I'm now a far more sorted individual.'

Jack looked at me with affectionate scepticism. His bright blue eyes studied my handbag with its faded, patchy brown leather, and the families of shredded tissues dangling from the pockets. The deformed, empty water bottle poking out the top, the clusters of crumpled notes that were leaking out of the sides, and the not-quite faded Biro marks on my hand, a shrine to yesterday's unfulfilled reminders. And finally he clocked my dark blue jumper which was back-to-front, a fact which I only realised myself when I got home and saw the care label showing through, and said, 'Yes, I see that. You're looking particularly smart and together today. I'm impressed.'

I thanked him for his kind appraisal and quickly moved the conversation along. For a few moments beyond, we were having a real laugh, almost like old times. But it was a shortlived respite – soon enough he'd steered us diligently back to the getting-back-together conversation.

'Jack,' I said wearily, 'I said I wasn't interested in talking about it. Can't we just catch up, and be friends?'

'Please, Am. Just give me three minutes.'

I thought about this for a moment. 'If you really must – have it your way,' I relented weakly. 'But not a second over.' So maybe just a small part of me was a little bit curious.

'Look, don't take this the wrong way,' he began again, as though he was beginning a new wave of attack, marching about the courtroom, 'but I've been thinking lately about those last few weeks we were together. And I've realised that, in my defence, you were never, ever in. You were constantly out working. Or if you weren't actually at your desk working, you were at a works do of some sort. You never had any time for us.'

Wide-eyed, I listened as he went on, 'And, when I called you to see how you were, or wanted to make plans, you would always try and get me off the phone; made me feel like I was so way down on your list of priorities. I felt so neglected . . . surely you can understand why I felt vulnerable to straying?'

OK, there goes the bell, I thought. That's your lot. 'OK, Jack, I don't think I can listen to any more of this. Time's up.' I started fishing around for my bag and my scarf. I was drunk, but not too far gone to know that I had to keep my distance from his fairytale logic.

'But I'm not finished. You have to hear me out. I've not even got to the best bit of my defence yet –'

I struggled not to burst into laughter. 'It's not a courtroom, Jack! You can't persuade your way back into my heart. No matter how well thought out your logical reasoning, and no matter how purple and forceful your rhetoric.'

At this he looked as though he might break down into tears. 'OK, then. Sod the rational reasons for you taking me back. What about my feelings?'

I looked away, avoiding his eyes. I couldn't face him then. I couldn't look at him as he told me how he'd never felt this way about another girl. I stared straight down into my almost empty third glass of wine. Focused my attention on the little chip in the edge of the rim, and on the bubbles resting on the surface of the wine, while Jack declared that he would never, could never love another woman the way he loves me. I began to feel faint and slightly nauseous. I stood up. Swaying slightly, I started trying to climb into my coat. I hastily gathered up my things, causing a tide of bag, hat, scarf, papers and tissues to rush out all over the floor.

'Goodbye, Jack. It was nice running into you again.' I crouched down, quickly raked together the most essential of my belongings, and walked over to the door. Jack stood up *and raced over to me, bringing my red woolly hat with him and placing it on my head with an almost parental tenderness. 'Just tell me you don't feel the same, Am. Just say it.' He looked deep into my eyes, put his hand half on my cheek, half on my neck, resting it there for a moment, in that way that had always felt so right.*

I looked up at him, praying for my inner resolve to come back and help me. 'Jack, you broke my heart!' I heard someone shout. I looked around at the bar, the noise levels having suddenly dipped, and eventually I realised that it was me who had just shouted these words. Clearing my throat, I continued in a softer tone. 'Listen. No lawyer's speech, however poignant, can ever undo what happened.'

I saw a sadness appear in his eyes that I'd never seen before. 'I'll never be able to see you in the same way. I'm sorry you still have feelings, but I don't, Jack. It's too late.'

His eyes glazed over with tears and I felt mine doing the same. I went to kiss him goodbye on the cheek. It felt genuinely horrible hurting him. Gutted me to see him so upset, in the same way that it breaks your heart to see your mum or your dad cry. But that's when I realised, that's all he would ever be to me now. Like a relative or a friend. Someone who knows me really well; in some ways better than I know myself. I know now that he's not the one for me. The reason? The spark. When he stole a goodbye kiss from me just before I fled hurriedly away – even though he kissed me with all the passion in the world – for me, the spark had all but gone out.

15

Performance and Cocktails

Twelve hours later, Duncan and Amelie were back at their desks, staring at each other's shoes, and listening to the loud Indie music that was pumping down the corridor from the studio. The pitch was now less than two weeks away, and still neither of them were any closer to The Moment of Eureka they were dreaming of. Duncan checked the clock on the wall and then looked around the room, at the dog-eared A3 pads on their desk, the ball-pond of screwed-up papers on the floor and the cryptic scribbles pinned to the wall. He grimaced. 'Diana Ross it is, then,' he said dejectedly, and stood up. 'Right, I'm on a coffee run. Would you like one, Am?'

Amelie was still thinking about the night before with Jack. Her head was thumping – both with the amount of alcohol she had endured on an empty stomach again – and also with the shocking reality that she had just told the one true love of her life to leave her alone, and never come back, in so many words.

'You OK, Am? You look a little pale,' Duncan observed.

It was for the best, she told herself. Of course it was. Onwards and upwards, she thought. On with the Fast Love brief. 'What, sorry, Dunc?' she asked. 'I'm fine, thanks. Coffee would be lovely.'

'And a croissant, or something else to eat?' Duncan went on. 'You're looking rather gaunt, my sweet, are you forgetting to eat again?'

'No, I'm fine, thanks. Really just not hungry at the moment. See you in a bit.' At which point Duncan's phone bleeped, making Amelie jump.

'Hello?' Duncan answered. 'Oh, hey there!' He blushed a little, and sauntered away while he spoke. 'How are you doing?'

Amelie was just calculating who might be making Duncan blush when Sally popped her head around the corner, looking more radiant than Amelie had seen in a long time.

'Hello, lovely! How are you?'

'Great, thanks.' Waiting until Duncan was out of earshot, she asked, 'Hey, do you know who Duncan's on the phone to? He just went beetroot when he answered the phone!'

'Ah, must be SJ,' said Sally. 'He's been on another couple of dates with her.'

Amelie felt bemused. She wondered why Duncan was suddenly being so secretive about his love life, and why she was the last to know about its recent developments.

'Anyway, have you got time for a chat?' asked Sally, sitting down on the bean-bag next to Amelie's chair. 'I want to tell you all about my date with Derek. I think I'm really starting to like him! He's just such a hoot, and this sounds totally lame, but I feel like he's really starting to make me think about life in a new way!' she gushed, while munching on a large bag of cashew nuts.

'Really? That's great,' said Amelie, hoping Sally wasn't about to go all born-again on her just yet. 'Well, who would have thought it, Sal. You with a militant Christian!'

'Who'd have thought it – me with a media salesman,' she added. 'Weird, huh?' Sally munched away, offering Amelie some nuts, but she declined, thinking to herself how strange it was that Sally really did seem to have found her spiritual match – the love of her life – at a speed-dating event. Maybe Love in the Fast Lane *can* sometimes deliver its promise, she thought.

Just then some tufts of brown hair appeared from around the corner; followed shortly by Josh's tanned and chiselled face.

'Ladies . . . May I interrupt your chat for just a second?'

Amelie nodded, and Sally held out her bag of nuts to Josh, who also declined.

'Just to say, girls, that I hope you're all ready for this weekend?'

'What's this weekend?' Amelie looked puzzled.

'You know – Wing? The team-building weekend?' Josh said, as though it was surely the highlight of everyone's calendar. 'Well, Fleur's going to email round later, so everyone knows what they need to bring. And the minibus is leaving on Friday at half two . . . with or without you, Amelie, so please try and be ready on time.' He grinned and walked away to find Fleur, to see if she would ask reception to send him up an apple in the lift.

Amelie watched Josh walk out of earshot and turned to Sally. 'I'd completely forgotten about this weekend. What a nightmare.'

Duncan returned to their room with a bag full of croissants and coffee. 'What's a nightmare?' he asked, wide-eyed, and pushed the bag towards Amelie. 'With or without chocolate?'

Taking Duncan's cue, Sally dived in for a *pain au chocolat* on her way out of the office, commenting, '*Why* is it that love hasn't suppressed my appetite yet? What's the hold up? Oh well, cheers, Dunc. See you guys for lunch.' And she skipped away. As she did so, Max popped his head round their door, having just emerged from the lift.

'Anyone order an apple?' he asked. Seeing Amelie and Duncan's blank expressions, he elaborated, 'This Granny Smith was just sitting on its tod, on the floor in the lift. Felt kind of sorry for it,' he added, about to bite into it, just as Josh strode past and rugby-tackled him for it.

Seeing all this eating going on, Amelie decided to try and be hungry. 'Oh go on, then,' she said, 'with.' And she took a nibble out of a *pain au chocolat*. 'So, the nightmare,' she said as they went to sit at their desks, 'is that it's the Wing Thing this weekend. This Friday night, it starts, and we don't get back until Sunday! I was kind of banking on working on the Fast Love pitch this weekend.' Amelie looked down at her diary, the pages of which were scored with red scribbles, highlighted meetings and exclamation marks. She leafed through the pages and frowned. 'I can't work on it tonight as I'm seeing Charlie's play. Next weekend is out, as it's Claire's wedding . . .' She turned the page to reveal where she had scrawled 'Fast Love pitch' in big pink capital letters. 'Well, that's it, then, we're doomed.' Amelie stared desolately out of the window into Soho Square. 'We won't get anywhere with the ideas we've got at the moment . . . Josh will realise we're past it already, have us fired and replaced by a new, even younger team. Basically, we're on the streets already – I may as well go and ask Jules over there if he wants any help flogging *The Big Issue*.'

'Don't worry, kid . . . we'll be fine.' Duncan tried to reassure them both. 'We'll think of something.'

'But how the hell will we manage it? There's no time left!'

* * *

SEPTIMUS: Oh, we have time, I think.

VALENTINE: Till there's no time left. That's what time means.

SEPTIMUS: When we have found all the mysteries and lost all the meaning, we will be alone, on an empty shore.

THOMASINA: Then we will dance. Is this a waltz?

SEPTIMUS: It will serve.

And with that, Charlie stood up ceremoniously, taking centre stage. The elfin girl next to him, dressed in a beautiful Regency dress, jumped up with excitement and yelled, 'Goody!' At this, Septimus took Thomasina in his arms carefully, and began to lead her around the stage in a romantic waltz. Amelie, sitting forward in her seat, felt a tear rise to the surface of her eyelids as she sat entranced, through the final minutes of *Arcadia*. It was the first time she had seen Charlie perform, and she had found herself unable to take her eyes off him all evening. His Septimus was certainly the most smouldering she had ever seen.

Watching him dance around the stage, sensing that the audience was following his every step, she admired how well the Regency attire flattered his brooding Byronic good looks. By the time the curtains fell, she decided that she was definitely seeing Charlie in a new light. The best thing of all, she kept reminding herself, was that she was no longer thinking about Jack.

After the play finished, and Amelie had joined in with the rapturous applause, she walked around to the stage door, feeling her stomach constrict with butterflies at the prospect of seeing Charlie again so soon after his stint as the irresistible charmer Septimus Hodge.

When Amelie reached the stage door, Charlie's face was barely visible through the crowd of admirers encircling him. Amelie could scarcely believe what she was seeing: little-known Charlie Stanton of Carphone Warehouse sandwich-boarding infamy was now suddenly signing autographs on people's programmes. His hair was still swept back in its Regency style, but he had since changed into a crisp tailored blue shirt, and Amelie couldn't help thinking he looked even more attractive than ever. As she called out his name, he looked over casually, his face breaking into a smile.

'Ah, Amelie, hi . . .' Charlie looked a little harassed at having all these people around him, some of whom looked less like groupies and more like they might be important industry figures. He gave an awkward grin. 'Sorry, everyone, this is Amelie. Um, Amelie, I'll just be a minute here . . .' He began to look uncomfortable but smiled through it. 'Can I meet you for a drink over the road, in a few minutes?'

If Amelie was put out she didn't show it. 'Sure, why not,

come whenever you're ready,' she said, and Charlie looked relieved. 'I'll be in that pub around the corner that we went to last time we were round here,' she added, but Charlie was already elsewhere. 'How long have I been with Malcolm?' he was saying to a tall blonde with glasses. 'Four years . . . ever since I left drama school, to be honest,' he said, turning to face a glamorous brunette who was pressing him for more questions. Amelie watched him nodding excitedly, taking business cards, and saying, 'Yeah, well, always looking for a change . . . definitely, that's great, thanks.' She walked away, leaving the chorus of networking to fade out into the distance as she headed down Haymarket.

An hour later, Amelie was sitting in a smoky pub booth, alone, texting Duncan and trying to decide whether she was a mug or not, when Charlie came bounding through the door, panting, with a manic look in his eye. Amelie looked up and smiled.

'Sorry, Amelie. I'm so, so sorry! My phone went dead, and I couldn't not talk to those people . . . Have you been OK? I'm so glad you waited . . .'

Amelie shrugged and said, 'Well, I thought Septimus was worth the wait. Charlie, on the other hand, I'm not so sure about . . .' She smiled jokingly. 'Seriously, though, I'm impressed! You were brilliant,' she said, standing up to give him a kiss on the cheek.

'Thanks! I was rather good, wasn't I?' Charlie said, and Amelie fought to detect a trace of irony on his breath. He went on, speaking rapidly, without pausing for breath, 'I haven't played the part in so long I thought I'd forgotten it – but I just jumped straight back into it! Oh, I loved it out there! I felt so alive again. It's been so long!'

'Great,' Amelie said. 'Can I get you a drink? You seem a little wired.'

'Yeah, that'd be lovely. I fancy a cocktail – maybe a Mojito?'

Amelie strolled up to the bar and joined the queue. After ten minutes of being pushed about at the sweaty bar, she looked back towards Charlie. He was chattering excitedly away on his mobile, the grin on his face the widest she had ever seen. Amelie decided to pass the remaining minutes at the bar by replaying the handsome memory of Septimus dancing around the stage. Smiling again as the barman brought her their drinks and her change, she went over to join Charlie.

He looked up and dropped his mobile quickly, an expression of guilt washing over his face. 'Sorry, my phone found a new lease of life.' He picked up his Mojito and took a large sip. 'That was my co-star, Isabella. You know, the one who played Thomasina?'

Then Charlie put his drink down ceremoniously, leaned in towards Amelie, clasped her hands in his, and lifted them into the air. 'You'll never guess what!' he belted excitedly.

'What?' Amelie leaned backwards, wondering to herself whether it was two lines of coke that Charlie had hoovered that night, or if it was closer to three.

'You know the lady I was talking to at the stage door?'

'Which one? There were so many,' Amelie said dryly. Her dryness was lost on Charlie, who went on chattering excitedly. Judging by his eyes and the speed he was talking at, she decided the answer was probably four. What was that saying again? she wondered . . . Charlie by name . . . ?

'She was only a top agent from ICM! You know – they

represent *all* the giants. If you get into them, you're *made*, you are!'

'Yes, I think I've heard of them,' Amelie said slowly, delicately sipping her Miss Magenta.

'Well, she was being dead nice to me back there, gave me her card and that,' Charlie explained, taking another large swig of his cocktail. 'But it gets better . . . Bella has just told me that after I left, she overheard Frances – that's the agent's name – overheard her talking to another guy about how she might have a slot, *and* that I'm just the sort of actor she is looking for! How exciting is that. ICM!'

'That's fantastic, well done you,' said Amelie.

'And to think, my own agent didn't even bother to show up tonight! I guess he's going to get a shock before long . . .'

After ten more minutes of Charlie talking about his agent and agents-to-be, Amelie broke the conversation to say, 'So anyway, did I tell you, I'm going away this weekend?'

'Oh, no, you didn't. Where to?'

'Some remote village in Buckinghamshire. It's this ridiculous team-building weekend that my new boss is taking us all on. Nuts, but I guess it will be nice to get away from London for a bit . . .'

'Oh, well, I'll miss you,' Charlie said, the Byronic grin breaking out on his face again, and a cheeky glint appearing in his eye. Seeing that their drinks were now empty, he said, 'Um, do you fancy making a move soon? I'm feeling kind of done-in. We could go back to mine for a nightcap?'

Facilitating Creativity

'Is that everyone?' Fleur Parker-Jones called out two days later across the interior of a large grey minibus, before walking down the aisle to pat people on the heads and count them for the second time. A minute later she paused, shook her head, and said, 'Mmmm, I think we're still missing one.' She looked around, her beady eyes falling on Duncan, and landing on the empty seat next to him.

Duncan was just about to speak up when they heard a cry from the distance, and the sound of somebody running and panting.

'Sorry, sorry, sorry, everyone! I'm here now. I *was* ready on time, early even, but then I realised I'd left . . . um, well . . . sorry.' Amelie noticed that everyone was staring at her blankly, and stopped chattering. She climbed on to the minibus, her cheeks flushed and her hair frizzy from running. She sat down next to Duncan, her bags balancing precariously on her lap. 'Sorry,' she whispered to him quietly.

'Do you want me to put your bags and coat up on the rack?' Duncan offered.

'Yeah, thanks, sweet, that would be great,' she said, sitting down and curling up in her seat. 'Right, I might just get a bit of sleep now, I'm totally shattered.' Amelie closed her eyes, leaned against the bus window, and was asleep in seconds. Duncan looked at her, bemused by her narcoleptic prowess, and turned to face the seats behind him, where Max and Sally were engrossed in a game of Top Trumps. The minibus pulled away into the Soho traffic, and headed out for the M40.

Some hours later, Amelie awoke to the sounds of rowdy singing from the back of the bus. Looking out of the window, she saw that the bustle of London had long since passed away, and even though it was now dusk, she could just about make out a darkened vista of charming green meadows and peaceful countryside. She turned to Duncan and rubbed the sleep from her eyes. 'Hey – are we here yet?'

Duncan looked out of the window as they drove past more fields and meadows, past an archaic-looking church, through some tiny cobbled streets, and down a winding alley lined with independent shops and cafés, until at last they pulled into a driveway outside a sprawling country inn.

'Looks as if we might be,' he said, just as Fleur's voice boomed out over the bus: 'Everyone, this is Wing. Welcome to Wing, one of north Buckinghamshire's oldest and most charming villages.'

Sounds of exaggerated excitement abounded as she went on, 'OK, we're just going to park up, then we'll show everyone to their rooms, after which we'll be meeting for a slap-up meal in the restaurant.'

At this point Josh took the microphone from Fleur and added, 'And then we'll go for a quick nightcap in the bar – but no hedonistic late-night drinking sessions, people . . . we've got an early start tomorrow!'

The next day at 8 a.m. sharp, the LGMK creative department were assembled in the reception area of the Wing Manor Inn, waiting for their team-building guru from Creative Blockbusters to arrive. Amelie, hiding from daylight in her brown beanie and pink aviators, looked from her watch to Duncan and laughed, 'Well, it's five past early. Shall we give him another five minutes and then go for a wander? I mean, if we can all make it here on time, and *he* can't even be bothered to show . . .'

She turned to Josh, who was looking out of one of the reception windows towards Leighton Buzzard in the distance, craning his neck to see whether their trainer's car might be approaching over the winding lanes through the hills. 'Still no sign of him?' Amelie asked Josh. 'Maybe we could all go for a nice walk? It's such lush scenery out there, isn't it? Lovely to be out here, away from the Big Smoke.'

'It is nice, yes,' agreed Josh. 'But I'm sure Bob will have factored in some time outside for us all.'

Just then there was the sound of a screeching motor on the gravel drive outside the inn, and everyone turned to peek through the window at the bumbling, bespectacled middle-aged man who emerged from an old maroon Ford Fiesta. The LGMK creative department watched with raised eyebrows as he fumbled about with a stack of papers and files, stood by the passenger door, and loaded them up high in his arms, before slamming the door and causing most of the papers to cascade to the ground. He bent down to pick them up, scrambled around on the ground for a few moments, before standing up again. Banging his head on the car in the process.

'Introducing Bob, the keeper of all our creativity,' said Duncan sceptically to Amelie and Max, who broke out into laughter.

Rubbing his forehead, Bob looked towards the bay windows of the Wing Manor Inn, saw the collection of suspicious urbanite faces peering out at him in amusement, gave a meek wave, and walked towards the front door.

'Morning all!' he spoke in a soft Welsh accent, once he was inside. 'I'm Bob. Bob Satchell. How are we all today?' he said in his best rendition of chirpy, looking around the room at all the weary and jaded faces. 'Sorry I'm ever so slightly late!'

Moments later, the receptionist showed them all through to the open-plan training suite, where A-Ha's 'Take on Me' was blasting merrily from a small red eighties-style Sanyo ghetto blaster. The teams filed tentatively into the room, which overlooked a view of lush green meadows, winding streams and grazing cows. They sat down hungrily to a breakfast of coffee, pastries and name badges.

Moments later, it was time for the round of 'introductory fun and frolics' as Bob Satchell described it, referring to that particular bullet point on his Creative Blockbusters clipboard agenda. Bob, smoothing back his diminishing comb-over and adjusting his lopsided spectacles, stood up and asked if everyone could please move away from the tables and form a wide circle.

'So, I hope you all enjoyed your breakfast and are

getting excited. We're going to have a lot of fun today and tomorrow! Now, as you may have seen in our brochure, at Creative Blockbusters, we like to cultivate a NO FEAR policy. All that really means is, by the time we get into the programme of exercises which I've tailor-made for your agency, none of you should be feeling in the least bit uneasy or shy.' Bob grinned devilishly and climbed up on to the makeshift podium. 'Now, if everyone's ready, we're going to start with a few "Get-to-Know-You" games,' Bob said, miming little speech marks with his fingers. 'We'll start with an old favourite of mine. It's called the Torpedo game. Does anyone know this?'

A sea of mute, blank faces gave Bob his answer. 'No? Well, it's very simple. All you have to do is walk towards another person while saying their name, holding your arms out in front of you – like this.' Bob proceeded to jump theatrically down from the podium, holding his arms in front of him like a traffic cone, and walking around the room. He then looked pointedly towards Chloe, who immediately blushed scarlet. Squinting to read her name badge, Bob then marched towards her with his arms outstretched in the torpedo format, bellowing, 'CHLOE!' at the top of his voice.

Poor demure Chloe looked as though she might burst into tears. Bob, standing closely in front of her with his sweaty little torpedo hands just inches away from her face, went on to shout, as though Chloe was of simple mind, 'Now! Now!'

Bob looked expectantly at her while she stood quietly and became increasingly red. 'Come on!' he yelled again. Then, impatiently, he explained, 'You know, now it's your turn to do the same as I just did, but to another person in the group.' Bob – along with everyone else in the room – stood still, patiently waiting for Chloe to oblige him. Duncan looked at Chloe sympathetically, and smiled encouragingly at her.

'J-Josh,' she stammered awkwardly, her feet gripped to the floor.

'And now walk towards him,' encouraged Bob.

'Right, sorry.' Her eyes formed little daggers as she forced her arms into the torpedo pose and strutted towards Josh, calling out his name.

'That's it! Now, Josh, your turn.'

Josh followed suit, calling out, 'Max!' and marching towards Max, who then yelled, 'Sally!' who yelled 'Fleur!' and so on, until the room looked like a delirious mass of parading daleks at an intergalactic cocktail party.

This went on for an unfeasibly long time, until Sally finally interceded: 'I don't know about anyone else, but I think – perhaps – we've got that game pretty clear in our heads now?'

Josh looked surprised at Sally's outspokenness towards Bob, who in turn looked subdued by this slight struggle in power. 'Right you are,' admitted Bob, 'OK. Good! On with the next activity then. Everyone back into the circle.'

Amelie saw with trepidation where this day was going. Where the whole weekend was going. She sighed, crept into her place in the circle next to Chloe, who appeared to have just about recovered from her recent ordeal. Cringing inwardly, they all listened as Bob explained the rules to Zip, Zap, Boing! before announcing that now it was Amelie's turn to begin.

Amelie fought back tears of fury as they started to play the game. She pointed across the room at Duncan, with her right arm stretched firmly out in front of her, shouting, 'ZAP!' as loud as she could, looking back at Bob for his approval. He shot back a look of pride that she had got it right first time, and then waited for Duncan to respond. Duncan followed punctually with a shy and quiet 'ZIP!' while he pointed at Fleur, who was next to him. Fleur responded with 'ZAP!' across to Josh, who was opposite her. Josh shot a 'ZIP!' to Amelie who was just next to him. Amelie fought back at Josh with a 'BOING!' which bounced off him and to the next person, and so on.

'Marvellous, *marvellous*!' screeched Bob with Welsh glee. 'Keep it going, faster now, faster!' While Bob smiled like an excitable child, the Zips, the Zaps and the Boings shot around the room, and no one around him was any the wiser as to why they were playing this ludicrous game, and what it could possibly be teaching them about creativity, team-building, or anything else in the entire world.

After ten more minutes of this, Bob had the teams sit down at the table. 'That was great, everyone. Hope you're all feeling nice and warmed up now. Right, what we'll do now is talk about what we just did, and discuss what it signifies.' Armed with a bright pink marker pen, Bob marched up to the white-board and in huge capital letters, wrote a single word:

CREATIVITY

Looking around at the room, he spoke painfully slowly, carefully kneading every syllable, 'Now, we're here to dissect what this word means. To see how we can best FACILITATE it into our every working day. To make it come about when we need it to, like the flicking of a switch. What we'll look at today in particular is the enigma of the CREATIVE SPARK, and the many ways there are to ignite it. We are going to study the creative spark as though it were under a microscope, and in doing so learn many things about ourselves.'

Amelie wanted desperately to be somewhere else. Anywhere else at all would do. She wanted to grab Bob with both arms, to shake him, speed him along. This isn't helping us to write ads, is it? she wondered. As Bob waffled on and on, Amelie couldn't help but become fascinated by the huge tufty wart on his chin, which seemed to grow and grow in direct proportion with his verbosity. Suddenly that was all there was; she could no longer concentrate on what he was saying. In an effort to distract herself from the wart, Amelie felt her concentration drift away. Soon enough she stopped hearing what Bob was saying, closed her eyes and checked out of Training Suite 1. Before long she was fully occupied with the dazzling memory of Charlie in his Regency costume, and the rest of their night together on Wednesday, which had resulted in her staying over at his for the first time. It had been a lovely night, she recalled through the cocktail haze. Despite it having been a frighteningly long time since her last fling with a man, as she remembered it, things had gone as well as could be expected. She smiled to herself, remembering the moment when, after waking next to an empty space in his bed, she had instantly assumed he had bolted on her. Before long she had realised that he had actually been busy downstairs, crafting egg soldiers for a surprise breakfast-in-bed. For the last few days, Amelie had been sporting a strange grin on her face that her friends could barely recognise. Looking at Amelie and Sally together, you couldn't be blamed for thinking that speed-dating had successfully worked its magic on them both. Amelie smiled to herself at this idea, but then realised that she was still no closer to finding the kernel of truth with which to break the back of the Fast Love campaign. Remembering where she was again, Amelie decided to try and foster an open mind: perhaps this escaped lunatic might have some nuggets of creative wisdom with which to save herself and Duncan from their doom, before crawling back to his asylum, as he undoubtedly should.

Tuning in again to Channel Bob, Amelie saw that he had now become even more animated, and was rapidly pacing the room. 'If I want you to learn only one thing today, it's this: it's only through PLAY that we can truly unlock our creativity.' He began to shift around on the spot, growing more and more excited. Max and Duncan looked at each other with alarm, and then at Josh. Josh was now looking strangely at Bob, and deciding that he should almost certainly have opted for the more expensive package; the one which that other competitive team-building company had emailed him. At any rate, this day certainly wasn't panning out quite as he had imagined it would; it was nothing like how they did things down under. Josh looked up again and ran his hand through his hair as Bob's sermon continued apace.

'Now, one fundamental which I want to teach you is that, contrary to popular belief, creativity can actually be best facilitated when we are put under the most *rigid* of conditions. So, by being given many *restrictions*, we can actually function far better, and our creative juices flow much more easily.'

Although this wasn't news to anyone in the room,

Amelie suddenly had a strange realisation. Perhaps this was a profound metaphor for speed-dating itself? As in, with speed-dating, the romantic spark is allowed to flourish, but only under controlled, restricted conditions. Yes. The rigidity of the speed-dating set-up is actually the perfect breeding ground for romance to blossom; just as structure is vital to the creative process itself. Was there something in this idea, Amelie wondered? It was highly likely that there wasn't anything in it at all, but nevertheless she noted it down in her journal, which she saw with regret that she had neglected since 1 February; since the evening with Jack.

Bob carried on pacing the room, an aura of mania orbiting him. 'As I showed you earlier, play should be unrestricted. It's vital that you leave your inhibitions at the door. Unlock your creativity! Playing is key! Don't hold back from the games. Resistance is futile!' Getting louder still, Bob went on, 'Spontaneity! It's about doing things just for the sake of it; for the pure unadulterated *curiosity* of it. Let *go*.'

Noticing the pained expressions around the table, Bob drew to a close. 'OK. Now we're going to play a word game. I just want you to open your minds to what I ask you – no matter how wacky or zany – and give me your most open, creative responses as we go round the room.' He turned to Fleur, leaned in uncomfortably close, squinting to read her name badge, and asked, deadpan, 'Tell me, Flower, what goes faster: a table or a chair?'

Fleur looked at him like he had just held a knife to her throat and asked her to hand over her Gucci handbag, her iPod and her mobile phone in one go. She said, as bluntly as she could muster, 'This is ridiculous.' Then, looking at

Josh, she added, 'I can see you guys are all set here, so I'm just going to leave you to it now, OK?' She turned back to Bob and explained slowly, 'Sorry, I'm not a *creative*. I'm a creative PA – I don't actually need to be here. Thanks for the fun and frolics, though.'

Chloe, who had been staring daggers at Bob all morning since his previous invasion of her personal space, took this opportunity to rise out of her chair, look to Josh for his permission, and then cross the room to join Fleur. If Bob felt upset then he didn't show it. Rather he nodded stoically and prepared to carry on with the show. Fleur smiled back at the fettered creatives and strolled happily away. 'Lunch is at 1 p.m. Have fun till then, people!' With that she trotted off towards the rolling countryside, Chloe on her tail, leaving the others staring longingly out at their freedom.

'OK, people, try this one for size: which is male and which is female – the tomato or the pineapple?'

A few hours later, the teams were heading back to the training suite after lunch, looking refreshed after a hearty dinner and beers. Returning to the room, they saw with dismay that Bob was sitting at the table, a sadistic grin on his face, surrounded by multicoloured bits of paper in all shapes and sizes, together with an array of different felt-tipped pens, crayons and jotter pads.

Round two involved a game where they all had to get in to their creative teams, decide what animal they were, and then act this out to the rest of the department. This lasted an unthinkably long time. It was so painfully slow that Sally began to dream of tearing her hair out, and felt sure that the others must surely be sharing her thoughts. Amelie realised with terror that time had never, ever gone slower. The speed dates had flown by at hyperspeed compared to this. Keep calm, keep your thoughts to yourself, she thought. You don't want to get on the wrong side of Joshua Grant, who, psycho that he is, is probably thinking today is a great success.

Thankfully they were then allowed a short tea break, during which, after seeing Bob go to the bathroom, Josh bought everyone a round of double shooters, 'By way of an apology, guys. Really and truly sorry. I had no idea it would be like this.'

'OK, everybody back sitting in a circle, on the floor this time,' said Bob, back in Training Suite 1 half an hour later. 'We're now going to play Pulse. This is where you sit around in a circle and squeeze your neighbour's hand, and follow the pulse round, and then back again. OK?'

Everyone did little to conceal their cynicism, but being of slightly lighter spirits after their shooters, flopped down on to the floor in a circle and held hands. Bob planted himself in between Amelie and Duncan, much to the former's dismay. Holding her breath, Amelie observed that Bob, now at a closer proximity, also had a halitosis condition to add to his collection of unsavoury characteristics. Bob clasped her hand tightly in his, and Duncan's in the other, and said, 'I'll start the ball rolling, so to speak.'

Once everyone in the room was holding hands, and had resumed their poses of looking with sceptical hatred at their team leader, Bob squeezed his right hand extremely hard, sending a shudder through Amelie, making her jump. She couldn't remember when a man had made her feel as uncomfortable as this, at least not since speed-dating. Could this day *get* any sillier? she wondered. As she did so, she noticed that both Josh and Bob were looking at her expectantly, and she realised it was up to her to continue the pulse around the circle. 'Right, got it,' she laughed awkwardly, and lightly squeezed Josh's hand. Josh looked at her and then sent the 'pulse' onwards.

Moments later the pulse had been through the chain, through Sally and Max, through all the other teams, and through to Chloe (who had returned with Fleur for this round of games, both of them having suffered an outbreak of guilt). Chloe looked bashfully at Duncan and squeezed his hand. He looked over at her and gave a shy smile, praying inwardly that he wasn't going red owing to this much contact with a girl he didn't know very well. Next he squeezed Bob's hand again, wondering how long this deeply uncomfortable game was going to last.

The 'pulse' darted through the circle a few more times, and soon became increasingly fast, with multiple pulses circulating in different directions. At one particularly frantic point, Amelie felt Josh squeeze her hand unusually intensely, at which she shot him a sharp look of surprise. He looked at her and mouthed an apology at this lack of judgement. Fleur, across the room, noticed this and squeezed Max's hand extra hard, shooting a meaningful look in Josh's direction. Duncan, meanwhile, was staring at them all, an odd expression on his face. Aside from Bob, everyone in the circle was once again united in one thing – a complete failure to understand the point of the game, just as with all the others they had endured that day.

Moments later, Bob stopped pulsating, and stood up, 'OK, that's great, you can all stand up now. So, how was that for everyone?' he asked excitedly. Everyone picked themselves up off the floor, and looked down at their feet, avoiding Bob's eyes.

Josh stood up and took a deep breath. 'Well, I'm sorry to say, Bob, that this game struck me as a little similar to all of the other games we've played today.'

'Oh really?' Bob commented. 'I thought it was very different to the others . . . that's why I always save it until later on –'

Josh shook his head. 'No, you misconstrue me. By *similar* I mean that this game, like all of the others, is terrible. Worse than pointless. It hasn't helped me to feel in any way more creative.' Josh looked around at his many creative teams, to see them all nodding their heads in acquiescence. 'And I think I speak for us all when I say that. In all fairness, Bob, I can't see what you are trying to achieve by showing us these games. A) they don't seem to have achieved the goal of building teams, as it were, and B) we're already creative. Maybe these activities are designed for people who aren't . . . maybe they're tailor-made for suits, accountants, lawyers . . .' He trailed off, trying to think of the right words to end with. 'In a nutshell, I'm thinking of the words, "coal" and "Newcastle"?'

Bob was sunken. Beads of sweat appeared on his forehead, and his eyes began to appear more shiny than before. 'I see . . .' he said, fishing into his briefcase for a wad of A4 forms. 'Well, if I could just leave you with these customer-feedback forms, you can say anything else you need to at the end of the course tomorrow.'

'I'm sorry, Bob. That won't be necessary. Perhaps your hit rate is better with the other people you are used to working with . . . but . . . I've just made the executive decision to terminate the course, in favour of a night's drinking and a morning's stroll through the countryside tomorrow. I can't help feeling that would be money and time better spent. And I fear that if I don't do this right now, by Monday I may have no department left.'

And with that, the LGMK creative collective filed out of Training Suite 1, leaving a befuddled Bob Satchell to pick up his multicoloured games and to mop the perspiration on his brow once again. Amelie looked back at Bob and felt a strange shred of sympathy for him; a sympathy that was complicated by her intense gratitude towards Josh. She now couldn't help but look at Josh with fresh eyes – thinking she couldn't have put it better herself – as they all headed into the pub for a night of team-building in the old-fashioned, ad land way.

Driving back the next day with their hangovers in tow, Josh was pleased to see that all the teams now seemed closer than ever. As the grey minibus filled with noisy, bantering creatives wound through the calm woodland scenery and back towards the heavy smog of London, Josh decided that the weekend had been a success after all – even if, ironically, it was the hatred for poor Bob and his cavalcade of soul-dampening frolics that had brought them all closer together.

Acting Up

*Hooray – am finally back from the bad day in Bedlam that
was The Wing Experience. Never in the history of the world
has time gone by as slowly as it did in the training suite with
that deranged dinosaur Mr Bob Satchell. Thank heaven
Josh came to everyone's rescue and heroically told him
where to stick his team-building nonsense. Can't help
thinking have new-found respect for him now.*

*The remainder of the weekend was actually really good
fun. We all went for a long walk around Wing, visited Ascott
House, a country retreat with some lovely antique
paintings. We all felt rather uplifted from seeing so much
nature and beauty. Before long and much to everyone's
relief, the spirit-crushing memories of Zip, Zap, Boing! had
passed away.*

*While we were on the walk around the village, and on the
way to see one of the oldest churches in England (which*

dates back to the seventh century, by the way), I fell into step with Duncan and Chloe. Can't say for sure, but I think that I noticed a few interesting looks being exchanged . . . starting to think there might be some kind of spark between them (and Duncan hasn't mentioned Sara-Jayne for ages, whom I thought he was still meant to be seeing a lot of). Still, as far as I can see, both Chloe and Duncan are too shy to act on it at the moment.

Then, over a long Sunday lunch in a gorgeous country pub, something else caught my eye. Fleur seemed rather withdrawn – by that, I mean not her usual snappy self. Also got the distinct impression she was doting around Josh and hanging off his every word much more than he was reciprocating. Ever since the team-building antics, I've noticed she seems to have the hump about something and is ostracising herself from the group more than usual. Once, I saw her sitting in the corner of the hotel canteen, reading a magazine on her own, so I asked her if she wanted to come and join Duncan, Chloe and I on our walk. She pretty much bit my head off, said she was waiting for Josh, and then looked at me really oddly, as though I'd said something deeply offensive. Don't know what her problem is – she used to be so easygoing when she was on reception. Now she's PA she's suddenly become really tightly wound; all defensive and prickly, and I can't help feeling it's me she's got some kind of issue with. Or maybe it was just the two days without her hair straighteners and manicure set, burning a hole in her reserve, and I'm being paranoid. Who knows . . . will see how it goes back at work this week. Ah, better go, that's Charlie on the phone – seeing him tomorrow; really looking forward to it . . .

Work, Wednesday 9 February, 11.53 p.m.

Made fatal mistake tonight of taking Charlie to the theatre. Ollie – an actor friend of mine from college – was performing in a West End play I've been wanting to see for ages. I thought Charlie would like to see it as it's had amazing reviews, and I also thought he'd like to meet Ollie, who was playing the lead – you know, contacts, networking and all that stuff?

Wrong on both counts! I really enjoyed the play, a biting satire about a book publisher and his array of sordid affairs. And I think Charlie enjoyed it too, at least, from what I could tell in those few scarce moments when he wasn't shaking his head and tutting to himself about the standard of the acting. When I asked him what he thought of it in the interval over a round of drinks (which, not to make too much of this but, I paid for again), I could see his face scrunch up awkwardly as he tried to think of the words, 'Yeah, it's really good. Great writing, great direction.' He sank a third of his pint, then added, as though he was trying in vain to suppress the words, 'Your friend's OK. But some of the other acting I'm not too fussed over.' And then I thought, here it comes . . .

'You know, that guy playing the lead, why did they have to get him in to do it? He's not adding anything new to the role, is he? It's just because he's famous!'

'He has been in a load of films and TV shows,' I agreed, 'but I don't see why you should hold it against him. I still thought he was brilliant.'

Charlie frowned in distaste, shifted about in his seat jitteringly. 'Nonsense. Any "unknown" could have taken that part and played it much more interestingly.'

'Like yourself perhaps?' I teased.

'Why's that so funny?' he snapped. 'And besides, I'm not that unknown, you know, I have had a recurring role in Doctors before.'

'Hey, chill, I was just saying . . .' I edged away from Charlie and his rapidly inflating ego, thinking that recurring 'taxi driver number three' probably didn't allow you into Z-list territory just yet. But, not wanting to upset him, I kept schtum.

'Look, it's just because they've all probably got shit-hot agents, and none of those swines from last week has called me back or replied to my letters . . . I'm sorry, Amelie. It's just such a horrible existence, being an actor. Your hopes are up and down like a yo-yo every day . . . you're made to feel about as important as the shit on someone's shoe, and yet you keep on going, keep on pushing at it, because you have to. I'm sorry to go on, Am, it's just – I feel so stuck. I can't give up – it's chosen me, this life. I can't do anything else. It would be unnatural to even try. And the trouble is, I know so many really talented people, Am, and there're just never enough parts to go round for us all. I just feel I've put in the years, I really have, and I really deserve a break, you know? It's not like I'm any less talented than anyone on that stage!'

As he drew his stirring monologue to a dramatic finish, Charlie looked at me, his once-cheerful cheeks etched with misery, and his brown eyes dilated with sadness (or coke, it's hard to tell which these days). Really felt bad for him; wondered what I could say that would help him. Just then I heard a loud bell ring, and, for a horrible second, thought I was at another speed-dating event. Was our time nearly up? I suddenly found myself thinking, as we went back into the theatre for the second half.

After the curtains went up and I'd risen with the rest of the audience (well, all bar one) for a standing ovation, Charlie and I went for a drink around the corner. I then made the second fatal mistake of the evening and invited Ollie to join us. Just as I was getting my money out to pay for our drinks at the bar, I felt Ollie appear by my side. He leaned across me and took his wallet out to pay, ordering himself a pint in the process.

'Thanks, mate,' I said. 'Great to see you – and well done, you were brilliant.' To which he replied that it was the least he could do, and thanked us both for coming.

'Charlie loved it too,' I lied.

'Where is Mr Speed-Dating Stud anyway?' Ollie teased. We both looked over at Charlie, who was sitting down in a booth and playing some sort of video game on his mobile.

'Come and meet him. He's lovely,' I said numbly to Ollie, fearing that a slow and painful few scenes were just about to commence.

At first I decided to try and avoid all talk of acting by bringing up some harmless talk about the shark-infested world of advertising. 'So,' I tried, 'only a week to go now until the dreaded Fast Love pitch. Duncan and I have been talking about which recruitment agencies to go and see, after it all falls apart and the agency goes into liquidation . . .'

Charlie's knee-jerk response was, 'Oh don't worry – you'll be fine – you'll come up with a moment of genius any day now.' He pinched me affectionately around my midriff and then moved the subject swiftly on.

'So, Ollie,' Charlie began, a hint of competitiveness in his tone, 'where did you train?' That was the one question I had been hoping he wouldn't ask, and obviously the one

question he had been itching, writhing about in his seat all night, waiting to ask.

'Oh, just around the corner from here,' Ollie said modestly. Charlie looked at him as though expecting him to spell it out for him, after which Ollie added reluctantly, 'RADA.'

Charlie's face fell. 'Oh right,' he said. 'I went to the Guildhall,' he said, before adding helpfully, 'you know, the one where Ewan and Orlando went . . .'

Ollie nodded sagely. But then there was one other question, which I was hoping Charlie wouldn't ask. But from experience with nights out with him and his actor friends, I knew there was precious little chance that any of us would get away without the inevitable acting-community question.

Cue Charlie: 'And who are you with?'

'Romantically speaking?' Ollie attempted humour, foolishly. Charlie frowned and looked impatient. Ollie added quietly, almost apologetically, 'Right; agent-wise, I'm with ICM.'

Charlie forced a smile; said how great that was. I tried in vain to move the conversation on to some other topic, but I could tell that Ollie and Charlie now seemed set on comparing careers all night. I gave them one more shot at changing the subject away from acting, but no such luck. After half an hour or so of listening to them calculate their success/failure ratio, my mind began to wander back to the Fast Love pitch, and I began to feel guilty for not having put in enough hours. I looked back at them, heard the immortal phrase 'working on my craft'; felt the final nail shoot into the coffin, and decided I couldn't take any more. Weirdly, it made me feel like I was missing my work. I looked at my watch. We were only minutes away from Soho Square. I decided to slip away to the office and leave the luvvies to it. If I stepped on it I could get there before the security guard left at 10.30.

Which brings us up to speed. Here I am, scribbling away at my desk like a sad old bastard, in a deserted ad agency, with a glass of red wine and a cigarette for company. In fairness, though, I was starting to think the time could be put to better use. I mean, right now, the Fast Love campaign needs my attention more than Charlie does. And to be honest I'm starting to lose my patience with how most of the times I've seen him he's been coked off his head, or if not, he's on the verge of being so – I've become really good at sensing the changes in his personality; almost like there's a switch being flicked or something.

That said, there is still something about him – something I really do like. He's also done a fabulous job of taking my mind off Jack, for which he should be highly commended. He is still loads of fun to be around, even if sometimes, just every so often, he can take things too far. A bit like a small, excitable child right before his mum utters the words 'It'll end in tears.' I guess that makes him loveable, but what if it gets exhausting after a while? I think it's all impinged by the coke – sometimes it's really hard to extract who the real Charlie is, from when he's not high on something or other. I'll never forget the moment the other day when, literally two seconds after sex, he turned to me with a deadly serious expression in his eyes and said, 'Oh my God. I've not shown you my Millennium Falcon yet, have I?' Then he leaped out of bed and began frantically jumping about the room, diving into his cupboards and drawers to see where he had put it. All I could think to say was, 'Well, that makes a pleasant *change from. "How was it for you?" ' and got up to use the bathroom.*

Reading this back again, I think I'm being a little harsh on him. So he has a few warts, but Lord knows so do I. Maybe he's not 'The One', but it's early days, and what's the harm in just seeing him for now, having some fun together? What are the rules – how long should you stay in a relationship with someone whom you don't think is quite The One? Even if you know there are things you like about them (and things that infuriate you about them), how long should you give it? Is it better to be single and waiting patiently for Mr Right, or to stay with someone because they make you laugh, because you're having fun with them, and you're still young? And anyway, aren't all relationships basically killing time until something better comes along?

Really want to believe that this could still go somewhere, that somewhere in all this I'll be able to see that speed-dating does work. I mean, it's worked wonders for Sally – will quiz her about it tomorrow. Still determined to find the solution – maybe Google will have something useful to say about it all.

Work, Thursday 10 February, 9.03 a.m.

As it happened, I didn't get very far with Googling. Shortly after typing in the word 'spee' I nearly jumped out of my skin. Josh was suddenly standing in my doorway.

'What are you still doing here?' he asked, wearing his black beanie, and climbing into his coat.

'Oh, hello,' I said, a little freaked out at seeing him, having assumed I'd been alone all that time. 'I only just got here, really; I was out in Soho, you know, just passing, and wanted to put in some quiet time on the Fast Love stuff.'

Josh looked both confused and impressed. 'Any brainwaves?' he asked, looking at my empty glass of wine.

'Oh, too many to mention,' I lied, and he could tell. 'What about you, have you really been here since five-thirty?'

He nodded. "Fraid so. Been working on some big ideas I've got for the agency. All will be revealed in time,' he said, an enigmatic look in his eye. Then he jangled his car keys, 'Anyway, I'm not such a tyrant of a boss that I'm going to leave you here working on your own after midnight. Can I give you a lift somewhere?'

For some reason I wanted to resist. Partly because I wanted to make the point that I was so dedicated to my job that I was going to carry on working through till dawn, and partly because I suppose there's a part of me that still doesn't quite trust him; that still hasn't got used to him being around. But, facing the fact that my ideas were definitely not flowing, I decided to call it a night, and accepted.

I'm not normally one for being impressed by expensive cars and things like that, but I have to admit that his car is pretty nice. It's a black convertible Golf – practical but sexy. I guess. If you're into cars that is, which I'm not. Anyway, as we were making our small-talk, it struck me how little I knew about this man who was my new boss. I didn't even know where he lived. He lives in North London, incidentally; near Camden somewhere. So my place was sort of on the way, which was good. Hated to think I was putting him out.

As he was chatting away, I started to think, Maybe he's not quite so bad. Maybe I've been overly harsh on him until now? So I decided to start asking him about himself, too. Soon we were chatting away amiably. He was telling me about growing up as a happy-go-lucky country boy on a farm in Perth, before his dad died and he moved to Sydney to be closer to his mum's side of the family. And I was telling him about the adventures I'd had backpacking, living in the Pommie ghetto otherwise known as Bondi Beach, before heading out to Thailand, where it turns out we very nearly crossed paths. I'm not sure we've got our astrology right, but there's every chance that we were at the same Full Moon beach party, at the same time, the same month, in the same year. Weird! I just hope he didn't have the misfortune to witness my chundering in a quiet corner of the beach after one too many of those lethal cocktail 'buckets'. Likewise, he assured me he wasn't one of those vile men peeing in the ocean like it was some communal toilet. It's kind of strange to think we might have been sitting in the same bar at one time and not known it. Maybe we even saw each other but didn't realise it at the time? Perhaps we shared a cocktail 'bucket' or two? Passed the same spliff around under the same sunset. Or maybe not. But it's funny to think about it, to realise what a small world we're in.

Anyway, back to the issue at hand. Speed-dating. And how to sell it. Duncan and I are being really productive today, working on a whole new batch of ideas which he's come up with, based on an analogy with cars. It's all rather ridiculous, and I'm partly responsible, as the idea came about unwittingly when I said that Sally had found love 'in the fast lane'. That was all it took for Duncan to go back to his vision of Cartoon Cupid. The idea of little Cupid speeding along in a little car, motoring away; putting his foot down. Incredibly lame, I know, but we're going to show them to Josh later and he's going to decide which ideas will go into the pitch, out of all the work the other creative teams *have come up with. Weirdly enough, Josh reckons the standard of work has already gone up as a result of the weekend away. As though somehow Bob's insane team-building games had the desired effect on our creative juices – that or the cocktails we had in the bar afterwards . . .*

Either way, I don't think our new ideas are any better than the Diana Ross ideas I came up with before. Seriously doubt any of them have got the edge that's needed to fend off whatever the other agencies will pitch in with. But then I get the impression that Duncan's lost interest; that he's starting to feel disillusioned with the job anyway and is past wanting to invest any more of his time. If Duncan's passionate about anything at the moment, it's not work, it's not women, and it's not cars. What's his big infatuation at the moment? Scratch-cards. I truly don't remember the last time I saw him without one. And his current winning/losing ratio really doesn't justify the time and money spent. In all seriousness, how can he afford them all?

Work, Thursday 10 February, 9.27 a.m.

Oh dear God. He said he was going out for a coffee a minute ago and he's just walked into the office with a batch of ten scratch-cards. Is this getting silly yet? I mean, worryingly silly? Am going to bite my tongue for now, but if it gets any worse over the next week, I'll have to do something. Go and get some addiction pamphlets to leave lying around, or something . . .

Anyway, there's one thing the weekend in Wing did make me think about. I'm starting to wonder whether maybe I'm also losing faith in the advertising circus – maybe I'm getting jaded? I don't suppose doing pitches like this can be helping; but I can't help wondering if the reason I can't get to the heart of this campaign is simply that my heart's not in it any more. Maybe my spark's just gone out, never to return?

Ah well, on to much more exciting things . . . my oldest friend is getting married the day after tomorrow – can't believe how fast it's come around. Really looking forward to it. I just know she's going to be immensely happy, and she's going to look amazing in her dress. Dunc and I are getting the train down to Penarth after work tomorrow, which means, dauntingly, the pitch has to be all sewn up before we go . . . Suspect tonight is going to involve another all-night work session. May not get time to write in here again now that it's all nearly over . . . So, I can only hope that Duncan and I have done our best as far as Fast Love's concerned, and that we won't be cast out on to the streets as of next week. Either way, thanks for listening. Over and out.

Wedding Bells

'**M**orning has spoken!!' shouted Amelie with sprightly enthusiasm.

Saturday morning, 7 a.m. The sun was rising over Claire in her parents' house in Bristol's Clifton district. From what Amelie could see as she drew open the curtains, the sky was a warm, bright blue, and seemed full of promise for a crisp but sunny February day.

'Good morning, Ms Wilson. How are you feeling today?' Amelie sang chirpily, planting a kiss on Claire's cheek, and a steaming mug of coffee on her bedside table.

'I – oh my God – it surely can't be morning already,' Claire moaned, pulling her duvet over her head. 'I've not even been to sleep yet!' Claire's eyes quinted at Amelie, who was already dressed and showered. Gradually, Claire's eyes opened a little wider, and she looked confusedly at Amelie. 'Who are you, speaking to me in this – this energetic, smug, "I've had sleep and you haven't" kind of way? You're never this perky in the morning . . . leave me alone!'

'Why haven't you slept, sweetness?' asked Amelie, ignoring Claire's stream of unconsciousness and stroking her forehead to try and bring about some calm.

Claire shook Amelie away and frowned. 'Well, I couldn't sleep for worrying about today. And then I started getting all stressed about not being able to sleep, and by then I was so uptight and restless that I gave up on sleep altogether, and then all of ten minutes ago I think I finally dropped off.' Claire looked at the clock on the wall and gave a double take. 'And now it's time to get up, and I'm going to look like a werewolf going down the aisle! No one's going to want to marry me with these dark circles!' she hollered as though it was all Amelie's fault. Claire's face then creased up with new levels of anguish at having caught sight of herself in the mirror on the wall.

'Calm down,' said Amelie in her best soothing voice. 'We've got four hours to make you look a beautiful, radiant picture, OK? So drink your coffee and then we'll get to work. What would you like for breakfast?'

'I couldn't possibly eat a thing. I'm far too scared. In fact, just call the whole thing off!' Claire yelled melodramatically, disappearing into one of her pillows.

'Listen to you – you sound like you've been taking neuroses lessons from me!' Amelie leaped on to Claire and began thwacking her over the head with the other pillow. 'Come on!'

'Piss bloody off!' But after a minute of pillow-beating, Claire surrendered. 'All right!' She stood up, feeling the room wobble as she did so, and added, 'OK. I'll go through with it. But only 'cause you're making me.'

*

After four hours spent battling with irons, hair straighteners and the traffic between Bristol and Cardiff, they made it to the city registry office on time. Just.

Dan, standing on the stage in the small white room and looking resplendent in his black Ralph Lauren suit, had his eyes fixed firmly on the door to the hallway, waiting nervously for Claire and Amelie to emerge.

A few anxious minutes passed by. Everyone in the room held in their breath. At three minutes past twelve-thirty, the door opened and Claire appeared, looking every bit the picture Amelie had promised she would, wearing an exquisite white empire-line dress which trailed behind her; as did her wavy blonde hair, which she wore long, laced with little white flowers.

Of the whole of Claire and Dan's family and friends, not one person could take their eyes off Claire. Considering how last-minute the wedding plans had been, Amelie couldn't believe how well it had turned out; how angelic a bride she looked. Taking her seat among the audience, in the first live wedding she had ever seen, Amelie watched, her heart in her throat as they began to say their vows, and felt a sad smile spread across her face. When it was Claire's turn to say her vows, Amelie couldn't help finding it strangely enchanting, hearing her elfin voice saying those much-fabled words. Having grown up on a strict diet of infidelity and divorce, and after nurturing years of cynicism towards all things love and marriage, suddenly Amelie was surprised to find herself feeling moved by what she was seeing – almost as though something in her outer shell seemed to be softening. Once the formal vows had been read, the registrar spoke the final words, 'You may now kiss the bride.' Despite having been worn out by decades of girlie movies, in Claire and Dan's case these words now seemed invested with a new lease of life, and didn't even sound clichéd to Amelie.

As Dan took Claire in his arms for a long, lingering kiss, from the other side of the room, Duncan looked over at Amelie. He blinked. He craned his neck to see if he was imagining it. Looking again, he watched as a stray tear slipped down Amelie's cheek. No one else had seen this apart from him, and as Amelie hastily dabbed at her eyes with a shredded tissue, no one was more surprised than she was.

After a short break, Lydia, Claire's best friend from university, took to the stage and began a farcical rendition of Pam Ayres's poem 'Yes, I'll Marry You'. As she acted out each line, bringing to life every joke with her comedic movements up and down the stage, the room exploded with laughter, and a happy tear rolled down Amelie's face.

Following this, Claire's sister Veronika took to the stage. Rustling nervously with a sheet of paper, she began to read quietly from Shakespeare's Sonnet Number 116. Looking like a much younger clone of Claire, Veronika read charmingly, if a little robotically. Through Veronika's stumbled, barely audible words, Amelie strained to hear the lines 'Love's not time's fool, though rosy lips and cheeks within his bending sickle's compass come; Love alters not with his brief hours and weeks, but bears it out even to the edge of doom . . .'

As Amelie's eyes filled again, she dabbed at them frantically, feeling bewildered at how sensitively she was reacting, but feeling a hardness in her gradually dissolving. She knew that since birth, her parents' actions had unwittingly indoctrinated in her the view that marriage was to be avoided at all costs. That it would only ever end in tears and heartbreaking paperwork. But now, looking at Dan and Claire with pride, she saw that maybe there was another side to it all. She wasn't ever going to settle down and commit to Jack, but, just because he had broken her heart and shattered her dreams, it didn't mean that she could never let anyone else in again; or that she wouldn't ever find happiness with someone else. Ten minutes later, having wept discreetly through most of the second half of the ceremony, Amelie felt cleansed, as though the whole experience had cathartically removed her of her heartbreak, her bitterness, her gravity, leaving behind nothing but a healthy heart, and an open mind.

After the ceremony, the wedding guests all made their way over to Penarth, where Dan's parents were hosting an intimate reception party at their house. Arriving at the charming Victorian mansion, Amelie was startled by the scenery. Wide-eyed, she took in the magnificent grounds. Leaving her coat in the hall, she headed towards the back of the house to the conservatory, which had been elegantly decorated with flowers and balloons. An extravagant buffet lay stretched out on tables, and guests were nibbling hungrily on quail-egg muffins here and bite-sized mush-room tarts there. Amelie looked through the bay windows and admired the sublime backdrop of the landscaped gardens, and the blue-grey waters of the estuary which ebbed and flowed in the distance. She was itching to go and explore, but the guests had now almost all arrived, and she could sense the anxiety of unspoken speeches lingering in the air. Spotting Duncan in the kitchen with the champagne, she went to join him.

'How are you coping, sweetie?' Duncan asked her, his words loaded with pathos.

'Fine, thanks . . .' Amelie said slowly.

'Recovered, then, have you?' Duncan teased.

Amelie's brow crinkled, but she said innocently, 'What do you mean?'

Duncan leaned in and whispered, 'I saw you, Ammie – sobbing like a baby in there.' He looked around to ensure no one was listening. 'I don't think anyone else did . . . your secret's safe with me!'

Amelie's face flushed as she whispered indignantly, 'I was not!'

'Don't deny it – I saw you!' Duncan challenged. 'I never knew you had it in you! Wow, who'd have thought it? Amelie Holden: the last of the true romantics. I think it's lovely . . . Don't be embarrassed.'

'Oh shush, now. So maybe *some* people were crying, but I honestly wasn't; I just had something stuck on my contacts. Still really not getting on well with these new Dailies that Sally recommended. They're so hard to keep flecks of dust out of! Anyway . . .' Amelie trailed off and pushed a platter of smoked-salmon blinis towards Duncan's face. 'Have one of these. They're to die for,' she said, as though this had concluded the conversation.

Just as Duncan dived into the canapés, they heard a little bell ring out, and the room hushed to reveal Claire's father – a stout, balding man with glasses – clearing his throat.

'Evening, everyone. It's marvellous to see you all here – thank you all for coming at such short notice!'

Everyone cheered, and then Claire's parents gave a short speech, before Dan stood up to say a few words. 'Hi, everyone, thanks again for coming; we're really happy to see you all here.' He turned to Claire and looked at her adoringly. 'So, I just want to say a huge thank-you to Claire for not standing me up. I still can't quite believe that I've managed to trick her into marrying me.'

Amelie saw Claire blush, the first of many, as Dan went on to narrate in full detail the story of how he and Claire had met in their second year at Bristol University. He talked in jovial and vivid detail of how he had pursued her diligently for over a year before they had eventually got together. After twenty minutes of poignant anecdotes that were specifically designed to make Claire blush and the audience coo, Amelie noticed that Claire, who was never a fan of being the centre of attention, seemed to be praying for the tide of embarrassing memories to please come to an end. Her eyes looked pleadingly at Dan and then at Amelie, who gave her a warm, encouraging smile. Eventually, Dan drew to a close and looked expectantly at Claire to take over. After Claire had offered her own, humble version of a speech, they eventually kissed again, to the sound of rapturous applause. Amelie stood watching the newly-weds, admiring the sparks that were flying in the air between them. Dan's father raised his glass. 'To Claire and Dan. We wish you all the best for a radiantly happy future.'

The room stood up in unison, raised their glasses, and cheered, 'To Claire and Dan.' Amelie cheered with them, but as she did so, a pensive look appeared on her face. Something they had said in the speeches seemed to have hit a nerve. She couldn't think now what it was, but there had definitely been a moment. Someone had mentioned something which had struck a chord, made her think. But now the moment had passed and she couldn't think what it was . . . hopefully it would come back to her later, she mused, and downed the rest of her glass of champagne.

Moments later it was time to cut the cake. Instead of the traditional split-level wedding cake, Claire had asked for a five-tiered affair consisting of fifty little chocolate pots, bursting with white, dark and milk chocolate dippers, and loaded with a rich and sticky mousse. So instead of actually cutting the cake, she and Dan stood by the tower of indulgence, posing for photos while they handed out the edible little pots to all their friends.

After some time, the opening beats to Lou Reed's 'a Perfect Day' kicked in. Dan took Claire into his arms and led her into the lounge, where his parents had cleared a space for a makeshift dance floor. After a few minutes of people admiring the newly-weds' dancing, Dan's parents took to the floor to join them. Claire's parents, by contrast, having been divorced for fifteen years, stood at opposite ends of the room and stole glances at one another, as they had been doing all through the wedding. Amelie smiled as Dan began to dance with his mother, and Claire began to dance with Dan's father. It was all rather charming, or sickening, depending on how you looked at it.

After the next few slow songs, Amelie noticed that the music was gradually becoming more upbeat, and was almost veering into cheesy territory. As it did so, the dance floor began to fill out. Claire's four-year-old twin cousins came on to the floor, and Amelie watched from the sides as Claire danced around with them. At the same time, Dan was dancing with Claire's mum, who was laughing and looking a little embarrassed. Meanwhile, Amelie was watching Claire's father and noticing that he couldn't take his eyes off Claire's mother. Amelie couldn't help reflecting that even after fifteen years of divorce, it still looked as though there was some trace of a spark between them.

As the evening moved on, Claire and Dan grew more intoxicated, as did the family and friends encircling them. Amelie and Duncan eventually joined everyone on the dance floor. Before long they were all dancing together in a big circle, kicking their legs up in the air to anthems like 'New York, New York' and 'Isn't She Lovely?' With Claire's every leg-kick, she felt her garter slipping further down her leg, and she frequently found herself having to discreetly raise it back up again, hoping no one else was noticing. But then to her dismay the 'Can-Can' music came on, and after the third time of it slipping down her leg, past her knee this time, she decided to pull it off. Then everyone exploded with laughter as her three-year-old cousin Robert grabbed the garter and planted it on top of his blond curls, and started dancing around the centre of the circle, with his cheeky blue eyes laughing; a born entertainer. And Amelie thought, at last, I've met the man of my dreams.

Some hours later, everyone was gathered in the front garden. Claire was glowing with happiness as she delivered her final thank-you speech.

'Seriously, we've both had the most incredible day and night. So we'd just like to say a huge thanks to everyone for making the pilgrimage down here at such short notice. It wouldn't have been the same without any one of you. I promise to send as many postcards to people from the Cook Islands as we can!'

'Speaking of which,' interrupted Dan, looking anxiously from his watch to the wedding car that was parked by the drive, 'it's time we weren't here . . .'

'He's right,' said Claire. 'Oh well, I guess all that's left to do is this . . .' And Claire fumbled around with her bouquet. 'Here goes, ladies!' Claire turned around and tossed her bouquet behind her. As the girls fell into a ladylike scrum, it was clear where the bundle of flowers had landed. In the hands of Lydia, who smugly exclaimed, 'Oh! I won't be needing this, I'm already happily married to Charles, aren't I?' She grinned up at the tall dark man next to her. 'How about I pass it on to the girl next to me?'

Everyone seemed to agree that this would be best, all except the girl next to her, who feebly attempted to refuse the offer. Claire's bouquet now belonged to Amelie, who forced a radiant smile on to her face as people laughed and cheered. Moments later, she was brushing a bittersweet tear away from her cheek as the wedding car containing Claire and Dan drove them away to the airport. Cries of 'Goodbye!' and 'Good luck!' trailed after them, Amelie cheering loudest of all, and waving her oldest friend away.

Shortly afterwards, the guests returned to the house to carry on with the party. Duncan and Amelie, saddened by having bade farewell to the newly-weds, made the executive decision to drink more, and to attack some of the remaining smoked-salmon blinis. After a few hours of this, Amelie looked around the room and saw that it had begun to thin out. By 2 a.m. they were among the last survivors. Most people had either left in taxis or crept away to stake their claim on the last of the guest bedrooms. The other remaining revellers were strewn over the sofas, watching DVDs and eating bacon butties served up by Claire's mother. Amelie scanned the unfamiliar faces and commented, 'It feels weird that they've gone already, doesn't it?'

'Yeah, it really does,' Duncan agreed. After polishing off the last of his second chocolate pot, he suggested they go for a walk down to the sea.

'That sounds lovely,' agreed Amelie. 'Yeah, we can take this bottle of wine with us and finish it on the pebbles. I think we've missed any chance of a bed to crash in tonight, so we might as well prolong the inevitable.'

Leaving the house via the back door, they began walking through the moonlit gardens. Past the Chinese fountains and willow trees, past the ponds and the quaint little summer house, and down to a dark iron fence draped in ivy. Amelie gave the gate a big push, and it flung open. Quietly they walked through to the little pathway which led them down to the sea.

At they set foot on to the meandering path, they were silent for a few minutes, until Duncan asked, 'So, you didn't think of inviting Charlie today?'

'Well, no,' replied Amelie. 'I knew it was just a small wedding, and I didn't want to add to the expense for Claire and Dan. I'm kind of glad now – it's nice just to be here with you and all of Claire's close friends.'

'Yeah, it has been lovely, hasn't it? And I don't feel like we've hung out together properly in ages.'

Amelie nodded and gave Duncan an affectionate hug. 'I know, I feel the same! I feel like it's just been work, work, work with us, and this speed-dating thing has kind of come between us in a strange way. I'll be so glad when it's all over on Monday!'

'Me too. I still can't get over the timing of it, though – the pitch being on the fourteenth of February. What are the chances? They must have rigged it from the beginning!'

Amelie laughed in acquiescence. 'I know. As if Valentine's Day isn't already the most pointlessly ridiculous day in the history of the world . . .'

They reached the beach and began walking along the pebbles. Amelie uncorked the bottle of Shiraz and poured out some wine into plastic cups. 'So, will you be seeing SJ on Monday, then? You really aren't keeping me informed enough on how it's going with her! What's the latest?'

Amelie couldn't help noticing Duncan wince at the sound of her name. He took a swig of wine and looked out at the sea. 'Well, to be honest, I'm not sure it's really going anywhere any more. Before now, I was already thinking it may have run its course. But the ceremony today has really drawn a line under that for me. After seeing Claire and Dan, and how right for each other they are.'

Amelie nodded sympathetically. 'I know. It really got to me, I'll admit it; I've never seen anything like it, apart from in tacky films and TV shows . . . OK, you were right, I was weeping like a baby!'

Duncan laughed and pinched her affectionately. 'It's OK, you know. You're only human. You don't have to justify why you cried.'

Duncan looked at Amelie closely, a fondness in his eyes, and went on, 'It's got me thinking, though. Sara and I, we're having a laugh and all that, and she's gorgeous . . . she's the whole package . . . but today I thought to myself, though I know it's too early on to be even thinking this stuff, I just can't imagine us tying the knot, going the long haul and all that. She's just not the person I would imagine myself settling down with.'

'But that's ridiculous,' Amelie said sternly. 'You guys have fun together, don't you? Why d'you have to go and spoil it by worrying about the future? Who knows what'll happen?' She fished into her pocket and dug out her pack of Marlboro Lights. 'Ciggie?'

Duncan took one gratefully. 'Yeah, I know it sounds mad. But it's like now the sense of purpose just isn't there or something, and now I've thought about it, all I can think is that – and don't freak out about this – if I can't see her as the mother of my kids, then in all fairness, what's the point?'

'Kids!' Amelie nearly spat out her wine. 'What kids!?'

'I know, *not till we're at least thirty*, I know, we agreed – but all I'm trying to say – very inarticulately – is that she's just not The One, Amelie. And I'm getting tired of playing the game now. If I know she's not The One, then what's the point in pretending, and just killing time with her?'

'It's not pretending, Dunc. It's just having fun, being young and irresponsible while you still can. Lighten up.' Amelie took a large swig from her glass, and began to feel the beginning stages of inebriation.

'I don't need to lighten up . . . I just think the moment's passed. Besides which, she's so superficial, Amelie. Do you know her favourite TV programme is *The Simple Life*? She actually said to me the other day that she seriously admires Paris Hilton; thinks she's a great role model for our times. I mean, what's that about?!'

'It does seem a little puzzling,' admitted Amelie.

'Also, I really can't handle how domineering she is. She can be so bossy; she's so adapted to getting her way all the time.'

'That's a bit harsh, isn't it?' defended Amelie.

'Well, listen to this!' Duncan said, taking another swig from his wine, and growing more animated. 'Did I tell you she got mugged the other day? It cracks me up!'

'Dunc, that's not very nice! Getting mugged must be horrid!'

'For any ordinary person, sure. For any normal person to get accosted by a team of big scary muggers in a dimly lit street in Stockwell, the normal thing to do would be petrified, accept it, and just let the fuckers get on with taking whatever they want. I mean, you don't mess with them, in case they actually use their knife, or whatever weapon they've got. But not our Sara-Jayne. When a cluster of big scary guys cornered her on the Clapham Road the other day, and demanded she hand over her whole Prada handbag, with all her valuables, she just looked at them all doll-eyed and said, "Oh, but how will I get into my flat?" So they looked around and said, "OK, take out your keys, quickly."'

Amelie giggled, and Duncan paused to light their cigarettes. 'Then she goes, "Oh, thanks so much. Do you know, there's a couple of vital work numbers in my phone that I'd be totally ruined without – do you mind if I just write down a couple of them quickly? I won't be a minute." To which they agreed. And then, while she searches for a pen, she starts arguing that wouldn't it be much quicker just to whip out the SIM card? So then she's stood there in this alley with these three hooded geezers, quickly trying to force open the back cover of her phone. And then, it gets worse! She can't get it open, so after fumbling about for thirty seconds or so she asks them if they can open it! And then one of the guys just goes, "Oh, fuck it, just take the phone, innit."'

Amelie laughed as Duncan went on. 'As if that's not taking the piss enough, then, just as they are about to head off, Sara goes, "By the way, I love that handbag more than life itself, and I'll never find another one like it. By all means take it, but . . . just promise me you'll give it to a careful owner who appreciates its worth!"'

'And then the chief hoody guy just looks at her like she's a total lunatic, but like in a weird way he totally he respects her, and so the next thing is, he's tipping the contents of the handbag upside down into his rucksack, before throwing her the handbag and pegging it down the road!'

'That's hilarious!' said Amelie in disbelief.

'I know! Least effective mugging ever!' laughed Duncan.

'Good on her, though, I say!' said Amelie.

'But you see what I mean? You don't cross Sara-Jayne and get away with it! Imagine me being with someone that controlling – I just don't think she'd be right for me, you know?'

Amelie leaned in to Duncan. 'Maybe . . . I guess I see what you're saying.' Amelie thought for a few seconds. 'But don't worry, you can always go speed-dating again.'

'Not in a million!' They collapsed into hysterics, and lay back on the beach, staring at the stars.

'What time is it? I'm starting to feel a little ruined,' said Duncan after they had got their breath back.

Amelie looked at her phone to check the time. It was

4.30 a.m. She saw that she had two unread text messages. The first was from Charlie. She opened it and read:

Sweetpeach, how ru? How is wedding? Lookin fwd to seein you next. Got a meeting Sunday night in town – might pop in and surprise you Sunday if you like x x x

The second was only three words long, from Jack: *I miss you*.

Amelie sat staring at her phone, thinking how numb she felt about the second text, and how unsure she felt about the first.

'Am? What's the time?'

'Sorry, hon?'

'The time?'

'Oh, sorry.' She looked at her phone again and said, in a daze, '4.31.'

'Christ, it's that late?' Duncan asked, shocked. 'So, what's wrong? Who's messaged you?'

'Oh, just Charlie. Just not sure what to do about him – bit like you – I'm not sure where it's going.'

'Oh well, just play it by ear. Take each day as it comes. And all those other clichés people say at times like this. Sorry, Am, I'm knackered. I think I'm gonna go to bed. Are you coming?'

'Oh. I'm quite enjoying it out here. But yeah, I guess we have to go to sleep sometime.'

'Ah, bless you. You never want the night to end, do you?'

'No – I'm such a big kid, aren't I?'

'Yeah, but that's why we love you,' said Duncan, enveloping her in a warm hug.

'Ah, thanks, Dunky. Love you too. Shall we go in, then?' They linked arms and walked back up to the house.

Some time later, Amelie and Duncan were lying fast asleep in the hallway outside the kitchen, having staked their claim on what by then were the only few unoccupied square inches in the house. Not wanting to wake anyone up to enquire after bedding supplies, they had employed their drunken survival instincts in fostering a patchwork quilt of tea-towels, muslin cloths and aprons, under which they were currently snoozing happily.

Suddenly Amelie flung her head in the air. She sat firmly upright, sending the 'I'm supposed to be retired' apron that was shielding herself and Duncan from the cold, flying.

'What the—?' asked Duncan, rubbing his eyes, and emerging slowly from his slumber. Seeing the redness of Amelie's cheeks, he asked with concern, 'What the hell's the matter?'

Amelie jumped up. 'I've GOT IT!!!!!'

She started pacing up and down the hall, getting faster and faster, in accordance with the brainwaves which ebbed frantically through her mind, her eyes lighting up with a manic delight.

'Got what?' Duncan asked impatiently. 'What on earth are you talking about?'

'I've got the perfect idea! The eureka moment! It's finally bloody well arrived! Thank goodness for that!'

Duncan shook his head from side to side, and said calmly, 'What, Amelie? Slow down. Sit still. Count to ten with me. One, two, three . . .' He saw that she most definitely wasn't going to do any of the above, and asked nervously, 'What are you talking about? Please, please, for the love of God, tell me you're not referring to the pitch which is TOMORROW, Amelie?'

'What else is there?' she asked, genuinely curious. She began hunting around for her shoes and her overnight bag. Finding it underneath her coat, she noted with dismay that there were clothes and toiletries scattered all around it haphazardly, and that some kind of hair product had leaked all over the insides.

'Duncan, I've had an idea which I *know* could really stand out from the competition. It could really work. We need to get back to London now so we can work on it. Come on. Uppy-getty. I'll tell you on the way.'

Duncan shook his head, adamant. 'Am, there's no time to do any more work on it. The ideas we've done are fine. Simmer down; come back here and get some sleep.' Duncan tried to speak soothingly, tried to stop this madness. 'Amelie, you're not thinking straight. Your head's full of booze. Come back to bed.'

She stood over him and his inefficient duvet of multi-coloured tea-towels, staring down at him in astonishment. She couldn't believe he wasn't supporting her. 'Don't you even want to know what the idea *is*?'

'Not particularly. Life's too short to go back and bust a gut over this, Amelie. We gave it our best shot; there's no point in wasting our Sunday doing this.'

Amelie looked at Duncan as though he had just strolled out of a spaceship. 'Wasting our Sunday? No point? Duncan – what are these words coming out of your mouth?'

As she ran around the corridor, frantically gathering together her clothes, she explained to Duncan the Big

Idea, which she had arrived at in the middle of the night. To her mind, it was a culmination of all the ideas they had touched on, and what was so great about it was that it had simplicity – it had an elegance, with so much potential. If they could only get back and work on it together, he would see that it would be worth it.

The trouble was, as much as Duncan could see that it was a moment of genius, the half of him that wasn't the same as Amelie just couldn't see that it was worth going the extra mile for. Try as he could, he just didn't see the point. It was a shame she hadn't thought of it sooner, that was all. Three minutes later, Amelie and Duncan were in the middle of the biggest fight they had ever had.

'Why do you always do this?' Amelie hollered. 'Quit, the minute we get close to something that could be out of this world? Could be ground-breaking? Award-winning?'

'Why do *you* always do *this*? You never know when to call it a day! I love you to bits, Amelie, but Jee-sus, you're a fucking nightmare! Can't you see? You're at your best friend's wedding in fucking South Wales. It's 6 a.m. on a Sunday morning. You've downed the equivalent of three bottles of wine. Get some perspective! The ad campaign – stick a fork in it, Amelie, it's done!'

'It's not "done", Duncan. It's not *done* until I say it is!' Amelie shrieked. Then, realising how early it was, she lowered her voice, trying to suppress her anger.

'How can you just lie there, Duncan, knowing we've still got time to fix up the campaign, and rewrite the pitch with these new ideas? Why are you always such a minimalist? Say we lose our jobs tomorrow! How can you be satisfied knowing you took the easy way out?'

'I'll forgive myself,' snapped Duncan. 'Easily. Because I'll be comforted by the knowledge that at least *I* know when to stop! That I have a clue how to balance my life – that I'm not a work-obsessed lunatic like you are!' Duncan rolled over on the floor, threw the Nigella apron back over his head, and shut his eyes. Amelie stood, her mouth wide open and her eyes brimming with tears. She couldn't believe what Duncan had just said. She sat down on the floor, and a tear rolled down her cheek. Did he have a point buried in there somewhere? She thought for a few seconds about what to do. Her head was buzzing, and her heart was pounding. Minutes later, she stood up. Her choice was made.

'I'll do this, Duncan. With or without you. I can't believe I'm saying this to you now – not when you've been my partner for six years, but I'm going to do this. I have to try and save our jobs if I can. I really don't want to give up everything we've worked so hard for!'

Duncan said nothing. His usual way of ending an argument, by just ceasing to talk, without even reaching any kind of verbal conclusion. This usually drove Amelie insane with frustration, when she was so ready to shout more things at him, and he just stopped, left everything hanging mid-sentence. This particular morning was no exception. Amelie tried in vain to ignore the rising cyst of anger within her as she rummaged through a pile of coats on the floor, desperate to find her missing shoe.

'*Where* is it? For fuck's sake, Duncan, if you're not going to help me save our jobs, then the least you can do is to please help me find my other shoe! Red, pointy, shiny!'

Duncan didn't move. Amelie carried on stuffing clothes into her wheelie suitcase; gathering up her belongings and stuffing them into her handbag. Sighing, she discovered the culprit of the leakage: a half-empty bottle of Frizz-Ease that was drooling all over her freshly clean jumper and the jeans in her bag. 'Great. At least all my clothes won't be frizzy any more. ARRRRGH!' She ran off to use the bathroom, exasperated, dialling for a taxi as she hobbled down the hall in her one red shoe.

A few minutes later, with clean teeth and a fresh face, she re-emerged. She had been planning on dressing in her clean clothes, but now they were drowning in Frizz-Ease, this seemed impossible. Instead, she zipped shut her wheelie bag and straightened out the creases in her wedding frock. She pulled her black jumper-dress over her head and shoved on her left shoe, which had happily re-emerged from under her jumper. Grabbing her bags, she ran out through the front door, closing it quietly behind her.

Fifty-nine seconds later, she ran back into the house, raced into the kitchen, and began opening drawers and cupboards. Duncan stirred in his sleep, poked his head out from under his aprons and towels, and watched as Amelie found a piece of scrap paper, and stood pen in hand, thinking rapidly. Duncan watched her through the hole in the towel as she scribbled a barely legible note, deposited it on the kitchen counter, and went running away again. At the sound of the front door closing, Duncan closed his eyes and went back to sleep.

Dear Mr and Mrs Proud Parents of Dan,

Thank you for an amazing wedding, and for all your wonderful hospitality. Hugest apologies – have had to suddenly dash back to London, hence brevity and shameful failure to say farewell in person.

All my love,

Amelie x x x

P.S. V. sorry for inappt. use of aprons and towels. Replacements in post first thing Tuesday.

Inspiration Bound

Cardiff Central, Sunday 13 February, 8.03 a.m.

Freezing. Have literally never been this cold. Currently sitting outside locked waiting room on Platform 1 of this desolate, godforsakenly cold train station; waiting for the delayed first train back to London. Am sitting here in my creased blue wedding frock, stinking of smoke and booze, possessing not sleep but instead one of the most ferocious hangovers known to man since the beginning of time. The really awkward thing is, I think the brainwave I've had for the Fast Love pitch – thoughtlessly timed though it is – might just be too good an idea to let go to waste. Unfortunately, Duncan just didn't see it that way. And even though I'm mortified that he's not coming back with me, I'm actually kind of looking forward to getting home and working up the ideas . . . it's a relief to know that after weeks of creative block, I've now finally got some small semblance of a spark back.

Because that's what I've realised it's all about. Everything. It all comes down to the spark. Whether you've got it or you haven't. And spending all this time with all these different people this last week has made me see that. Seeing Jack again has been a headfuck – truly confusing – but I've come out of it the other side now, and I know for sure that I'll never take him back. When he kissed me back then in Little Italy, although it felt really nice – familiar, warm, lovely – in all honesty there was no chemistry. Maybe it was there once, but it's definitely not there any more. It was like kissing my brother, and I don't even have a brother. And, I couldn't help noticing, seeing Claire's mum and dad together again, that, even though they've been divorced for fifteen years, there still seemed to be some kind of charge between them. Even now, after everything they've been through, and yet they're both still single and unhappy. Charles and Lydia (Claire's friend from uni, that is) – they were both at the wedding, and although they've only been married a year, they really didn't look that happy; barely looked at one another all night – and when they did it only seemed to be to exchange looks of mutual boredom with one another.

Seeing Duncan with Chloe in Wing – I knew there was some kind of energy there. I think they'd make a great couple, if they'd only pluck up the courage to act on it. And Charlie – seeing him again . . . still not sure how much mileage there is with us long-term, but I know there's a big physical attraction going on . . . and I guess that's my best offer at the moment.

But the most stirring thing of all was yesterday – seeing Claire and Dan look so ridiculously happy together. Have never seen so much genuine love and affection displayed in

Make or Break

Five hours later, a bedraggled Amelie, wet through from the rain, her face streaked with window-pane creases, finally arrived home. She threw her bags to the floor and slumped on to the sofa. Felt her eyes close and her body sink gratefully into the comforting recesses of the cushions. Minutes later she was almost asleep. But then she remembered. Less than fifteen hours to go. Vital work to do. Then, and only then, would sleep be permitted. Amelie forced her body to be vertical again, cradled her throbbing head in her hands, and went to make herself an extremely strong vat of coffee.

She put on Miles Davis, who always helped ease her into the right mindset at moments like this. Sitting down at her desk, armed with coffee and muesli, she unplugged the Internet, and switched off her mobile phone and landline. And waited.

Five minutes later she was still staring at a blank lay-out pad, drumming her fingers away on the desk. Nothing. She decided to switch the Internet back on and do some picture research to get her started.

By 5 p.m., she hadn't moved from this spot, but was surrounded by a whirlwind of paper. The floor was a mosaic of coloured run-outs, research print-outs, half-finished A3 marker-pen scribbles and badly drawn storyboards. Already she was exhausted, yet there was still so much to get through.

Just then the doorbell rang. Duncan! At last he's come to his senses. Amelie leaped into the air with relief, and her heart began to beat more calmly, now that she knew they would be able to work together on the pitch, and also that she would have one of her best friends back.

When she opened the door to reveal Charlie standing there, she could barely conceal her disappointment. 'Surprise!' He reached out to embrace her, a huge grin on his face, and handed her a bag of brownies. 'How's my little wordsmith doing?' He kissed her on the cheek, flashed his vastly dilated pupils at her, and headed through the hallway into the flat.

'Um . . .' Amelie didn't know what to say. This was the worst-timed impromptu visit ever. 'Hi! *Thank* you for these,' she said, looking into the bag and smelling the freshly baked brownies. 'They look amazing, how thoughtful of you.' She put them down on the counter in the kitchen. 'Would you like one?' she called back to Charlie who was making himself comfortable on the sofa.

'No thanks, not hungry just yet. Soon, though.'

'Right . . . coffee, then?' Amelie asked forcefully, as though the quicker she fed and watered him, the sooner he might want to depart again.

'In a bit, yeah. Come and sit with me, lovely. Haven't seen you in ages!'

Amelie walked back into the lounge and sat down next to him tentatively. He leaned over brashly and kissed her, enveloping her in his arms. Amelie responded accordingly, but soon she felt increasingly restless, and kissed him back superficially before pulling away.

'What's wrong? Aren't you pleased to see me?' he asked.

'Yes, of course. It's just that – I don't mean to be rude – I'm right in the middle of something.' She indicated the swamp of papers and scribbles that was the lounge floor.

Oblivious to the hint, Charlie chirped away, 'What are you in the middle of? Can I help you with it?' He got on to his hands and knees and started wading through the layers of drawings and scribbles. Amelie felt herself becoming uptight, and stood up. 'No, leave it, it's fine, thanks.' She watched him pick up one of the storyboards and start to read it aloud, acting it out, in an attempt to be entertaining. Amelie's face creased up with tension. 'I'd really rather you didn't move that. These papers are all in a certain order, to help me think. It's for the pitch tomorrow – I've had a total rethink – I've got a ton of work to get through.'

'Oh, OK. I'll just sit here and wait till you're done, then. I've got the paper, I'll sit and read.' Then he added theatrically, in a jovial mock-Irish accent, '*You won't even know I'm here.* Promise!' And with that he opened up *The Stage*, started to leaf through it and put his feet up on the coffee table. Amelie shook her head numbly and went to sit down at her desk.

She was just getting into the flow of a press ad she was writing, when she felt something on the back of her neck. She raised her hand to quash the offending bug or fly. Then she realised that it was no fly; it was Charlie's fingers, gently attempting to massage her neck. She let him continue for a few seconds, felt the tension gradually seeping out of her neck. She closed her eyes and let her head flop down. After a minute of this, she felt the fingers move down on to her shoulders, and now there were kisses on her neck. Soft little kisses. Gradually the kisses changed in strength, and Charlie worked his way up her neck towards her cheeks, growing more forceful, before trying to move Amelie round to face him. He kissed her more urgently on the lips, before attempting to pull her up out of her chair. Amelie almost swayed; was almost swept along in the moment, but then something inside of her snapped, and she pushed him away.

'Wait, no . . . Charlie, stop.' She stood up. 'Sorry, I can't do this now . . . I've really, *really* got to work.'

'Can't you just take a break for a bit?' he said in an almost whine. 'It's ages since I saw you last. Just come and chill out for a bit with me on the sofa, then I'll help you with it afterwards and we can get it done in half the time.'

Amelie shook her head. 'You know that's not going to work! Look, if you want to stay, fine, just sit there and try not to disturb me. I might not be too much longer.'

She turned back to her desk and thought, Hold on. Who am I kidding? There's a hideous amount to get through. She picked up her pen, began to tweak the headline again; tried to pretend that there was no other presence in the room.

Ten minutes later, Charlie's mobile sang out at full volume, to the tune of *Ghostbusters*. He answered it and began chatting away noisily. Amelie put her pen down, turned around and stared mini-daggers at him. He looked back, pulled out a pack of cigarettes and mouthed that he was going to go outside. Moments later, to Amelie's infinite joy, the flat was all hers again.

But it wasn't long before the doorbell rang again. Amelie groaned, threw down her pen and went to let him in.

'Thanks . . . Hey, that was Isabella. She said we might be getting to take *Arcadia* on tour soon – the funding's finally come through!'

'That's great . . . brilliant!' said Amelie, pleased for him but also praying that Charlie wouldn't go on into more detail just yet.

'Don't worry, I'll be as quiet as a mouse now. Honest. Squeak, squeak,' said Charlie, sitting back down on the sofa.

By six Charlie had read and circled every relevant casting ad in *The Stage* newspaper, and devoured *FHM* from cover to cover. His stomach was now beginning to rumble. 'Hey, are you hungry, Am? What shall we make for tea?' He got up and went to forage in the kitchen cupboards for food.

Amelie put her pen down impatiently. 'I live in a Bridget Jones house, I'm afraid,' she shouted from her desk. She was in the middle of another inspirational flow, and prayed that Charlie wouldn't say too much else and bring her out of it again. 'There's never any food in. But help yourself to the brownies, by all means. And coffee.'

Charlie re-emerged from the kitchen, stood behind her

watching her for a while, and then said, 'Hey, I've just realised,' as though he'd heard a sudden newsflash, 'I don't even know if you're ticklish or not!' Then he started to try and tickle her, pounced on her roughly, teasing her under the arms and her midriff, pinning her down. Amelie squealed with laughter but her face was unsmiling. She was growing more and more irate. Charlie was strong; she had to struggle hard to fend him off her. But after a few seconds she succeeded. Standing over him, she hollered, 'OK, that's it!'

Charlie looked visibly afraid. '*What*'s it?'

'You've got to go. Really. You've got to get out of here and leave me to it. I can't take your childish antics any more.' Amelie looked pale from lack of sleep, and her eyes were black and devoid of all emotion. 'I don't mean to be rude, honestly, but this pitch is too important to me, and I'm just getting fuck all done with you clowning about all around me. Please can you just go.'

Charlie looked like someone had just stamped all over his train-set and then run off with his light-saber. 'Fine. I'll go, then,' he said sulkily. 'I'm gone.' He stood up and walked away from her. 'To think, I thought it would be a nice surprise for me to come round and bring you fresh brownies – how wrong was I!? Jeez . . . I've never met anyone so work-work-work as you. You're like obsessed or something – I've come all this way to see you . . . and . . . you can't even spare me a second of your precious attention!'

Amelie felt as though she might explode. 'You're one to talk! I've never, ever managed to hold down a conversation with you that didn't involve you, your acting, your agent or agents-to-be! Charlie, you're a nice bloke and all, but you're one of the most self-absorbed people I've ever met!'

Charlie's face screwed up in distaste; clearly unable to comprehend anything he was hearing. 'Well, that's really rich, coming from *you*.' He moved away from her, shaking his head, looking increasingly angry. 'You know what? I thought you were really nice when I met you – but – I'm not so sure I like this new Amelie Holden I'm seeing. Tell you what, speed-dating doesn't work after all – and you can quote me on that in your stupid ad campaign! You can stick your speed-dating, Amelie! Strike that – you can stick your any kind of dating full stop with me! You've just blown it with Number 27.'

And with that, he marched into the kitchen to reclaim the bag of brownies that was rightfully his. Then, on his route back to the door, he began trampling all over the patchwork of papers, rustling them around with his feet for what he considered dramatic effect. Amelie stared after him, her mouth wide open. Grabbing his copy of *The Stage*, Charlie stormed out of the flat, slamming the door as loudly as he could. As the walls of the flat shook with the impact of his temper, Amelie sat down on the sofa, feeling shaky, yet strangely relieved.

A short while later, Amelie was drifting back into her advertising bubble, trying to block out the memory of the last few hours. She knew she had behaved like a bitch, but she also knew that she had just lost patience with Charlie to the point where she couldn't remember any of the reasons why she had wanted to be seeing him any more. She had seen through his pitch, his performance, and now she realised that all along she'd been attracted to Charlie the performer – Orlando, Septimus, whoever – and when it came to getting to know the real man behind the façade, she realised that she wasn't the right girl for him after all, and he certainly wasn't the right guy for her.

After everything that had happened during the last few months, she couldn't help thinking back with amusement at her protestations back at the beginning of the year. She thought back to that day in the bar in Hoxton with Claire, when she had vowed that this year she was going to focus only on her career. Instead, what had she done over the last month? She'd ended up going on date after date after date, all of them failing to bear fruit in the end. Still, she was nowhere nearer to finding any close contenders for the title of 'The One'. No, she'd been right first time – this year was going to be the year of her career – maybe next year she would think about looking for love again. For now, she had work to do.

As Amelie typed and doodled away, she became gradually more unable to suppress the two painful truths that were fighting for attention in her mind:

1. She could not, for the life of her, draw.
2. There was no way she was going to be able to get this pitch ready on her own.

It pained Amelie to admit it. Even after all the effort she had put in, and even though the essence of the ideas was there, still the actual execution of the campaign was a train-wreck. This was now entering crisis territory. How could she go in there tomorrow and present these half-formed thoughts, these shambolically presented scribbles? But on the other hand, how could she give up without even trying?

Sighing, Amelie turned on her mobile phone, half hoping that Duncan would have messaged her to apologise by now, to say he was going to come over and help. But no, there was only a text from her mother Lucy, wondering why she hadn't called her in so long. Amelie felt a twinge of guilt, but knew she would be able to call her after tomorrow and make up for it then. Instead, she dialled Duncan's number, but it went straight to answerphone. She thought about leaving a message, but then hung up before giving herself the chance. There was only one person she knew who would be willing or able to help now. Last resort.

She looked through her address book and punched in the number. He answered on the third ring.

'Hello?'

'Hi! It's Amelie. Are you busy?' Without giving him a chance to answer, she chatted on at hyperspeed, 'Listen, I need your help. I've had a total brainwave on the Fast Love stuff, and Duncan is trapped in Cardiff so he can't help out – is there any chance you can come over and see whether there's anything we can salvage?!'

'I'll be there in half an hour.'

At seven twenty-nine, Josh Grant was standing in her doorway, his car parked out the front of the flat.

'HI!' Amelie screeched, manic from the caffeine intake, and excited that Josh had come to the rescue. 'Come in! Come in!'

She beckoned him into the flat, asking, 'Can I get you a drink? I was just about to make more filter coffee.'

'Actually, I bought us some Red Bull leftovers from

Wing – it sounded like we had a big night ahead of us. I might crack into one of these now. Have you eaten yet?'

Amelie had completely forgotten about food. 'No, but I'm not hungry – there's just too much to think about right now. I'll put these in the fridge, though. Can I bring you any food?'

Amelie walked into the kitchen as Josh declined the offer, which was fortunate, she thought – remembering that she had no food in the house to offer him. As she fixed some coffee, Josh stood looking around the flat at the disconnected trails of drawings all over the floor, and then he began to study the travelling artefacts and photos which adorned all the walls. He looked closely at the pictures, recognising some of the beach resorts in Goa and the waterfalls in Laos that he had also been to. His eyes kept falling back on to one particular photo. It was a slightly faded, sun-swept picture of a smiling Amelie on Bondi Beach, with a circle of friends around her, lounging in front of a deep blue sky. With a smoothie in one hand and a chick-lit novel in the other, she looked more innocent and carefree than he had ever thought her capable of. Still, she had the same sparkle in her eye that he was gradually getting to know so well.

Amelie came back into the room and felt herself blush. She couldn't believe he was looking at that photo of her in that horrid ancient pink bikini. 'Oh no, don't look at those, they're so old! I really must redecorate in here.'

'Are you serious? I think they're great. Especially the ones on the beaches. I miss the sea more than I can say.'

Amelie nodded in sombre agreement and handed Josh a coffee.

'Thanks, that's lovely,' he said. 'Didn't ask for one, but

thanks. So, what's the big idea, then?' Josh looked up at Amelie expectantly. 'Let's have it! I've been so intrigued on the way over here.'

'Oh no – I hope you haven't got too excited – I don't want you to be disappointed if you don't think it's all that good . . .' Amelie looked at him nervously, but then remembered the feeling she'd had when the idea had first popped into her head. It was also important to remember that it was a 5 a.m. idea. In her experience, a 5 a.m. idea was always a special idea.

Standing in front of the now neatly co-ordinated piles of paper, she told Josh about her insights into speed-dating. How this weekend, all her experiences both in dating and in real life had suddenly come to a head, leaving her with a kind of epiphany about the whole process. How in the end, out of all the other qualities, it all came down to sparks flying. 'You see, the Fast Love USP is that it's all about searching for the spark . . . the test for chemistry feature . . . this makes perfect sense, because, as everyone knows, you either have it with someone or you don't.'

Josh looked at her meaningfully and nodded. 'Yep – that all makes sense. Carry on.'

Amelie smiled and went on, 'Sorry, I ramble when I'm nervous. Anyway, that's enough preamble. What I've got here are loads of little ideas for how we can carry out the main concept into all levels of media.' She gestured towards all the drawings and mind-maps behind her. 'But it all ties in with My Big Idea . . .' Amelie paused, looked at Josh nervously, and grinned. 'The best, most memorable way to demonstrate the product truth – is this.'

Amelie stood back from the piles of drawings, and held up the centrepiece of the campaign. She gave Josh a moment to take it in, looked at him, her heart in her throat. She hadn't realised how much his opinion mattered to her until now. Suddenly she was terrified that he wouldn't like it, that he would think less of her. Or worse, he would think that she was insane for dragging him out this late on a Sunday, caffeinated and hyperactive, babbling to him about sparks. The more Amelie thought about it in her head, the more embarrassed she began to feel at how deluded she had been acting. Duncan was right – she did have her work/life balance all wrong. So much so that she had now lost all perspective and could no longer judge for herself when an idea was good or not. She hung her head down, waited for all eternity, and finally said, to break the silence, 'OK, I'll get your coat. You think I'm a psychopath. I'm incredibly sorry for wasting your time. I've clearly not been to bed yet, and I do still have a lot of booze pumping through my veins – please try and accept that by way of an explanation. I'm sorry – I'll clear all this up, and I'll see you tomorrow. Oh well, at least I can finally get some sleep.'

She bent down and began collecting up the papers on the floor, shaking her head and tutting to herself, when Josh, who still hadn't spoken a word, grabbed her arm to stop her. The strength of his fingers stopped her from rambling any further.

'I love it,' he said quietly.

Amelie froze. 'Really?'

'It's genius. Total genius. I love it. You're a star, a total star.' He moved his hand from her arm, and Amelie suddenly looked shattered with relief. Josh leaned closer and gave her a warm embrace by way of congratulation. 'Seriously. Well done. I can't believe I never thought of it before. It's brilliant. So simple! And if the client goes for it, it could get the agency a whole load of PR . . . it could really raise our profile again!'

Amelie grinned excitedly, feeling elated inside. 'You think we should work on the presentation? It's all a total mess at the moment, as you can see . . .'

They knelt down on the floor and began sifting through the drawings. Josh creased up with laughter at how much work Amelie had done. 'What are you like? You're obsessed, lady!' he teased her, but there was a look of admiration in his eyes.

Josh looked through all her storyboards and mocked-up ads, slowly dividing the wheat from the chaff, and discarding some of the papers to one side. Amelie watched him work, listened to him comment on her ideas, and agreed with nine out of ten of his creative judgements. Before long they had only the highlights, which they sat down to work on. Josh showed he had a flair for drawing as well as writing, so he took over the art direction in Duncan's absence. Amelie worked on her Mac, writing and finessing the choice of words they were going to use in all the different ads, and in the Powerpoint presentation. As Amelie typed; cutting and pasting her words around the page, Josh neatly drew up the different visual elements of the campaign. In the hours that passed until the birds began to sing, Josh had added many clever twists and turns into the mix. Amelie showed him her work for him to check, and he showed her his, every time, he had a new idea. Every few minutes, a 'That's so great – you're a genius!' or an 'Of course! I love it!' came from either one of them. By the time the sun rose, the medley of both their imaginations had created a five-star campaign.

As the chorus of milk floats, morning birds and early morning traffic descended upon them, Amelie stood up, pressed the print key, and declared ecstatically, 'Well, I think that's it! We're done.'

'Brilliant,' Josh said, standing back and admiring their work now that it was finally complete. He looked over at Amelie, a broad grin on his face, and ran a hand through his usually thick, prominent tufts of brown hair, which had now become flattened and tousled from all the hard work and perspiration.

'Well, I'd better be getting off home,' Josh said. 'Get myself freshened up before the pitch. I'll carry all this stuff in, as I've got my car.'

'That would be great, if you don't mind.' Amelie looked at him gratefully. As she helped him get all the work ready to carry, she thought to herself that, after the craziness of the day, and after Josh's chivalry in coming to help her out, she would be sorry to see him go.

'We make a good team, though, don't you think?' Josh said tentatively, reading her mind as he moved towards the front door.

Amelie smiled thoughtfully and retrieved Josh's coat from the cupboard. She handed it to him and said, 'No one's more surprised than me . . . but yes, I think we do. Thanks for coming to my rescue.'

Josh put his coat on. 'Nonsense – thank *you*. For rescuing the agency. Wait – what am I saying, tempting fate like that? I mean, we've no idea how this will go down in the pitch this morning, or what the competition will show them . . . But, that said, I think we're really in with a chance now. Thanks, Amelie.'

Amelie smiled with relief and said, 'No worries. I couldn't let this one go. Hope it's worth it! Well, I'll see you at work!'

And then Josh put out his hand. 'It's a lovely idea. Really, you should be pleased.'

Amelie didn't hear what he said; she was staring at his hand, which was stretched out in front of her, wondering why it was there – whether she should put hers out to join it. Did he want to shake her hand? Will it be rude if I don't shake his hand now that he's extended it? she wondered. In slow motion she went to put hers out, and said, 'Thanks.' But just as she did, his hand moved away; it was too late, and now her hand was left dangling. She wondered why this was suddenly so awkward, but now that she had extended her hand she felt even sillier taking it back, and all the while she was thinking how bizarre it was that she should now be so hung up on etiquette of all things. Clearly this was a product of her sleep and sobriety deficit, she thought, as her hand hung limply in the space between them. But then Josh brought his hand back, took hers in his, and it felt as though they were holding hands, not shaking them. Amelie felt the need to say something, to explain away this moment of contact. 'Thanks for all your help. Thanks for everything,' she said, stilting her words, looking at their still-entangled hands. 'So, I'll see you in the morning?' And she shook his hand formally, as though they had just closed a business deal. 'Well, later this morning, I mean,' she added, noticing it was now 7.00 a.m.

'Yes,' Josh said, businesslike, and pulled his hand away.

'I'll call an urgent meeting first thing, so we can get everyone else on board with the new ideas.'

'Yes, that would be good. See you in a couple of hours,' said Amelie.

Josh smiled at her, and they linked eyes for a moment. 'See you, then,' Josh said. He opened the door, stepped into the hall, and Amelie waved him out on to the street. As he drove away, Amelie stood for a moment and watched the dawn rising over St John's Wood.

Pitching for Passion

Date: 14 February, 8.06
Sender: Grant, Joshua
To: Everyone (all agency)
Importance: High
Subject: Urgent FAST LOVE meeting, ground-floor conference room, 9.30 a.m.

Morning all,

As of last night, big changes are afoot regarding the Fast Love creative work we have chosen to present to the client today. Amelie Holden and I have been working until this morning on what I believe to be a fantastic reappraisal of the creative brief, and which I think could well give us a running chance of winning the account.

Please be in the conference room by no later than 9.30 so I can brief you all on the new creative work.

The clients, one Eva Frey (Marketing Director), Ted Matthews (Financial Director) and Maggie Rose (MD), will all be arriving here at 12.15, for a quick slap-up buffet, before we present the work to them. Please, please, make sure the reception area, toilets and stairwells stay as tidy as they are now, and if you need to go out for a cigarette this morning, do try and time it before or after the clients' arrival, so you aren't all haphazardly lining the entrance to the building when they come in.

One final thing – if you've volunteered to help with the decoration of the conference room, please be down there by no later than 10.30. Chloe and Fleur have got all the materials together; it's going to look great by the sound of things.

See you at 9.30, thanks,
Josh

P.S. Happy Valentine's Day all.

Reading this email an hour later, Amelie's eyes were bright with adrenalin; she couldn't help smiling at the postscript. Much to her surprise, and for the first time in years, she had been faced with a Valentine's card when she got to work. She hadn't opened it yet, however, she was saving it until she was ready to drink her cappuccino. Now that she was, she tore through the envelope, and opened up the card.

For Amelie, Queen of Quirky,
With all my love,
?

That was all it said. She didn't recognise the handwriting
particularly, but then Jack could easily have made an effort
to disguise his handwriting. In fairness, she had nothing to
compare it to – they had never bothered with Valentine's
cards even when they were going out. Amelie had always
protested against how horribly commercial it all was; Jack
had always chastised her for being a hypocrite and working
in advertising, and the same old argument had prevailed
every year.

So maybe it was Charlie, Amelie thought. But surely
not, after last night's debacle? Although he could always
have posted it beforehand. Amelie's head began to hurt
with all the detective work and the not-knowing. After a
moment, she concluded that, on balance, it was most likely
to be Jack. In which case, it was very nice and all, but
nothing had changed. She put it to one side and went down
to the briefing.

When she arrived, Josh was already explaining the new
ideas to the teams. They were largely well received,
although there was now some anxiety among the troops at
the last-minute u-turn. However, the consensus was that
the new ideas were definitely worth going the extra mile
for. Seeing Amelie walk in, Josh opened his mouth, looked
at her, and delivered his bombshell: 'Although we'd
normally expect the account managers to present the work,
in these special circumstances, I've decided that Amelie
and I will deliver the pitch between us.'

Amelie froze. She stared intensely at Josh, thinking,
How dare he do this to me at the last minute?

Creative, she was, yes. Ask her to think of a good idea, a snappy headline, a witty strapline – no problem, she'd do it gladly. But ask her to stand and articulate herself in front of a room containing in excess of five people, and Amelie would crumble, like a burnt bagel stuck in a toaster. Ever since the time at Brownie camp when Brown Owl had made her stand up in front of a whole group of Brownies and Guides and present to them her life story (so far, aged seven). Feeling excruciatingly shy and in desperate need of the toilet after drinking two whole beakers full of orange and pineapple squash, Amelie had stood up on stage, stammered for a few seconds, flushed a deep shade of scarlet, and eventually said, 'I can't remember my life story. I was born, then nothing much has happened since. As everyone laughed and booed and pointed at her, Amelie ran off to the toilets, her long brown braids flapping around in the air, her eyes welling with tears. Ever since that day, when asked to present anything, throughout school, college and her working life, she recalled that idiotic Brown Owl moment and felt the same humiliation all over again. She always insisted to anyone new she met that it must have been decreed at her birth: 'Thou shalt never ask Amelie Holden to speak in public. Terrible things always happen as a result – it can only ever end in tears.'

She ran up to Josh at the end of his address. 'Josh! I can't believe you never mentioned this to me! Sorry, but public speaking is my biggest, worst fear. It's a bad, bad idea getting me to speak.' She looked at him, intense lines of fear spreading over her oval face. 'If you put me on that stage, I'll fuck everything up. You've seen the first *Bridget Jones* film? The jaw-droppingly embarrassing incident with *Kafka's Motorbike*? Salman Rushdie? Well, quadruple that – and you're still nowhere near to the intensity of awkwardness I'm talking about . . . Seriously, I beg of you. We'll lose the business, you'll never want to see me again . . . I swear to Cupid.'

Josh tried to suppress a smile at Amelie's neurotic monologue. 'Don't worry, you'll be fine,' he said comfortingly, resting his hand on her arm.

Amelie shook her head. 'No really, you don't understand.'

Josh looked at his watch and thought for a moment. 'OK, how about I do the opening, the introductions, and start off the speech. You can just chip in when I look at you, and when you want to. If you find you're not comfortable, just give me some kind of sign, and I'll take over . . . how does that sound?'

Trying to feel optimistic, and remembering her job was still at risk, Amelie decided that this seemed a reasonable compromise, and smiled cautiously. Maybe he wasn't so bad after all. 'Thank you – I appreciate your understanding.'

'No problem,' Josh said, winking at her, and they made their way out of the conference room towards the lifts. 'Let's meet for a coffee to go through my notes just before they arrive.'

As they walked past reception, there was a commotion coming from behind the desk. Chloe, Fleur and Sally were talking excitedly, gathered round an exquisite bouquet of bright red roses and daisies. When they saw Amelie approaching, they each broke into smiles. Fleur was the first to announce, 'Amelie. You've got a special delivery here.'

Amelie walked slowly over to them, and flushed red when she saw the big bouquet. 'Oh my gosh – how ridiculous. They can't be for me?' They all nodded and Chloe handed her the card with her name on it.

'So . . . open the card!' shouted Sally.

'Yeah, we want to know who they're from!' peeped Chloe. Fleur was looking at Josh meaningfully, but he was avoiding her gaze.

Amelie shrugged as though it was all slightly beyond her, but opened the envelope. Josh hung back behind her and went to call the lift. Amelie sensed him walk away, and turned around to see him watching her. Their eyes met for a second, and then she looked away to see the writing on the card.

> *Amelie,*
> *V. sorry for being such a D*** yesterday.*
> *Break a leg today, as we say in theatre-land.*
> *Happy Valentine's Day.*
> *Call me later x C x*

'Well?' asked Sally impatiently. 'It's Jack, isn't it? Now, even if it is, hon, you know better than to let him affect you, don't you?'

'No, they're not from him,' Amelie said flatly. 'They're from Charlie.'

'Oh, that's nice, isn't it?' cooed Chloe, and this was followed by similar noises of appreciation from the other girls.

Amelie heard the sound of the lift opening, and looked back to see Josh getting in. She looked back at the girls and said distractedly, 'Oh, well, it's a bit strange, really – we've just broken up, and I thought we'd agreed last night that we weren't ever going to see each other again!'

'Oh, that *is* rather awkward,' said Fleur. 'Still, better to receive unwanted flowers than to receive no flowers at all.'

Two hours later, Conference Room 1 was unrecognisable. The huge meeting table in the centre of the room had been dissected into sixteen small table-for-twos, arranged around the room. Each table-for-two had a red tablecloth, a small scented candle and a mini-vase with a single red rose in the centre. Every chair was angled slightly towards the stage, where a small podium had been erected. While Beethoven's *Appassionata* played in the background, Chloe and Fleur danced in between each table, laughing as they lit each candle and handed out the scorecards and pens, which they had had printed for the occasion. They carried out trays of love-themed nibbles and placed them on the side tables. Now, with half an hour to go before the directors of Fast Love arrived, the room was ready.

Four floors above them, Amelie was pacing around her room, worrying what she was going to say. She had just been to see Josh – between them they had had some good ideas for what to say in the pitch, but Amelie still had a knot of fear in her stomach that she might just freeze up with stage fright when her moment came. She thought of Charlie, wondered what he would do in this situation, being a natural performer. She considered calling him but decided that would probably be a mistake. Suddenly, she couldn't help feeling annoyed with herself for coming up with the new ideas – if she hadn't done, she could be relaxing and enjoying herself down there, digging into the free pink champagne. Instead, she had a huge, horrible test to pass – one final pitch. She checked herself in her hand-held mirror, touched up her lip gloss and mascara, and was just about to go down to the conference room, when her Mac pinged to indicate new mail.

Date: 14 February, 11.36
Sender: Natasha.Webster@imaginativeselection.co.uk
To: Holden.Amelie@LGMKLondon.com
Subject: Developments

Dear Amelie,

Hope you are well. Further to our meeting last week, please can you give me a call, either today or tomorrow latest? Something has come up that I think might be of interest to you.

Best,

Natasha

Intriguing, thought Amelie, eager to know more. She clicked reply and started composing an email, but then the sensible sixteenth of her suggested that perhaps there wasn't time. The minutes were rapidly jumping by and she was going to be late for the presentation if she didn't stop faffing and leave immediately. She turned off her screen, glanced out of the window at the couples in Soho Square, and straightened out her red jumper-dress. Just as she was walking out, Duncan was in her path and went charging into her by mistake.

'Oh, sorry!' he exclaimed.

'No worries,' Amelie said coolly, wondering where he

had been all morning, but not wanting to admit to having any interest. She looked at him, her eyes blinking the words 'Excuse me, you're blocking my path', at which Duncan stepped aside.

Meekly, he said, 'I know it's a bit late, but good luck, Amelie. I know how much you hate speaking in front of an audience, so . . . all the best. I'll be crossing my fingers for you.'

Amelie gave a lukewarm smile as she said, 'Thanks,' and walked away.

Down in the reception area, Chloe and Fleur were busily scribbling name badges for people, insisting that everyone in the building from Manuel the handyman to Dave in IT must wear one. 'We *all* need to show a united front and show we're committed to the spirit of Fast Love!' said Chloe, who, after six weeks at LGMK, had now become firmly indoctrinated into the twin languages of ad-drivel and marketing-speak. Spying Duncan coming out of the lift, she took an empty name badge and wrote his name in big capital letters, before striding up to him and pinning it on to his shirt.

'Oh, you shouldn't have. Why, thank you,' teased Duncan, embarrassed but happy to have the attention from Chloe. He smiled at her and was about to say something when there was a loud buzz on the front door of the agency. Duncan and Chloe stepped apart from each other and looked through the revolving doors at the three people standing outside in the rain.

'It's them! Fleur, they're here!'

'Quick! Everyone!' Chloe picked up the intercom, and spoke into it loudly and firmly. 'Everyone to Conference Room 1 now. Client is here. Conf Room 1 now please.'

Emil Myers, Managing Director of the agency, having flown in from Singapore only that morning, strolled into reception. Dressed in an elegant dark blue suit, he nodded to Chloe and they both went to greet the guests as they came through the doors. Chloe smiled and presented them with a large fragrant bouquet of red roses, as she chirped, 'Hello, and Happy Valentine's Day!'

There was an awkward silence as the three faces eyed the flowers suspiciously and quietly nodded hello. Maggie, a red-haired lady with glasses, took the flowers and said, 'Thank you,' with a sweet smile. Emil extended his hand to them one by one. 'Hello, Emil Myers; Managing Director of the agency . . . or the "M" in Lewis Gibbs Myers Kirby.'

Maggie, the Fast Love Managing Director, seemed to be the quirkier, more approachable one of the three. Eva, the Marketing Director, was slightly younger and had a pretty smile, but seemed at first glance to be the bolshiest one of the group. Ted, the Financial Director, hanging back from the other two, seemed to exude a more serious, quietly contemplative air about him. He was evidently the brains and the mathematician behind the Fast Love business, and would generally only 'tune in' when it suited him to do so. The rest of the time you could never be sure whether or not he was really listening. Emil studied Ted, who was, even now, staring out of the window rather than at the agency or any of the people in it. 'Anyway, it's a real pleasure to meet you all again,' Emil added, smiling broadly. 'Do come through.'

Opening the door to the conference room, their footsteps fell on to a red carpet of rose petals, and they saw with delight that the room had been entirely transformed for their benefit. Maggie, Ted and Eva looked around in astonishment. The lights had been dimmed, curtains were draped all around, and purple and red throws hung from the ceiling. Rose petals were scattered all along the edge of the stage, and the effect of this combined with all the candles was suitably ambient and uplifting. Emil looked visibly impressed, even if the slightly po-faced Fast Love directors were trying their best to give nothing away.

'Hey, how you going?' said Josh in his thick Australian accent. 'Welcome . . . I'm Josh Grant, the Creative Director. And this' – he said, motioning to the tables made up of LGMK 'couples', chattering away, engaged in conversation, jotting comments down on their scorecards, pretending to be on speed-dates – 'is the creative hub of LGMK. Would you like a drink? Pink champagne anyone?'

Eva, Maggie and Ted nodded. As they took their drinks, Josh joked that they could sit anywhere they liked, that they didn't have to stick to the boy/girl regime if they didn't want to. Maggie and Eva laughed, obviously both rather charmed by Josh. Eva said, 'Oh, I don't mind, are you taken?'

If Josh was cringing inside he made a great effort to conceal it. 'No, be my guest. Maggie, you can sit with Emil if you like? We can always switch round after three minutes.'

As the lights dimmed, they sat down, clinked their champagne glasses and began to stuff themselves happy from the buffet. At 1 p.m. sharp, Fleur appeared on the podium and loudly rang the bell, signalling that it was time to begin. Amelie had ensured that they acquire a traditional school-playground bell for authenticity, and she couldn't help smiling on hearing that sound again.

Standing in the wings, watching Fleur officiously ring the bell, Amelie felt her stomach flood with hyperventilating butterflies as she watched Josh striding confidently towards the podium. Once the din had subsided in the audience, Josh launched into a charismatic opening speech, delivering the speed-dating preamble they had prepared earlier, before inviting Amelie to speak. Amelie walked slowly across the small stage towards the podium, her mouth feeling like a desert. Please, please don't screw this up now, she begged herself. She glanced anxiously at Josh, looked down at the iBook, prepared her thoughts, opened her mouth to speak, and saw with horror that the screen was entirely black. The computer was turned off. Surely she had turned it on only minutes earlier, and it should still be on? Where was the vital Powerpoint document they had prepared? Had Fleur been messing with the controls? She looked around the room, anxiety washing over her darkening cheeks. She saw that everyone was looking at her expectantly. How on earth was she going to fill the time while the computer loaded up? She had never performed a successful ad-lib in her life, not when she was seven, and certainly not now. Time was ticking by and she knew that everyone was waiting. Meekly she tried, 'Hello, everyone.'

'So . . . um, great to see you all here today.'

What else do people say in situations like this? she wondered desperately. Those people who can 'think on their feet', and are blessed with 'the gift of the gab' and other sayings like that . . . why wasn't she one of those? Looking blankly across at Josh, he smiled awkwardly back at her, tried to indicate something with his eyes. Then, mutely, he leaned over to the laptop, effortlessly hit a key and it flashed magically into life.

'Just went to sleep, that's all,' he whispered to her calmly, his eyes encouraging her to go on with the show.

Amelie smiled with incandescent joy at Josh, vowing to have his proverbial babies in gratitude, and opened up the Powerpoint. Never in all her life had she been so elated and comforted to see a few little slides. Rearranging them slightly, all too aware that the uncomfortable silence in the room wasn't getting any less awkward, she knew she couldn't stall any longer.

'Sorry, slight technical hiccup there, but it all looks fine now.' She smiled dumbly, feeling like she was exactly the sort of person she would hate watching, were she sitting in the audience. Her heart was beating so very frantically and loudly that she looked at Josh as if to check whether he could hear it thumping. It was hard to tell – he simply gave her a supportive wink and one of his trademark lopsided smiles. Gradually her fears subsided, replaced by a new feeling of almost-confidence.

Amelie looked down at her notes and began. ' "Love is the answer." ' She stopped, became aware of how much she was shaking, and prayed that the hotness in her cheeks wasn't too obvious. She took another deep breath, tried to steady herself from the off-the-richter-scale quakes that were charging through her, hoping they weren't as noticeable as they felt. She went on, forcing a calm expression. 'As everyone knows, that's John Lennon, and yes, you might say he had a point there . . .' Amelie paused, remembered to look up and make eye contact with the audience, and went on. 'In this increasingly nihilistic, agnostic, disconnected world we live in, you might say that love is the new belief system; the new faith. We all want to believe in the idea of fate finding us our one true love . . . or of Cupid nobly drawing his arrow and matching us up with our perfect partner for life.' Amelie stopped, remembering her English teacher Mr Williams and how he had told her in GCSEs that you should always speak as slowly as possible when presenting, and not gallop through your words. She took a sip of water and looked down at her notes, squinting to make out what she had scrawled earlier.

'Some . . . Some of us spend our whole lives waiting for this magic moment, all the time asking, *What if?* Praying that love will find us when we least expect it. After all, as another great philosopher once said' – Amelie paused, cringing inside, and wondering why all this hadn't sounded naff in her office, but now, spoken aloud in front of all these people, this next bit was surely going to sound faintly ridiculous; too late to backtrack now, she realised, and went on regardless – ' "You can't hurry love . . . You'll just have to wait." ' Amelie smiled through the cheesiness, and so – to her relief – did the audience. 'And yes, Diana Ross did also seem to have had a point. Who would want to disagree with her?'

Soft laughter darted around the room, and as Amelie looked around at her colleagues, she felt her cheeks cool down and she began to relax a little.

'Well, I used to agree with her. I used to think that it was all very nice and fluffy and romantic to just sit and wait for Mr When-You-Least-Expect-Him. But the trouble is, the times are changing. We now live in a completely different world. A manic, rushed-off-its-feet world that runs to its own timetable. A world that might not want to sit around twiddling its thumbs and waiting for Cupid to do his work at the leisurely pace he's used to. In this web-obsessed, low-GI, low-carb, text-messaging, iPod-wearing lifestyle that modern life dictates, let's face it, few people really have time to let romance blossom naturally. Hats off to all those who still do. But to those who don't, we need to show them that there is now a simple way of finding your other half. A way that works; a way that is safe, economical, flexible and, above all, great fun.' Amelie stopped, took some more water, and noticed that everyone was still looking up at her attentively, and seemed to be enjoying listening to her speak.

'And this way is speed-dating; which we at LGMK believe is an ingenious solution to the isolations of modern life.' Amelie paused, looked around the room again, then went on, 'So, who is our target? Our audience is every single man and every woman who knows what loneliness is. That's quite a lot of people, isn't it? So how do we reach them? With these ideas, which we're extremely excited to show you today.'

With that, Amelie and Josh prepared all the visual material, and began to talk through the concepts. Amelie realised that she was meant to be handing over to Josh at some point. But she felt she was in full flow now, and Josh was looking at her, visibly impressed by her surprising show of eloquence. His face told her to continue. She looked him in the eye, took a breath and went on.

'As everyone knows, one of the most important things in any relationship is the chemistry; the spark. It's either there or it's not. And that's what you really do get to test for when you go speed-dating, which you don't get to do with any other method of dating. Not with answering an ad in

Time Out or the *Guardian*. Not with Internet dating. Not with Burger Dating. Not with Dating in the Dark. And not with being set up by your friends on a blind date . . .' Amelie paused and looked around the room, surprised at how long she had been talking. She couldn't believe it. Maybe, at long last, she was over her fear.

'You see, the great thing about speed-dating is that you can cull the people you simply feel no sparks for. Let's face it, the 'three-minute test for chemistry' feature does make a lot of sense. Don't waste time emailing people before you've met them, before you know you have some energy between you. And so on. So . . . we decided to use this insight as the key thought behind our creative.'

Amelie began to unveil the work. 'There're numerous eye-catching ways to execute this, using both traditional media (TV and outdoor) and also ambient and viral techniques. Here's how we'd start things off; with a teaser direct-mail campaign.'

Amelie gestured to the big screen behind her, which showed an illustrated visual of some packs of sparklers and fireworks. She gave people a moment to look at this. From a distance, they looked like regular fireworks. On closer examination, you could see that the words on the packaging read, 'Fast Love.com. For guaranteed sparks.'

'The idea with these is that we'd send them out as teasers to as wide a demographic as possible; to start increasing general awareness very early on, before the above-the-line action all kicks off. The great thing about these ideas is that we know we're definitely not over-promising, because we know that with Fast Love, if you don't find your sparks the first time you go, you can go again and again for free, until you do.' Amelie stopped for some water, wondering to herself how many people would actually choose to go speed-dating more than once, in an entire lifetime. She kept this thought to herself as she went on with the performance.

'Anyway, we'd follow this up with a second mailing – this time with some of those magic candles that never go out.' Amelie clicked on to the next slide, revealing a picture of some candles branded with 'Fast Love. For sparks that never go out.' Amelie bit her tongue, wanting to apologise for how cheesy this idea sounded now it was out in the open, but she decided it was more professional to glide over that small detail. Looking at the audience grinning and laughing enthusiastically, Amelie thought perhaps they didn't seem to mind.

Next Josh held up some board-mounted mock-ups of some outdoor posters and TV storyboards. Amelie talked through them, completely in her stride now, possibly even enjoying herself.

'But now for the pièce de résistance,' Josh announced, and Amelie felt a wave of adrenalin wash over her, excited that they would finally be unveiling the big idea.

'So here's the final thought, with which we'd launch the whole campaign. It would kick off primarily as a publicity stunt, but could also have many other permutations. Ladies and gentleman, here is how we would launch the Fast Love brand in London, with a bang.' Amelie grinned confidently, trying not to wince at how saccharine she was beginning to sound in her head. Fleur, standing by the doors, dimmed all of the lights so that now there was only a small flicker being emitted from the tiny candles on each table. The large screen behind the stage flashed into life, presenting a panoramic view of the Thames – a brilliantly illuminated

Big Ben and St Paul's, a vibrant London Eye, and all the other glowing landmarks which lined the river. Gradually a fireworks display broke out over all of them, sending multicoloured sparks flying all over the sky.

'OK – now imagine there's a boat zooming up and down the river, with people handing out flyers and heart-shaped balloons. And then . . .'

Maggie turned to look at Eva, itching with curiosity to see what would happen next. Eva, her eyes smiling with excitement, turned to Ted, who was staring out of the window. She nudged him firmly, making him jump. He looked agitatedly at Eva for her having disrupted his daydream, but, obligingly, he turned to face the screen, just in time to see what was happening in the sky. Gradually, the Catherine wheels, rockets and fountains were beginning to change shape and to morph into letters. Circles turned into Cs and Os, star-shaped clusters turned into Fs and As, and so on until, one by one, the sparks in the air had all joined together, flashing in unison and spelling out the words FAST LOVE.COM.

The effect was enchanting. The room fell silent, and Amelie went on, her heart in her throat. 'Well . . . this is just a digital demonstration of the idea, and obviously it could be done in any other city in England, or the world, even. But hopefully you can see the point from this illustration, that this could be an unforgettable way to lodge the connection in people's minds – to make them associate Fast Love with finding the sparks they are looking for in their love life.'

Realising that she had finally run out of things to say, and struggling to believe how long she had managed to talk coherently for, Amelie stopped and took a deep breath. She looked out into the room of table-for-twos and saw with amazement that there was a raft of smiling faces looking back up at her. Then she looked across at Josh, who was wearing the biggest smile of all.

Josh moved closer to Amelie and thanked her for her presentation, before dispensing his closing remarks. After he had finished, a hearty applause broke out. Before long, though, the room had become awkwardly quiet, and it was time for the Fast Love team to depart. Maggie, Eva and Ted got up from their seats, said a brief thank-you, and said that they had to be getting off to their next appointment, and that they would be in touch. Although they appeared to have enjoyed the afternoon's entertainment, it now seemed that they weren't giving anything away from their illegible expressions.

Moments later, Fleur, Duncan and Chloe sprung into action. Switched the lights back on, drew the curtains, and pulled down the throws and drapes. Chloe darted around and blew out all the candles, while Duncan gathered up all the roses and forced them into a bin bag, all bar one, which he put to one side. Soon a sombre, anti-climactical mood had set in, and in no time at all, the speed-dating empire had changed back into Conference Room 1. 'Show's over now,' Amelie observed numbly, feeling exhausted yet surprisingly empowered for having finally conquered her greatest fear since childhood.

'You did amazingly,' Josh said, coming up behind her and patting her on the back. Fleur, from the other side of the room, caught his eye and gestured that she wanted to talk to him. Josh gave a half-nod, and began edging away from Amelie. 'Listen, really, really well done, Holden. We've definitely given it our best shot now.' As he walked away, he turned back and said, 'All we can do now is wait.'

As Josh went to talk to Fleur, Amelie wandered upstairs to check her emails, before then going outside to get some air. Job done, she thought to herself with incredulous relief. Literally, she thought, as she walked through the revolving steel doors, past the 'We think, therefore you buy' engraving, towards Soho Square, where she slumped down on a patch of grass.

Duncan came shuffling up to her, two cigarettes in hand, and sat down next to her. 'Here, a celebratory, please-be-my-mate-again ciggie.' He smiled meekly. 'That was completely fantastic, Amelie. Really. You should've seen their faces in there. I mean, I know the client has to confer for a bit, and maybe they've got more agencies to see, but I think it's pretty clear you won them round with that pitch.'

Amelie was silent. Her expression was as blank as the sky was clear. Duncan commented that she didn't much look like someone who had just won a five-figure pitch. She shook her head, took a drag on her cigarette, said nothing. Duncan looked at her pensively, nervously plucking weeds from the grass and playing with them.

'Am . . . I'm so sorry I fucked up and didn't back you with the new ideas. I've really let you down, I know.'

Amelie smiled enigmatically. 'It doesn't matter a bit, Duncan. I behaved like a monster too, and for that I know I should apologise . . . But you've always known my temper has a mind of its own.'

'Yeah, I know, but still, I shouldn't have given up on it all. I was just being a lazy bastard. Or a silly coward – one of the two. But, seeing you up there, after all the work you'd put in by yourself, I felt so useless. We're meant to be partners . . .'

'Honestly, don't worry about it, Duncan, I don't mind. And it wasn't just me – Josh did a lot of it. And . . . maybe we've won it – maybe we haven't – you know what? I've just realised that I don't really care any more. I know a week ago that was all I cared about, but now it's like, all of a sudden, I can see right through it. It was bullshit, what I said in there. I just gave them what they wanted to hear. I mean sure, speed-dating does have its good points; it's a great solution to loneliness, for some people. Well, OK, Sally. But all that spin I put on it in there, it makes me feel kind of sick now, playing it back in my mind.' Amelie stopped, and the sun went behind a solitary cloud. She pulled her coat tightly around her.

'I was just saying what I did because that's what you do in a three-minute pitch. It was all a bit of an act, like speed-dating – a performance designed to make the recipient buy into the product. You twist things, present yourself differently, just to make people love you.' She pulled on her cigarette, looked into Duncan's eyes. 'That's what ad land's all about, isn't it? And now I've seen that, I've suddenly realised, I'm over it.'

Duncan looked shocked, his face becoming overcast as Amelie went on, 'I need a change, Dunc. I love the ideas, I always will. But I'm finished with the game. I want to move on to something that feels a bit more real.'

Duncan sat up urgently, his eyes serious. 'What? What do you mean, move on?' He was desperate to hear more, but Amelie's phone rang, displaying a 'withheld' number. Amelie stood up, pressed OK, and moved out of earshot.

'Hello? Yes, speaking . . . right.' She strained her ears above the Soho din in the background. 'I see. Yes . . . yep . . . that's great . . . OK, yes . . . I'll see you then, then. Thanks. Bye.'

As she hung up the phone, Max leaned his head out of his office window, directed his decibels towards Soho Square, and hollered down at Amelie and Duncan, 'Guys! Result's here! Come back inside!'

22

Tick

Date: 14 February, 15.06
Sender: Grant, Joshua
To: Everyone (all agency)
Importance: High
Subject: LOVE AT FIRST SIGHT

It gives me astonishing pleasure to announce that the results from Maggie Rose (Fast Love's MD) have just come in.

Turns out they thought LGMK was their perfect match, and they have given us a great big tick. They would like us to handle all elements of their account, from below to above the line. This is an absolutely stellar result.

Drinks party on my balcony, commencing as soon after *5 p.m.* as humanly possible. Hope not too many of you will have to dash off to romantic engagements and that you will be able to join in as we all get suitably inebriated.

I just want to say a gargantuan thank-you to everyone who has been involved in this pitch. One person in particular, Amelie Holden, went way above and beyond the call of duty on this brief, and for that she deserves much praise and thanks. But I know what a big stress it's been for a lot of people. Believe me when I say all your hard work has been noted and will be duly rewarded.

Josh

Moments later Amelie received the same email again, forwarded from Josh, but this time with a little note prefacing it.

A,

Really was most impressive, what you managed to pull off – both on your own in the flat, and on the day itself. Imaginative, clever, cutting-edge . . . You should be extremely pleased with yourself. Just make sure you try and take some time out for a while now!

Beyond that though, I've been thinking about how to take things forward with you and Duncan – we can chat about it tonight at the drinks. I've had one or two thoughts.

Yours impressed,

J x

Date: 14 February, 15.18
Sender: Holden, Amelie
To: Grant, Joshua
Subject: RE: FW: LOVE AT FIRST SIGHT

It was a pleasure. Thanks for all your help too.

A

She thought about saying more. So many different thoughts were cartwheeling manically through her brain. She couldn't think what to say. After five drafts she had deleted them all and decided to keep it simple. She was starting to feel differently about things; she wasn't sure what really mattered any more.

Two hours later, the fifth-floor balcony at LGMK was full to capacity. The sun was setting in fluffy layers of pink and violet, and for February it was a mild, temperate evening. The champagne was flowing, the noise levels rising as people grew increasingly animated. The mood was jovial, and a sense of new beginnings and opportunity hung high in the air. Belle and Sebastian's 'Another Sunny Day' was blasting tinny but happy tones from the little stereo that hung precariously on the window sill of Josh's office.

Amelie stepped out on to the balcony, took a glass in her hand, and joined in the celebrations, despite having been running on empty for the last two days. She was exhausted from the lack of sleep, her clothes were hanging off her, and now that all traces of adrenalin had been eroded, she felt as though she was drifting through some bizarre shade of comedown. She also still had no appetite, despite the pitch finally being over. She had no idea why, but even now that the public-speaking episode was all over, her stomach was still full of anxious butterflies, and there was much activity in her restless mind. Concluding rationally that the only possible way out of this must be to drink more, she forced on her happy face, and smiled along with everyone as they cheered and clinked their glasses over and over again.

Duncan had been watching Amelie avidly ever since she had arrived. His mind was also working overtime, and he was ransacking his brain to know what she had meant earlier in the park. He repressed all these questions for now as she came towards him. He tuned back in to Max and Chloe, who were explaining to him the reasons why he wanted to buy a Porsche. Amelie joined them just in time to hear Duncan replying, 'No, I don't need a car, let alone one of *those* poncy things. Who wants a car in London? Surely more hassle than it's worth? No, I've got a few ideas up my sleeve . . .'

Max turned to Amelie excitedly. 'Hey, Duncan's got news!'

'Really? What's happened?' She looked nervously at Duncan.

'Well, it's been the day of big wins today.' Duncan grinned sheepishly and went on to reveal what he'd been bursting to tell her all day. That he'd finally got lucky on the instants. That he'd finally had the chance to look at the batch of scratch-cards he'd been clinging on to all day, ever since their meeting in the park. 'I only remembered them just now,' he exclaimed, 'and – you won't believe this – I've won!'

Amelie was shocked that his commitment to his habit

had finally paid off. To his face she said, 'That's amazing! Well done,' but in her head she was sifting through her mental filing cabinet, in search of any friends she had who might be able to recommend an addiction workshop of some sort.

'No, Amelie. I've *really* won . . .' He leaned in and whispered the amount in her ear. Amelie gasped in astonishment. 'Jesus!!!! That's amazing! Well, congratulations all round!' Everyone raised their glasses, clinked them together for the fifth time in the last hour, and poured more champagne down their throats.

Just as they did so, Josh came out on to the balcony, greeted them all and gave a congratulatory speech. Shortly afterwards, Duncan looked eagerly at Amelie; saw that Max and Chloe had drifted away and that she was now on her own. He made eye contact with her, and was about to start talking to her when suddenly Josh appeared in between them. Duncan watched as Josh went to Amelie and gave her a warm congratulatory hug. He overheard Amelie begin to talk nervously and vacuously to Josh about nothing very much in particular. Vowing to try and rekindle their conversation a little later, Duncan shrugged and went back to find Max and Chloe.

Soon Josh and Amelie were in the flow of a lighthearted conversation, joking about Josh's first few days in the agency. 'You know, I have to confess that I didn't take to you at first,' Amelie said, feeling the champagne in her becoming increasingly vocal. 'I guess I was being a bit childish, but I really got the wrong impression about you – thought you were a bit of an obnoxious Ozzie meathead!'

Josh looked wounded, but then he broke into a laugh, as Amelie went on to add hastily, 'But now I see how wrong

I was. I know we haven't worked together for very long, but you've been a great mentor to me, and I'm really grateful. I'm glad you came, now. I'm sorry if I was aloof to start with . . .'

'Aloof!' exclaimed Josh. 'You were an iceberg!'

'Sorry,' said Amelie, looking guilty and embarrassed. 'But I hated you for replacing my lovely Jana . . . I know, I know, it wasn't your fault. It can't have been easy coming in and taking over the reins from her – I'm truly sorry for making your life harder.'

'Don't be silly. On the contrary, you've made life interesting. I've enjoyed our little clashes over this and that. It kind of added . . .'

'. . . added some sparks to the daily grind?' Amelie smiled, finishing his sentence.

'Something like that,' said Josh, refilling Amelie's glass. Looking around to see who else needed refuelling, he saw that the balcony had begun to thin out. Evidently, most people had exciting Valentine's Day engagements to pursue. Chloe and Duncan were still on the balcony, leaning out over the rails together and sharing a cigarette. A few moments later, Chloe started putting on her coat, and Duncan came over to announce that they were going out to eat somewhere. 'Can't decide where to go for grub with my new-found fortune – Oxo Tower or The Ivy – what d'you reckon?' Duncan joked.

'Mmmmnn, there's a choice. Well, best of luck getting a table at either,' said Amelie, then wished them a good time. She gave Duncan a quick kiss on the cheek, and winked at him. 'Take care now . . . don't spend it all at once!'

As they walked away, Josh turned to Amelie and said

casually, 'So you're not dashing off on some exclusive Valentine's date?'

'Me?' Amelie laughed. 'No – I've actually been a bit of a monster the last few weeks. Burned my bridges with the last few guys – but for all the right reasons. None of them were the right one for me, it turns out. The single life just keeps calling me back; I think it's my natural state of being.'

'But what about Romeo who sent you the flowers today?'

Amelie's face fell. 'Shit . . . You just reminded me. I haven't even thanked him for them yet! I've been so busy, I plain forgot.'

'You're not that into him, then?'

'I was, to start with . . . but we had a huge blow-out yesterday. He drove me ever-so-slightly crazy, before you arrived. I totally lost my temper with him and was such a bitch to him I thought I'd heard the last of him. I'm so surprised to get flowers from him, after the names he called me!'

Josh laughed. 'He sounds quite smitten to me . . .'

'He's a funny one. But not *my* funny one, I don't think.' Amelie paused, her mind hovering over whether she should ask the next question or not. She went ahead with it anyway, 'So, what about you?'

Josh smiled awkwardly, and ran a hand through his hair.

'You're such a fan of doing that, aren't you?' Amelie teased. 'It's like playing with your hair is your favourite pastime, or something . . . well, besides talking in epigrams . . .'

'Hey – less of the cheek, lady! Thought you'd just agreed to turn over a new leaf as far as being nice to your boss was concerned? Anyway, proverbs are the driving force behind a productive, happy day.'

'There you go again!' she teased, and Josh laughed again. 'But seriously,' Amelie continued slowly, 'I thought you'd be taking Fleur out somewhere?'

'Oh, no.' Josh looked surprised. 'That's not been working out for a while. I kind of put a stop to things after the weekend in Wing. I just realised it was kind of unprofessional of me to be messing around with my assistant like that. I feel quite embarrassed about it, actually. Oh well, no point regretting it now. Hopefully it will all be forgotten soon enough.'

'So it was more to do with office etiquette than how you felt about her?' Amelie felt butterflies spring to life in her stomach again.

'Well, yeah, that too. It's funny, what you said yesterday, about realising that it all comes down to the spark. That's what made me see that I'd done the right thing calling it off. Sure, there're other reasons why we weren't good together, but ultimately, there weren't enough fireworks there for me.'

Amelie felt herself shiver, suddenly feeling the cold. 'I just need to pop inside and get my jacket. I'll be back in a bit.' She moved inside, shutting the door behind her.

When she got back to her desk, she saw that she had four missed calls. Opening her Outlook, she saw she had two new emails from Natasha at Imaginative Selection.

After quickly following up the messages and phone calls, Amelie decided to head outside again. She was just about to shut down her Mac when, in her champagne haze, she remembered something.

Date: 14 February, 19.45
Sender: Holden.Amelie@LGMKLondon.com
To: charliestanton@yahoo.co.uk
Subject: thank you . . .

Hi Charlie,

Thank you vvvvvv much for the lovely lovely flowers.
Really, really so so sweet of you.

OK – so I've been doing some thinking about
things . . . I think you are brilliant . . . but . . . I don't
think it'll come as a big surprise to you when I say that
I'm not sure it's really working out between us. Think
maybe we should call it a day . . .

I do feel bad about this, but I thought it better to say
something now before we get any more serious. Sorry
if that sounds rubbish.

A x x x

P.S. Will always look out for you. I just know you're
going to make it big one day.

Amelie read and reread this a few times, and tried her best
to check for mistakes. Feeling a twinge of sadness at yet
another one biting the dust, she sighed, closed down her
Mac and headed outside.

She pulled open the door and stepped out on to the
moonlit balcony, feeling awe-inspired by how handsome
London looked. It was now entirely dark outside, the stars

were out in full force, and the whole of the Thames was lit up just as it had been earlier, in the Fast Love digital show. Josh turned and smiled at her.

'Hey,' Amelie said, leaning over the balcony edge and looking out, admiring the kaleidoscopic colours along the Thames, and the iridescent buildings and monuments tracing its outline. 'It's so beautiful out here, isn't it? You know, if you look that way, you can see as far as the Wheel, and St Paul's.'

'I know,' enthused Josh. 'I love the view out here. This is where I come when I get disillusioned with London. Whenever I start to get homesick, I come and sit out here. Makes me remember why I left Australia; the Opera House has nothing on this.'

'Best city in the world,' stated Amelie patriotically.

'Amelie,' Josh began, in a more serious tone, 'I mentioned earlier that I'd been thinking about your career. Actually, it's a shame Duncan's already left, so he won't be here to hear this, but . . . I want to tell you that I'm going to recommend to the board that you be promoted to a senior team.'

Amelie was silent. It was all she had been working for this year, and yet, this was the last thing she had been expecting Josh to say. She looked dumbstruck, the colour fading from her face, as Josh went on.

'I think the standard of work and effort you've been putting in over the last few weeks proves you're more than worthy of this. You'll be given new responsibilities of course, it's not just a title change . . . And I'll also see that your salary is given a nice big upwards nudge too . . . But we can discuss all that tomorrow, when Duncan is back . . .'

Josh looked at Amelie for any clue of what she might be thinking.

'I meant what I said earlier. You have real potential.'

Amelie felt her heart sinking slowly. 'Wow,' she managed, despite the indecision that was spreading like a virus through her mind. 'That's – that's – amazing . . . I don't know what to say.'

'Don't say anything just yet. Just think about it. Take the weekend. Let me know your thoughts on Monday.'

'Thank you. Thank you – I certainly will.' Amelie felt her pulse quicken as she realised she couldn't keep her secret from him any longer. 'Josh. I'm sorry. There's something I really need to tell you . . .'

Josh was looking at Amelie, a new shade of intensity in his eye. 'There's something else I need to tell you too. He put down his glass, ran a hand through his hair, and looked uncharacteristically edgy. He looked Amelie in the eye. 'Listen, I must explain: what I've said just now, it comes with a kind of asterisk. Small print, so to speak. In fairness, you're highly unlikely to accept the offer I just made you now, once you hear what I've got to say. And that's fine, I totally understand. But I just thought I'd better be honest now, rather than entrap you into taking a job before you know the full story. So I'm telling you this now, so you can make an informed decision.'

Amelie felt her mouth begin to go dry, wondering what could be wrong. Her heart was beating faster. She said nothing as Josh went on, 'I know I've just been banging on about professionalism, so it's ludicrous of me to even think of saying these words . . . maybe it's the champagne in me, or the craziness of today, something in the air . . . but . . . I suddenly feel like I can't keep it to myself any longer.'

Josh stopped, as though he was struggling to think of the right words. Amelie's blue eyes were now dilating with alarm, poised to discover what could be so serious. What could make Joshua Grant, who was usually the pinnacle of composure, suddenly appear so worried and uncomfortable? He stammered on, 'I don't know how this has happened, and I know this is so, so improper, and tacky, and wrong . . . but . . . here's the thing . . .' He paused, took a breath, and added, looking down at the floor, 'Amelie – I think I might be falling in love with you.'

Her heart stopped. She looked down, avoiding Josh's gaze; not wanting him to see her face, which was breaking out into a strange smile.

'I can't stop thinking about you. I've not been able to get you out of my head. You've been there, your face, your hair, your smile, your ideas, your sparkle, in my mind, as soon as I wake up, all the time, until I go to sleep. Not that I've been doing much of that lately. Or eating. Or drinking. Or thinking about anything else. And . . . that night in your flat, working together on the pitch, I felt there was the most incredible connection between us. I don't think I've ever felt such an intense combination of admiration and attraction, and fascination, for another human being . . . I know you probably think I'm a total maniac, and I really shouldn't have said anything . . . I'm the sleaziest boss you've ever had, I know. I'm sorry. I'd better go.'

Amelie's voice box had tied itself up in knots. Suddenly she was seven years old again, back in that terrifying circle of bossy, extroverted Brownies narrating their life stories; suddenly she felt the same feeling of complete loss over the power of speech. As she stood there, mute and dumbfounded, an important realisation set in. The recurring butterflies in her stomach – they weren't just there for her inspiration, for her nerves. They were there because of Josh.

'Am?' Josh asked tentatively. Still she said nothing; her eyes were a confused whirlwind of emotions. 'You hate me,' Josh said factually. 'I can see that. I've deeply offended you. I'm so sorry, I'm the biggest bastard. You'll tell the board, and they'll have me removed. OK – fair dos – I deserve everything I get. I'll get my coat.'

'Shhhhh . . .' Amelie whispered. She looked up at him, and her face broke into an electric smile. Seeing this, Josh hovered for a moment, then edged closer to Amelie, cautiously putting his arms around her. He looked at her with new-found adoration as she planted a spontaneous kiss on his cheek.

'I won't have you removed,' Amelie said, pulling away. 'Not just yet.' She looked up into Josh's eyes, and smiled at him knowingly. He took her in his arms, kissed her knowingly back.

'So,' said Josh eventually, pulling away from Amelie and stroking her hair. They smiled into each other's eyes, and Josh said, 'What was it that you wanted to tell me?'

There Is a Spark that
Never Goes Out

Hurrah! We won the pitch! So that's it, then. 'THE END.'

Yet somehow there is still more to say. So much has happened in the last few days . . . Where to start? Am sitting in The Nellie, waiting for Duncan to arrive so I can drop my bombshell on him. My bombshell being that, despite busting a gut to keep our jobs this last month, and being offered a dream-like promotion as a result of winning the Fast Love account, I've now had a complete inner revolution and decided that after three years at LGMK, it's time to move on. I've made up my mind, and I'm heading somewhere pretty different. I didn't mean for it to happen, and honestly do feel pretty bad about it.

It all started when Duncan and I met up with some head-hunters a few weeks ago, when we were convinced our days were numbered. This one lady, Natasha, turned out to be really nice, and super keen. She said it's actually a good time for copywriters; that there's quite a lot going on. So she pushed me forward for this job that she thought I'd like – and I'd forgotten all about it until she kept calling me up this week and saying there was someone I had to meet. So I went along to the meeting, and it turned out to be for a really amazing, unique opportunity, and a job that I think I'd really love doing. Trouble is, it involves going solo, which means leaving Duncan, after six years of working together, since we first met in college. It's going to break my heart, but I know it's the right thing; it's been there at the back of my mind for ages. For the first time in my life I've made a firm choice about something without a severe attack of indecision. And I just know I definitely have to get out of ad land for a bit, or else I might start to go completely mad . . .

So, instead, I'm going somewhere a bit calmer, where I know I'll believe in what I'm writing about, and it won't be so much about the pitch, the game-playing, the back-stabbing. Where I'm going, I'll be able to get up in the morning and know that I'm selling something worthwhile, pleasant, life-affirming. So in a month's time, I'm off to the cosy old world of book publishing, to write book ads and dream up cover shoutlines. Big new chapter (sorry, inevitable), but I'm really looking forward to it. With any luck it might be less all-consuming than LGMK; I might try and leave the office every day at 5.30, start getting my priorities in order . . . Family. Friends. Flat. Life. Cat. Shopping. Exercise. Film. Decorating. Art. Theatre. Curtains. Love . . . Kids?

One step at a time.

Ahhhhggggh, Duncan has just arrived – here goes.

> *Home, Sunday 20 February, something like midday*

Life never ceases to amaze. The actual meeting with Duncan was worlds apart from the one I'd played over in my mind a thousand times before. He arrived late, we shared some wedges and beers, and slowly, after a deep breath, I broke the news to him. Told him how I'd been for my interview at the publishing house, and that the Head of Marketing had called me a few hours later to tell me he wanted me for the job, much to my shock. I told him how they'd given me until Monday to think about it, but that my mind was already made up.

Lovely, silly, Duncan. Far from being heartbroken that I wanted to leave him; on the contrary, he had news of his own to break to me . . . He'd been busticating throughout all of last night trying to tell me about it, but I'd been avoiding him, for fear of how he would take my own news. Turns out, the minute his little fingers had finished scratching away at the silver powder on the scratch-card and revealed the £77,000 winnings, he'd decided instantly what he wanted to do with it. I guess that's why they call them instants – they change your life in a matter of seconds. His big idea is to leave LGMK and go travelling around the world. First stop, Australia. He says he's always wanted to, and that the way Josh and I are always going on about our backpacking days hasn't exactly helped pin him down to grotty old England. The funny thing is, Duncan admitted to me that he's been feeling the same all along as

I have about ad land; wondering if he's cut out for it. He said to me, 'It's like relationships. Sometimes you both just know when your heart's not in it any more.'

It's true. In a strange way, the sparks between Duncan and I had kind of been fading for a while. But we've just been too good friends to admit it. So I wish him all the best – maybe we'll get back together one day. If I don't stay in publishing for ever, that is, or if Duncan doesn't get stuck on a fishing boat somewhere teaching people amateur diving. Or move into a hut on a desert island off the shores of Fiji; get a job painting people's caricatures, or something equally Duncan . . . For now, he's bought a one-way ticket to Oz, leaving in a month. As soon as we've worked out our notice, he's out of here, indefinitely. I'll be gutted to see him go, but at least I know he'll be well looked after. Chloe, whose visa happens to run out at the end of the month, is going back to Melbourne shortly after and has kindly offered to be his tour guide . . . Looks like I was right about those two. Seems Duncan's heart has finally found its happy place – as has Sally's. She's never been more loved up than she is right now. Derek's taking her to Milan this weekend, for their first of, hopefully, many mini-breaks. You've got to hand it to Fast Love, as far as those two are concerned . . .

Speaking of Fast Love, it turns out Charlie's luck has taken a turn for the brilliant, I'm pleased to say. He sent me a sweet email, saying that he'll keep in touch, but that he's just about to fly off on a fantastic round-the-world tour with Arcadia. At the same time, he's also nabbed himself a fabulous new agent, with 'someone even better than ICM' he says, who also just happens to know Russell T. Davies, the chief writer for Doctor Who *really rather well. Really happy for him – no matter what I said about him, he certainly has charm and talent enough to go far; I wish him all the best.*

There's one other thing. Little, tiny thing, really. The thing that happened with Josh at the after-party. It's still happening. I know, I know – he's always got on my nerves intensely . . . But truly am now starting to see him in a totally new way. Admittedly he's nice to look at. But, after spending so much time with him lately, working together on the pitch, and getting drunk together at the party afterwards, I realised, there's so much more to him. I guess some people just need a little more time to show the real them . . . You can't hurry some people. And I actually think we make a great team . . . I'm just finding out how great. Starting to think that maybe I've found my intellectual equal. I'm just so full of respect and admiration for him, for how much he's achieved so young, how inspirational he is – I think I'm already falling in love with his mind. And the sparks, when he kissed me! I've never known fireworks like it with anyone. Maybe it's true, then? Love does happen when you least . . .

Josh stirred from his slumber, opened his eyes, rubbed them a little, and turned over to see Amelie scribbling away again. Wondering what was so important that couldn't wait, he leaned over and tried to tickle her, but she carried on writing, her face determined to finish whatever point she was making. That was it. Josh rolled over, formed a new wave of attack, tickling her more aggressively this time, and throwing her pen across the room. He grabbed the diary from her hand, snapped it shut. Mid-sentence, she was in his arms, and the diary fell to the floor.

Epilogue

Tock Tick (One Year Later)

The old man on the bench was studying the film-wrapped sandwich on his lap; wondering whether or not it was safe to eat. Having grown jaded with the latest tedious antics on *Celebrity Big Brother*, the grey-haired man tossed his newspaper to one side. On closer inspection, he decided that the edges of green mould on his sandwich weren't too overt, depending on what light you looked at them in; and if he picked them away, the bread looked as though it might just about be edible. His stomach rumbled. The sun passed away behind a cloud, and he thought, Where else is my food coming from today? and opened his mouth.

As he bit into it; as he crunched away on the stale bread and lettuce, the sun came back through the clouds, and he watched its golden reflection in the water. As he sat watching the still waters of the Grand Union Canal, suddenly there was more movement between the bubbles in the water, and a canal boat went gliding past. He sat back on the bench and pulled his old green duffle coat tightly around him, drank in the enchanting views of Little Venice, and munched away on the last of his sandwich.

As he did so, a tall, good-looking man came into view. He was walking along the canal, looking at his watch. His dark brown hair was thick, and he wore it long, just past his ears. He was wearing a long dark trench coat, and after some time he found a comfortable spot of wall against which to lean, just by the Bridge House pub. Running a hand through his hair, he continued to check his watch, looking back towards the direction of Warwick Avenue, where a double-decker bus was just pulling up.

The old man continued to watch the tall dark stranger, intrigued. Ten minutes later, the expression in the dark-haired man's face changed. His eyes flickered, zooming in on something in the distance, before his face broke out into a wide grin. Then there was the sound of running, of pounding footsteps getting faster and louder; and then the sounds of panting and gasping for breath. Looking up, the old man saw a flustered but beautiful young woman, whose thick brown cascades of curly hair trailed in the air after her as she ran. He watched from afar as she fumbled along the canal-side, laden down with large carrier bags bursting at the seams; books and thick manuscripts leaking through the holes. He watched as her flushed, weary face broke into a radiant smile, as her eyes made contact with the tall, dark-haired man who smiled back at her and waved. She ran up to him, dropped her bags to the ground, and flung her arms around him.

'So sorry I'm so very late,' he overheard her say in between breaths. 'The bus didn't show for hours. Couldn't get on it . . .' she panted. 'Nightmare . . .'

'Don't worry,' came the reply, 'There's no need to rush. We've got all the time we need.'

Acknowledgements

Thanks to Scollett and Alex (the original and best Milky Bar Kid), for accompanying me on two surreally entertaining nights out in London, and helping to provide much of the material thereafter. To Clare Lomas, for unearthing so much hilarity in the wonderful world of singletondom. To Big Rick and Little Mark for macho prowess with all things flat-packed – without which all of this would have been composed on the floor. To Hannah for all the coffee and life/beret-swapping. For too many other reasons, thanks to Claire, Sarah and Martin, Kris Smoothie-Shrimpton, Luke Brown, Miriam Berry, and the 'RH' girls – Smorris, Auds, Soph, Jules, Lou, Becks and Sarah O.

Big thanks to Cat, Harrie and all at Headline for all your brilliant help and enthusiasm. Special thanks to Lucy, and wishing you all the Luck in the world with your new ventures. Thank you to Kate Elton at RH for helping turn this from a pitch into a reality. To Will Awdry of DDB for reminding me of the outer circle. To Rob for being an inspiration with all things words, ads and indecision. To John Simmons, and all the other wordsmiths of 26. To Sam Snape, and to Simon Kilgannon. And to all at archibald ingall stretton . . . for providing the finishing touches to ad land – even if (NB) any similarities to reality are a true coincidence and none of the characters (NB Anna B and Steve!) are based on anything but fiction – excepting a certain Granny Smith.

Special thanks and cwtches to Guy (the original and best Billy Bibbit), for making me laugh out loud, always. To Lauren for wonderment in every way. To my mum for tolerating so many direful early drafts. To my dad for saying he'll write his book one day and hopefully meaning it. And finally thanks to Evie, Emil and Camilla for always encouraging me, always being there.

NINA KILLHAM

Mounting Desire

Jack Carter and Molly Desire are just housemates. There could never be anything between them – they're far too different. **Aren't they?**

Jack, a successful romance writer, is looking for his soul mate. Molly, a fully paid-up sexaholic, views having to lodge in Jack's house as a necessary but very temporary evil.

For a while, it looks as though they're the exception to the oldest rule in the book: **the one that says opposites attract**. But then Molly takes to writing her own instantly successful steamy romances, and Jack is furious. As the sparks start to fly, it appears there's a whole lot more to their relationship than meets the eye. But could it be that two such different housemates could really be . . . soul mates?

'Truly a book to be devoured with relish' Jennifer Crusie, author of *Faking It* and *Fast Woman*

0 7553 3277 6

little
black
dress

SWAN ADAMSON

My Three Husbands

What's a girl to do when husbands just keep lining up?

Meet Venus Gilroy: twenty-five, carefree, irresistible, and with a nasty habit of getting hitched to the wrong guy.

Husband No 1: would have been a winner, if it hadn't been for the forgery and embezzlement charges.

Husband No 2: sometimes a girl has to realise – meeting a husband in a strip bar will never end well.

Husband No 3: Is the real deal. Isn't he? Surely sexy, rugged, *principled* Tremaynne is finally the right one for Venus?

With her insane mother, not to mention her two gay dads, plus porn-video-store-owner boss, all weighing in with advice, it's time for Venus to learn for herself – how you know that Mr Right . . . doesn't turn out to be Mr Wrong.

0 7553 3364 0

little
black
dress

little black dress

brings you
the most fabulous fiction
every month!

Sign up for news on authors,
titles, competitions and
a monthly email update at
www.littleblackdressbooks.com

You can buy any of these other
Little Black Dress titles from your
bookshop or *direct from the publisher*.

FREE P&P AND UK DELIVERY
(Overseas and Ireland £3.50 per book)

The Bachelorette Party	Karen McCullah Lutz	£3.99
My Three Husbands	Swan Adamson	£3.99
Daisy's Back in Town	Rachel Gibson	£3.99
Mounting Desire	Nina Killham	£3.99

TO ORDER SIMPLY CALL THIS NUMBER

01235 400 414

or visit our website: www.madaboutbooks.com

Prices and availability subject to change without notice.